if he had been with me

if
he
had
been
with
me

laura nowlin

sourcebooks
fire

Published by Sourcebooks Fire, an imprint of Sourcebooks.
P.O. Box 4410, Naperville, Illinois 60567-4410
(630) 961-3900
sourcebooks.com

Originally published in 2013 by Sourcebooks Fire

Library of Congress Cataloging-in-Publication data is on file with the publisher.

Printed and bound in the United States of America.
LSC 30 29

For my husband, Robert;
without you, I wouldn't have known how to write about true love.

one

I wasn't with Finny on that August night, but my imagination has burned the scene in my mind so that it feels like a memory.

It was raining, of course, and with his girlfriend, Sylvie Whitehouse, he glided through the rain in the red car his father had given him on his sixteenth birthday. In a few weeks, Finny would be turning nineteen.

They were arguing. No one ever says what they were arguing about. It is, in other people's opinions, not important to the story. What they do not know is that there is another story. The story lurking underneath and in between the facts of the one they can see. What they do not know, the cause of the argument, is crucial to the story of me.

I can see it—the rain-slicked road and the flashing lights of ambulances and police cars cutting through the darkness of night, warning those passing by: catastrophe has struck here, please drive slowly. I see Sylvie sitting sideways out of the back of the policeman's car, her feet drumming on the wet pavement as she talks. I cannot hear her, but I see Sylvie tell them the cause of the argument, and I know, I know, I know, I know. If he had been with me, everything would have been different.

I can see them in the car before the accident—the heavy rain, the world and the pavement as wet and slick as if it had been oiled down for their arrival. They glide through the night, regrettably together, and they argue. Finny is frowning. He is distracted. He is not thinking of the rain or the car or the wet road beneath it. He is thinking of this argument with Sylvie. He is thinking of the cause of the argument, and the car swerves suddenly to the right, startling him out of his thoughts. I imagine that Sylvie screams, and then he overcompensates by turning the wheel too far.

Finny is wearing his seat belt. He is blameless. It is Sylvie who is not. When the impact occurs, she sails through the windshield and out into the night, improbably, miraculously, only suffering minor cuts on her arms and face. Though true, it is hard to imagine, so hard that even I cannot achieve the image. All I can see is the moment afterward, the moment of her weightless suspension in the air, her arms flailing in slow motion, her hair, a bit bloody and now wet with rain, streaming behind her like a mermaid's, her mouth a round O in a scream of panic, the dark wet night surrounding her in perfect silhouette.

Sylvie is suddenly on Earth again. She hits the pavement with a loud smack and is knocked unconscious.

She lies on the pavement, crumpled. Finny is untouched. He

breathes heavily, and in shock and wonder, he stares out into the night. This is his moment of weightless suspension. His mind is blank. He feels nothing, he thinks nothing; he exists, perfect and unscathed. He does not even hear the rain.

Stay. I whisper to him. *Stay in the car. Stay in this moment.*

But, of course, he never does.

two

———

PHINEAS SMITH IS AUNT ANGELINA'S son. Aunt Angelina is not my aunt; she is my mother's best friend from girlhood, her best friend still—and next-door neighbor. Our mothers had been pregnant together that spring and summer long ago. My mother respectably so, married to her high-school sweetheart for over a year with numerous pictures of their wedding scattered throughout their house with a fenced-in backyard. My father was—is—never around because of his work, but Mother did not mind; she had Angelina. Angelina was pregnant from her lover. He was married and rich and far too old for her. He also refused to believe that it was his child. It would take a court-ordered DNA test a few weeks after Phineas's birth to get his father to do the honorable thing—buy Aunt Angelina the house next door to my mother, and after writing each monthly check, pretend that she and the baby did not exist for the next thirty days.

My mother did not work, and Aunt Angelina taught art at Vogt

Elementary across the street from her duplex, so the summer was theirs to spend. They told us that the summer of their pregnancies, Aunt Angelina would walk over from her duplex on Church Street— her stomach large and heavy, protruding, as if it were leading the way—to our large Victorian house on Elizabeth Street, and they would spend the day on the back porch with their feet propped up on the railing. They would drink lemonade or iced tea, and only go inside to watch *I Love Lucy* in the afternoon. They sat close together so that Finny and I could kick each other like twins.

They made such plans for us that summer.

Phineas was born first on the twenty-first of September. A week later, likely missing the one who had been kicking me, I came along.

In September people will tell you that their favorite season is autumn. They will not say this during any other month of the year. People forget September is actually a summer month. In St. Louis, this should be apparent to people. The leaves are still green on the trees and the weather is still warm, yet people hang smiling scarecrows on their front doors. By the time the leaves and weather do begin to change in late October, they have tired of autumn and are thinking of Christmas. They never stop; they never wonder if they already have it all.

My mother named me Autumn. People say to me "Oh how pretty," and then the name seems to glide away from them, not grasping all the things that the word should mean to them, shades of red, change, and death.

Phineas understood my name before I did. My name had what

his did not, associations, meaning, a history. His disappointment when our fourth grade class looked up names in the baby name books surprised me. Every book gave his name a different meaning and origin: snake, Nubian, oracle, Hebrew, Arabic, unknown. My name meant exactly what it was; there was nothing to be discovered by it. I thought if a name was of unknown origin and meaning, it could not disappoint. I did not understand then that a boy without a real father would crave an origin and a meaning.

There were so many things that I did not understand about him over the years, but of course, of course, of course, of course, they all make sense now.

We grew up in Ferguson: a small town in the suburbs of St. Louis, composed of Victorian houses, old brick churches, and a picturesque downtown of shops owned by families for generations. I suppose it was a happy childhood.

I was quirky and odd and I did not have any friends besides Finny. He could have had other close friends if he wanted; he was good at sports and nothing was odd about him. He was sweet and shy and everyone liked him. The girls had crushes on him. The boys picked him first in gym. The teachers called on him for the right answer.

I wanted to learn about the Salem witch trials for history. I read books under my desk during lessons and refused to eat the bottom left corner of my sandwiches. I believed platypuses to be a government conspiracy. I could not turn a cartwheel or kick, hit, or serve any sort of ball. In third grade, I announced that I was a feminist.

During Job Week in fifth grade, I told the class and teacher that my career goal was to move to New York, wear black turtlenecks, and sit in coffee shops all day, thinking deep thoughts and making up stories in my head.

After a moment of surprise, Mrs. Morgansen wrote *Freelance Writer* under my smiling Polaroid picture and tacked it on the walls with the future teachers and football stars. After consulting her, I agreed that it was close enough. I think she was pleased to have found something for me, but sometimes I wonder if she would have cared as much if I had been ugly as well as odd.

For as long as I can remember, people have told me that I am pretty. This came from adults more often than other children. They said it to me when they met me; they whispered it to each other when they thought I could not hear. It became a fact I knew about myself, like my middle name was Rose or that I was left-handed: I was pretty.

Not that it did me any good. The adults all seemed to think it did, or at least should, but in childhood my prettiness gave more pleasure to the adults than it did me.

For other children, the defining characteristic was another fact I had accepted about myself—I was *weird*.

I never tried to be weird, and I hated being seen that way. It was as if I had been born without the ability to understand if the things I was about to say or do were strange, so I was trapped into constantly being myself. Being "pretty" was a poor consolation in my eyes.

Finny was loyal to me; he taunted anyone who dared torment

me, snubbed anyone who scorned me, and always picked me first to be on his team.

It was understood by everyone that I belonged to Finny and that we belonged together. We were accepted an as oddity by our classmates, and most of the time they left me alone. And I was happy; I had Finny.

We were rarely ever apart. At recess I sat on the hill reading while Finny played kickball with the boys in the field below. We did every group project together. We walked home together and trick-or-treated together. We did our homework side by side at my kitchen table. With my father so often gone, The Mothers frequently had one another over for dinner. A week could easily go by with Finny and I only being separated to sleep in our own beds, and even then we went to sleep knowing the other wasn't very far away.

In my memory of childhood, it is always summer first. I see the dancing light and green leaves. Finny and I hide under bushes or in trees. Autumn is our birthdays and walking to school together and a deepening of that golden light. He and his mother spend Christmas at our house. My father makes an appearance. His father sends a present that is both expensive and unfathomable. A chemistry set. Custom-made golf clubs. Finny shrugs and lays them aside. Winter is a blur of white and cold hands shoved in pockets. Finny rescues me when other kids throw snowballs at me. We sled or stay indoors. Spring is a painting in pale green, and I sit watching from the stands while Finny plays soccer.

All the time that became known in my mind as Before.

three

I WALK TOWARD THE BUS stop with my book bag slung over one
shoulder. There are a few kids already there, standing loosely
grouped together but not acknowledging each other. I look down
at the sidewalk. My boots are spray-painted silver. My hair and
fingernails are black. I stop at the corner and stand to the side. We
are all quiet.

Our bus stop is at the top of the big hill on Darst Road. Finny
and I used to ride our bikes down this hill. I had always been frightened. Finny never was.

I look at the other kids at the corner while pretending that I am
not. There are seven of us. Some of them I recognize from middle
school or even elementary school; some of them I don't.

It is my first day of high school.

I go back to looking down and study the shredded hem of my
black dress. I cut the lace with fingernail clippers a week ago. My
mother says I can dress however I want as long as my grades stay

the same. But then, she still hasn't figured out that I'm not going to be one of the popular girls this year.

On the last day of school, Sasha and I walked to the drugstore and spent an hour picking out dyes. She wanted me to dye my hair red because of my name. I thought that was dorky but I didn't tell her; since our recent eviction from The Clique, Sasha has been my only girlfriend, my only friend actually.

"Hey," somebody says. Everyone looks up. Finny is standing with us now, tall, blond, and preppy enough to be in a catalog. Everyone looks away again.

"Hey," I hear one girl's voice say. She is standing somewhere behind me and I cannot see her. I should have said hello back to Finny, but I'm too nervous to speak right now.

––––––––––––

Last night at his house we had what The Mothers called an end-of-summer barbeque. While they were grilling, I sat on the back porch and watched Finny kick a soccer ball against the fence. I was thinking of a short story I started the day before, my first attempt at a Gothic romance. I planned on a very tragic ending, and I was working out the details of my heroine's misfortunes as I watched him play. When they sent us inside to get the paper plates, he spoke to me.

"So why did you dye your hair?" he said.

"I dunno," I said. If someone had asked me why Finny and I weren't friends anymore, I would have said that it was an accident.

Our mothers would have said that we seemed to have grown apart in the past few years. I don't know what Finny would have said.

In elementary school, we were accepted as an oddity. In middle school, it was weird that we were friends, and in the beginning, we had to explain ourselves to the others, but then we hardly saw each other, and we had to explain less and less.

By some strange accident, my weirdness became acceptable, and I was one of the popular girls that first semester of seventh grade. We called ourselves The Clique. Every day we ate lunch together and afterward all went to the bathroom to brush our hair. Every week we painted our nails the same color. We had secret nicknames and friendship bracelets. I wasn't used to being admired or envied or having girlfriends, and even though Finny had always been enough for me Before, I drank it up as if I had been thirsting for it for years.

Finny joined a group of guys who were vaguely geeky but not harassed, and I usually waved to him when I saw him at school. He always waved back.

We were taking different classes, which meant different homework. After a few weeks, we stopped studying together, and I saw him even less. Being one of the popular girls took a lot of time. After school they wanted me to come over and watch movies while we did each other's hair. On the weekends we went shopping.

When I did see Finny, we didn't have a lot to talk about anymore. Every moment we spent in silence was like another brick in the wall going up between us.

Somehow we weren't friends anymore.

It wasn't a choice. Not really.

I'm looking at my silver boots and torn lace when the bus pulls up. Everyone steps forward, heads down. We silently file onto the bus where everyone *is* talking. Even though I had no reason to think Sasha wouldn't be there, I am relieved when I see her sitting in the middle of the bus. She is wearing a black T-shirt and thick, dark eyeliner.

"Hey," I say as I slide in next to her, placing my book bag on my lap.

"Hey," she says. Since I refused to dye my hair red, she dyed hers an unnatural shade instead. We smile at each other. Our transformation is complete. Sort of.

I can say *exactly* why Sasha and I weren't friends with Alexis Myers or any of those girls anymore.

I didn't try out for cheerleading.

I had planned on it. I wanted to be a cheerleader. I wanted to be popular and date a soccer player—that what's cool at McClure High instead of football—and everything that went along with staying in The Clique. But I couldn't make up my own routine and perform it alone for tryouts, so that was that.

Alexis and Taylor and Victoria all made it onto the squad, but Sasha didn't. Officially, we weren't kicked out of The Clique, but all they talked about at lunch was cheerleading camp and the older girls on the squad who had seemed soooooo nice.

On the last day of school, Alexis and Taylor and Victoria all came to class with their hair in braids. They hadn't told us that it was going to be a braid day. We always wore our hair in braids on the same day. At lunch when we asked them why they didn't tell us, they just looked at each other and giggled. I figured they had finally realized the truth I had kept hidden; I was a Pretty Girl, but I wasn't a Popular Girl. I was different. I was strange. So I decided to give up and be the Weird Girl again, and Sasha followed me.

On the bus, Sasha leans toward me and says, "You look cool."

"So do you," I say. I turn to face forward and I see a girl walk down the aisle wearing the blue and red uniform. Her blond hair swishes back and forth in a ponytail. I am still feeling the pang of rejection when I see that she is sitting down next to Finny. By the end of the month, they will be going out, and my mother will tell me that Finny met Sylvie Whitehouse on campus while he was at soccer practice and she was there for cheerleading.

"What do you think people will say?" Sasha says. I almost tell her not to be so dorky.

"I dunno," I say.

four

———

FOR THE FIRST FEW DAYS, Sasha and I eat lunch alone on what I start to call the Steps to Nowhere. The cement steps descend from the front courtyard down a hill to a field of grass and weeds that is used for nothing.

Alexis and the others wear their uniforms and smirk every time they see us, as if our new look is hostile to them. A new girl, Sylvie from St. John's Catholic School, sits at their table. Nearly all of the freshmen are from the same public middle school, but there is a sprinkling of these new Catholic kids whose parents could not afford the higher cost of the private high schools. These kids have been with the same classmates since kindergarten and are lost and awed in the vast sea of McClure High. It is awkward the first few days as everyone tries to figure their places out. Then, slowly, everyone slides into new alliances and a pattern begins to be set that will be followed for the rest of the year, possibly for the rest of high school.

Sasha has met a girl from St. John's who wears a crucifix and a skull on the same chain. They have gym class together and walk the track side by side for a few days before Sasha invites her to eat with us. Her name is Brooke and she brings her boyfriend Noah and her cousin Jamie with her. The next day, more people show up—so and so's friend, someone from somebody's class who seems cool. Soon we have a group hanging out on the Steps to Nowhere. Some leave after a few days, finding other groups; a few stay. By the end of the second week, a group of friends emerges from the Steps to Nowhere.

There are four girls and three boys in our group. Brooke and Noah are already together, and they are devoted to each other. They even look alike, brown hair and freckles, and when they laugh their eyes crinkle.

That leaves me, Sasha, and Angie for Jamie and Alex. Angie, blond and a little bit chubby, still has a crush on some guy from her old school. Alex has pretty eyes, but he is short and the goofy, silly type, still a little immature. I can see by the way she looks at him that Sasha is my competition for Jamie.

I got butterflies in my stomach the first time I saw Jamie's face; his eyes are green and fringed with impossibly long eyelashes. Above that, his hair is dark, a little curly, and very messy. He is tall, skinny, and pale.

Jamie is animated and funny and he smirks a lot. He reminds me of Puck from *A Midsummer Night's Dream*. Jamie leads the other boys into mischief that the girls sit back and watch from the Steps, giggling. They play football in the field with Brooke's shoe, toss balls of paper inside open classroom windows, and sing songs in a style mocking the school's a cappella group. Jamie throws his head back and laughs when his mischief turns out as planned. I watch him and think of Peter Pan telling Wendy that he just has to crow when he is pleased with himself.

Sasha and I each try to hold Jamie's attention in our own way. Sasha teases him and displays her tomboy cuteness. I am alternately demure and flirtatious. She runs down the steps and participates in the boys' games. I smile at his jokes and look up at him from under my eyelashes. Sasha holds her hand up for a high five. I cheer for him from the steps. It is a battle, but we never cut each other. Sasha and I know that when it is over we must still be friends.

Slowly, yet at the same time suddenly, because it happens in only a matter of days, I pull ahead of Sasha. She makes a valiant effort for a few lunches, but it becomes obvious that Jamie is now courting me. He sits next to me on the steps. He offers me the rest of his French fries. He tickles me. He smiles up at me on the steps while he and the boys are playing shoe-ball, and my stomach flutters. *Jamie. Jamie. James.* Jamie.

One Monday afternoon on the Steps to Nowhere, Jamie takes my hand in his, as if it has long been settled that it is his hand to take whenever he pleases, and everyone acts as if this is normal. I hold his hand and look down at the concrete steps to try to stop from grinning and giving away my feelings. Inside, I feel like I am trembling; on the outside, I stay as casual as he is. Of course we're together, of course. Of course.

That day, Alexis and the others look at me with interest when Jamie and I walk down the hall past them, then turn away as if they couldn't care less. But they have to have noticed. He is undeniably gorgeous. Jamie is a dark-haired Adonis, a Gothic prince. And he is now mine.

five

———

JAMIE WANTS TO GO FURTHER, and I tell him that I'm not ready. We've been together since the third week of school, but it's only early November, and I'm surprised that we're having this discussion already. A few days ago on the phone, he said that he loved me; I said I wasn't ready to say that back, and now, lying next to him and staring at the ceiling, I'm wondering if this is why he said it.

"Okay, then," he says, and takes my hand in his.

We're both fully clothed still, and dressed in the eccentric uniform adopted by our group. We're not goths or hipsters, just odd. The girls dye their hair unnatural colors and the boys make an effort to look like they just rolled out of bed. We all wear boots and bite our fingernails. I know that we're just conforming in a different way, but this is not something that I have said out loud. What binds our group together is the shared statement that we are different—and therefore somehow better—than all of the "normal" kids at school. Especially better than the popular kids.

Now that I've actually been to high school, I have no desire to be one of those girls with the ponytails and the pleated skirts. I am thrilled to finally be allowed to be myself, even if it is still under certain confines. With my new friends, being weird is a good thing, as long as it's the same weird as them.

"Your house is so weird," Jamie says.

I turn and look at him. This is the first time he has seen my house on the inside. My parents are at my dad's office's fall festival. Jamie was sick the night of my birthday party, and Mom still hasn't convinced me to have him over for dinner.

"What do you mean?" I say.

"It's so perfect," he says. "Even your room." It is not a compliment.

I look around at the lavender walls and white wicker furniture. I shrug.

"My mom decorated it," I say, a half lie. She decorated the rest of the house, and it is perfect, just like her. Everything coordinates; everything is arranged precisely so. It could be in a design magazine with my mother sitting at the kitchen table with a vase of white tulips, not a hair out of place as she pretends to read the paper. We did my room together. In the magazine, I would be in a cheerleader's uniform. I would be smiling.

"You should get some posters or something," Jamie says. I roll on my side and lay my head on his shoulder. I think to myself that he is handsome in that traditional tall-and-dark way. He says he wants to pierce his eyebrow and I've been trying to convince him not to.

"Yeah, I'll probably do that," I say. I really like Jamie, even if

I'm not sure that I love him yet. He's smart and quirky, and he's the leader of our group. As long as I am with him, I can never be evicted again. He rests his hand on the back of my head and twines his fingers in my hair.

"I love you, Autumn," he says. Downstairs, the back door slams. We both sit up. "Is your mom home?" he says. I'm not supposed to be alone with Jamie in the house, especially since my parents haven't met him. I'm still surprised that he was able to convince me to let him come over. I look at the clock. They still aren't supposed to be home for hours. I shake my head.

"It's probably Finny," I say.

"Are you serious?" he says.

"Yeah," I say. I've told Jamie of my sordid past, of the popularity and the ponytails. I told it as a tale of escape. How I narrowly missed becoming one of *them*. He knows too that my mom is best friends with Finny's. I told him that we played together when we were little. There had been an old picture of Finny and I on my dresser that somehow survived our separation in middle school; for nearly two years, I only spoke to Finny when I had to, but it never occurred to me to take the picture of us down until this morning when I was getting ready for Jamie to come over. I hid it in the top drawer of my dresser under my socks.

Everyone knows who Finny is now, except they don't call him that. Everyone at school calls him "Finn." He was the only freshman to make varsity soccer. He and some of his formerly geeky male friends have now been absorbed into The Clique, but they don't call themselves that anymore. Having a name for your group is way immature now. It's strange that only a few months ago I considered these girls my best friends, and even stranger that Finny is becoming friends with them.

We were barely able to avoid having each other over for our birthdays. In middle school, it might not have been as big a deal, except my parties were all girls and his all boys. This year, our mothers thought that if we were having a mixed group, then we should invite the other as well. What they didn't understand was that this year, Phineas and I are separated by something far greater than just growing apart. We move on completely different planes of existence and bringing one into the other's realm would cause a shifting in reality that would upset the entire structure of the universe. Finny was popular now. I was a misfit who had found other misfits to fit with.

They didn't talk about this in front of both of us; my mother argued with me about it, and when I told her it was absolutely impossible that he come, my mother sighed and said, "What is it with you two this year?" so I knew he was having the same argument with Aunt Angelina.

"Why would Finn Smith be in your house?" Jamie says.

"He's probably getting something," I say.

"Like what?" he says. I shrug. I don't know how to explain. "Let's go see." I don't argue with him, even though my stomach drops.

Jamie hangs back in the hallway as I look into the kitchen. Finny is crouched in front of the open refrigerator, his blond head hidden from me.

"Hi," I say. He looks over his shoulder at me. Until middle school, we were always the same height. Somehow during those years, he shot up past me and is now six foot. It is strange to see him looking up at me.

"Oh, hi," he says. He stands up and faces me from across the room. He blushes lightly. "Sorry, the back door was unlocked, but I didn't think anyone was home."

"I didn't go with them," I say.

"Oh," he says. "Do you have eggs?"

"Um, yeah." I cross the room and open the refrigerator door again. Finny steps aside for me. Before I bend over, I see his eyes focus outside the room, and I know he has seen Jamie lurking in the hallway. "How many do you need?" I say.

"I dunno," he says. "Mom just said to see if you had any eggs." I stand up and hand him the whole carton. "Thanks," he says.

"No problem," I say.

"See ya," Finny says.

"Bye." I stay where I am and listen to him clatter down the back steps before I go into the hall again.

"Wow," Jamie says. "You guys know each other."

"I told you we did," I say.

"Yeah, but that was weird," he says. I shrug again and walk back toward the stairs. "Does he do that a lot?"

"He lives next door," I say.

"Yeah but—never mind." We don't say anything until we are back in my room. I lie down on my flowered bedspread first and he scoots in next to me. We kiss for a long time, and after a while, I push his hands away and we lie together in silence. I wonder if this is what it feels like to be in love. I'm not sure. Suddenly Jamie speaks.

"It's almost like you were supposed to be one of them," he says. "But somehow you're not."

"What do you mean?" I say.

"I don't know," he says. "Your room and him."

"Well, I'm not," I say. I start to kiss him again. I'm kissing him to make him stop thinking about it. The room once again is silent except for our breathing.

I'm thinking about it though. I'm thinking about going with Aunt Angelina to pick up Finny after soccer practice. I'm thinking about the cheerleaders asking me if he is my boyfriend. I'm thinking about sitting next to Finny on the bus the first day of school.

We could have ended up together, I realize as Jamie begins to grind his pelvis against mine. He would have told me that he loved me by now, but he wouldn't have asked about sex. Not yet.

I can see all of this as if it has already happened, as if it was what happened. I know that it is accurate down to the smallest detail, because even with everything that did happen, I still know Finny, and I know what would have happened.

"I love you," I say to Jamie.

six

──

THE DOLL IS CRYING AGAIN.

"I'm never having sex," Sasha says. She kneels between the clothing racks and lifts the doll out of its carrier. The saleswoman folding clothes by the register looks over at us. Sasha lifts the doll's shirt up and inserts the key dangling from the bracelet around her wrist into the small of the baby's back. It continues crying.

"That's what they want you to say," I tell her over the noise. I glance over my shoulder at the saleswoman. "I think she thinks that it's real," I say. A few moments later, the doll's crying winds down. Sasha still holds it slung over her arm with the key twisted in it. If she takes it out before two minutes are up, it will start crying again, and if the computer chip inside the doll records that she ignored it, Sasha will get a failing grade for the project and at least a C– in her Family Science class. Sasha looks over at the saleswoman and shrugs.

"Well, it's working," she says. "I'm never going to have sex."

"Does Alex know?" I say. I turn back to the sale rack and continue to flip through the clothes.

"If it starts crying during the movie, I'll break it to him then," Sasha says, and I smile. The boys are supposed to be meeting us later. It's been a good semester. I like our new friends and my new clothes. I'm going to have straight A's and B's when school lets out for Christmas, and our agreement said Mom wouldn't be allowed to say anything about how I dress as long as my grades didn't slip.

I hold up a black faux corset with thick lace straps. Sasha raises her eyebrows.

"I could wear it with a cardigan," I say. This time she laughs at me, but I'm serious. I like the idea of mixing something sexy with something schoolmarmish. I walk over to the saleswoman. "I want to try this on," I say. She looks up at me and nods. I see her eyes flicker over to where Sasha kneels, strapping the doll back into its seat. I follow her over to the dressing rooms and watch her unlock the door. "Thank you," I say.

"How old are you girls?" she says to me with her back still turned.

"Fifteen," I say. Sasha's birthday isn't until March, but I give her my age anyway.

"Hmm," she says and turns to leave. Part of me hates this woman, and part of me wants to grab her sleeve and tell her that I'm actually a good kid.

"It's a doll," I say. She turns to face me.

"What?"

"It's a doll. A school project," I say. She narrows her eyes at me and walks away.

It's an hour later at a cheap jewelry store, while Sasha is looking for a necklace for her little sister, that I see the tiara. It's silver with clear rhinestones, the kind they used to crown the homecoming court just two months ago. We laughed and rolled our eyes at the tradition, but at the time, I'd wanted a crown, just not what it symbolized. I pick it up and slide the combs into my hair to hold it in place. I admire my head, turning it back and forth in the mirror, then step back to get the effect with jeans and a T-shirt. I like it.

"What are you going to do with that?" Sasha says, coming up behind me at the register.

"Wear it," I say, "every day."

"Hello, Your Highness," Jamie says to me when we meet them later outside the mall's movie theater. I'm thrilled to have his approval. I reach out and take his hand and he kisses me hello.

During the movie, the doll starts crying again, and Sasha and I meet each other's eyes and start laughing. We laugh so hard that I have to go out with her into the hall while she sticks the key in the doll. We stand in the hall laughing together, her with her doll and me with my tiara, and people passing by give us all strange looks.

———————————

It was a good time for us, first semester. It was the sort of happiness that fools you into thinking that there is still so much more, maybe even enough to laugh forever.

seven

"So why have you been wearing that tiara?" Finny says. The way he says it reminds me of the way he asked me why I dyed my hair, but for some reason it pisses me off this time.

"Because I like it," I say. It is Christmas Eve, and we are setting the dining room table with my mother's wedding china. My father is drinking scotch in front of the Christmas tree. The Mothers are in the kitchen.

"Okay, sorry," he says. I glance over him. He's wearing a red sweater that would look dorky on any other guy but makes him look like he should attend a private school on the East Coast and spend his summers rowing or something. He's walking around the table laying a napkin at every place. I follow behind with the silverware.

"Sorry," I say.

"It's cool," Finny says. It's hard to make him angry.

"It's just that I get asked that enough at school."

"Then why do you wear it?"

"Because I like it," I say, but this time I smile and he laughs.

At dinner, The Mothers let us have half a glass of wine each. I am secretly giddy to be treated like an adult, and the wine makes me sleepy. My father spends a lot of time talking to Finny about being the only freshman on the varsity team. He seems pleased to have something to talk about with one of us, as if Finny and I are interchangeable, as if his duty to either of us is the same. It's easy to understand why he would think that way; the only time he is ever home for an extended amount of time is for the holidays, and Finny and Aunt Angelina are always with us then. Perhaps he thinks Aunt Angelina is his other wife.

Mom and Aunt Angelina talk about every Christmas they can ever remember and compare them to this Christmas. This is what they do every year. Every year, it's the best Christmas ever.

I wish I could always believe that it is the best Christmas ever, but I can't, because I know when the best Christmas was. It was the Christmas when we were twelve, our last Christmas in elementary school.

It snowed the night before Christmas Eve that year. I had a new winter coat and mittens that matched my scarf. Finny and I walked down to the creek and stomped holes in the ice down to the shallow water. The Mothers made us hot chocolate and we played Monopoly until my dad came home from the office and nothing mattered except that it was Christmas.

It hasn't snowed for Christmas since then, and every year there has been more and more other things that matter, and it has felt less and less like Christmas.

Jamie is spending Christmas with his grandmother in Wisconsin, and I am pleased to be missing him. It is a dull ache that I enjoy prodding.

Jamie, I think, *Jamie, Jamie, James,* and I remember his tongue in my mouth. I don't like it as much as I thought I would, but I'm getting used to it. I tell him that I love him all the time now, and he hasn't said anything else about having sex. He gave me a new journal for Christmas, and even though I haven't filled up my old one yet, I'm going to start it on New Year's. He'll be home by then and we'll spend it together. *Jamie, Jamie, James.*

"Autumn," my father says, "are you the Sugar Plum Fairy this year?" There is a silence at the table as I try to understand what he means. Then I see my mother bite her lip, and I realize he is talking about my tiara. He has not noticed that I have worn this tiara every day for the past three weeks. I take a breath.

"Yeah," I say. "Just thought I'd make the dinner a little more festive." He smiles at me and takes a bite of ham. He is pleased with himself. My mother says something to Finny, and slowly the conversation at the table resumes. After a few minutes, I excuse myself and go to my room.

I've bought some posters: Jimi Hendrix rolling on stage with his guitar, Ophelia drowned and looking up at the sky, a black-and-white photo of a tree without leaves. I like the effect they have on the lavender-and-white room, like the corset and the cardigan, like my tiara with ripped jeans. I don't look at the posters though. I lie down on the bed and look at the ceiling.

When someone knocks on my door, I pretend I'm asleep. A moment later, the door opens anyway and Finny sticks his head in.

"Hey," he says. "They said to tell you that we're done eating."

"Okay," I say, but I do not move. I am waiting for him to leave. He doesn't though; he keeps standing there like I'm supposed to do something. I do nothing. I look at the ceiling until he speaks again.

"It really sucks that he hasn't noticed," Finny says.

"At least my father's around for Christmas," I say. His expression changes only for an instant. Then it is as if a door has closed again.

"I didn't mean it like that," I say.

"It's fine," he says. "Everybody is waiting downstairs."

After he leaves, I lie in bed a little longer. I think about telling Finny how I don't care, and how it hurts, and how it doesn't really matter to me but I wish it mattered to my dad. I imagine that suddenly Finny is holding me and telling me it is okay, and he's saying that you can feel more than one way about a person. We go downstairs and he holds my hand while we watch *It's a Wonderful Life* together on the couch. When he and Aunt Angelina leave, he kisses me good night on the porch, and we see that it is starting to snow.

I swing my legs over the side of the bed, wipe my eyes, and go downstairs.

eight

THE PARTY IS AT MY house, because it is big and so my parents can meet Jamie before they go to my dad's office's New Year's Eve party.

Jamie was good with my parents. He shook hands, made eye contact, and didn't smell like any kind of smoke. Dad was satisfied. Mom was pleased, and I have a nagging feeling that it is because Jamie is so good-looking, as if she can now rest assured that I am not too uncool at school.

Sasha, Brooke, and Angie are going to spend the night. Alex's mom is going to pick up the boys after midnight. Until then, we are alone.

Brooke has stolen a champagne bottle from her parents' party. It's wrapped up in her sleeping bag, and it will only be after it is too late that we will realize it was safe to put it in the fridge.

We eat pizza and watch a movie. The movie is not great. The boys crack jokes and try to be the one to make the girls laugh the most. Jamie is winning, of course. I lean back in the leather couch and feel like a consort.

Afterward, we sit around and talk, and everyone is trying to be funny now. Mostly we talk about the other kids at school. Eventually the conversation turns to sex, as I am learning all conversations eventually will. None of us have had sex, and we are young enough that this is not embarrassing; it is simply a fact that time will remedy. We tease each other and exchange stories of who at school has done what where. We laugh and throw pillows at each other. Sex is something to joke about. Sex seems as possible, as real, as the world ending at midnight.

Midnight. I am as excited for the kiss with Jamie as if it were our first. I've only been kissed at midnight once before, and I am eager for this kiss to replace that kiss, to be a kiss that I will remember forever.

At eleven-fifty, we raid the kitchen for pots and pans. At eleven fifty-five, we stand at the front door and ask Jamie for the time every thirty seconds. For some reason we have decided that his phone is the most reliable.

And then, as it always does, the moment comes and passes, and even as part of me is once again surprised that I feel no different than I did a moment before, I am running across the lawn with the others, banging my pot and looking up at the stars and illegal fireworks my neighbors are setting off. We scream as if we have heard wonderful news. We shout a happy new year to each other and the trees and the others we cannot see out there, shouting at the sky like us. We scream as if this display of joy will frighten all our fears away, as if we already know nothing bad will happen to us this year, and are happy for it.

"Jamie, come kiss me!" I shout. I toss my pot and wooden spoon on the grass and hold my arms out to him. He swaggers over and pulls me to him by my hips. The others bang their pots. It is a good kiss, just like all our other kisses. The others drop their pots and exchange their own kisses. I pick up my pot and spoon again, and during the relative quiet before we begin to bang again, I realize we are not alone.

Thirty feet away, Finny and Sylvie and Alexis and Jack and all the others are banging on their pots and laughing at the sky too. Finny and I meet eyes, and he looks both ways before waving at me surreptitiously. I wave back, my hand no higher than my hip, terrified one of his friends will think I am waving to them. At that exact moment, everyone else seems to notice the others, for we are immediately in a competition that no one will ever acknowledge out loud. We are having more fun than they are. We love each other more. We are louder. We have more to look forward to this year than they do. We scream and shout and kiss some more. The boys begin their a cappella impression, and we hold out our arms and spin in the street.

And of course, we are having so much fun that we don't even notice them standing over there.

Then Jamie does something that proves once again why he is our leader.

"Time for the champagne!" he shouts, and we scream a chorus of agreement that drowns the street in our elation. We run up the lawn laughing before they can retaliate. We are so over banging pots in the street; we have way cooler things to do inside.

We drink the warm champagne out of water glasses and act like it is no big deal.

Tipsy for the first time in our lives, we begin to dare one another to kiss. Brooke and Angie kiss. I kiss Noah. Sasha kisses Jamie. And then we decide that each of us must kiss all of the others in order to seal our eternal bonds of friendship. We giggle and cluster together. Did I kiss you? Have we kissed yet? Oh my God, I kissed Alex twice.

Afterward we wash all the glasses twice. Jamie and the boys take on the manly task of smashing the bottle on the driveway and sweeping up the pieces. When they come back inside, we all take breath strips and stand together in the kitchen. The girlfriends stand with their boyfriends in preparation of the impending separation. We hold hands and lay our heads on their shoulders, sighing how sleepy we are. The boyfriends smile at us indulgently. Angie sits at the kitchen table and endures as she always does.

"Hey, did Finn Smith wave at us?" Noah says. Brooke opens her eyes and lifts her head up.

"Yeah, I saw that," she says.

"He was probably waving at Autumn," Sasha says.

"Why?" Angie and Noah say at the same time.

"They used to be, like, best friends," Sasha says. Everyone looks at me.

"He lives next door," I say. "Our moms are friends. Really close friends."

"They spend Thanksgiving and Christmas together," Sasha says. "Every year."

"Oh my God, that is weird," Brooke says.

"We're like cousins," I say. "If Jamie was one of the popular kids, you'd still have to see him, right, Brooke?"

"Me?" Jamie says. Everyone laughs.

"Still, it is weird," Sasha says. "For a little while in middle school, you guys still hung out sometimes, right? I mean you guys could still be friends even—"

"Hey, I'm not the one who tried out for cheerleading," I say, and I am no longer the center of attention.

"You did what?" Alex says, as if she has betrayed him. Sasha begs for mercy, pleading her youth, her inexperience, her naiveté.

"I knew not what I did," she says, her hands clasped in front of her. We listen to her case, and after she has been sufficiently melodramatic, Jamie pronounces her forgiven and we all hug her as Alex's mom knocks on the door.

The subject of our pasts is dropped for the night, and we unroll our sleeping bags and huddle together on the living room floor. We talk about our boys and which of the popular girls is the snottiest. We all disagree, each choosing the one we feel is our counterpart.

"Sylvie always looks so smug," I say. "I *hate* that."

"But Victoria glares at me," Angie says. "I mean, seriously. Like this." We all laugh at her impression, which resembles Popeye more than Victoria. Sasha and I are even more delighted, because we had both always thought her grimace was funny, even when she was our friend.

My parents come home before we have fallen asleep. They are

arguing and trying to be quiet about it, and the other girls pretend not to notice. After a few minutes, I hear my father go upstairs. A moment later, my mother pokes her head into the living room.

"Did you girls have a good New Year's?" she asks brightly. All the girls nod and say, "Yes, ma'am." She looks directly at me. "Did you, honey?" she says. I nod, but she looks at me strangely and leaves us.

Sasha probably would have added, if I had not stopped her, that Finny and I used to spend every New Year's together too.

nine

WINTER IS ALWAYS A DEAD time for me. I wish I were like the trees. I wish I could feign death, or at least sleep through the winter. My tiara continues its reign as a permanent fixture on my head. Before long, no one asks me about it anymore.

Second semester I trade gym for health class. On the first day the teacher, Mrs. Adams, tells us that she used to be a professional water-skier and leaves out the part about how she ended up a professional health teacher. It becomes apparent after the first month that every disease we study, she has known someone who has had it. Most of them were on the water-skiing team. Angie has the class with me, and Mrs. Adams becomes the frequent subject of our lunch conversations.

Walking to and waiting for the bus is now my personal hell. I stamp my feet, keep my head low and my shoulders hunched, and quietly hate the world for being so cold. I am careful to always stand with my back to Sylvie and Finny. I have never told anyone how much I hate seeing the two of them together; they would make too big of a deal out of it and think it meant something stupid. I just don't like her, and they annoy me.

Some mornings, I think maybe Sylvie is talking for me to overhear. When it's really cold out, I think the idea is ridiculous and that I am stupid for even thinking it. It's cold, and nothing matters except getting inside that bus and getting to Jamie.

"So I was thinking this weekend we should go to that party—you know which one I mean."

"Yeah."

"I mean, everyone is going to be there, so we should really go."

"Is Jack going?"

"*Everybody* is going, Finn."

"Class," Mrs. Adams tells us, "eating disorders are not something to joke about. I've seen what they can do to a person. One girl on my water-skiing team had anorexia. Another was bulimic. They were such beautiful girls, but these are not pretty diseases."

Jamie and I talk on the phone every night before we go to sleep. We talk about getting married someday and what sort of house we'll have and how many children. It surprises me how much he wants these things, such normal things, and nothing else.

Sometimes I am disappointed with love. I thought that when

you were in love, it would always be right there, staring you in the face, reminding you every moment that you love this person. It seems that it isn't always like that. Sometimes I know that I love Jamie, but I don't feel it, and I wonder what it would be like to be with someone else.

I love him the most when we fight and I am scared that he will leave me. After we fight, I want so much to be close to him, and the next day I want his hand in mine every minute. Sometimes he loves me more than I love him, and he wants me to pay attention to him, but I wish he would leave me alone so that I could go back to reading or talking to Angie about Mrs. Adams. Sometimes we both love each other a lot and it's hard to hang up at night, and I wish it could always be like that.

"Class, I was young once too," Mrs. Adams says. "I know about the pressures to have sex. Not just from your partner, but from your friends and the media and even your own body. It can be hard. But please, please be careful. I know you think that no one you know has an STD, but that's how they spread. I remember having to hold the hands of several of my teammates after they found out that they had an STD. One girl got herpes, and, as we've learned, that's one that never goes away. Imagine having that forever."

One morning, it sounds like Sylvie and Finny are fighting. They whisper back and forth, and Finny is suddenly saying a whole lot more than "Yeah."

Now that I want to hear what they are saying, I can't. I glance over my shoulder at them. Finny is standing next to her, glaring at the ground. Sylvie is facing him and clinging to his side as she looks up at his face. From a distance, it would be hard to tell that they're fighting.

"Please," I see more than hear her say. He shakes his head and doesn't reply.

Jamie gives me a promise ring for Valentine's Day. All day, whenever I see someone I know, I rush up to show them my hand and tell them that I have the best boyfriend ever. He gives me another tiara too. This one is gold and has more curlicues.

To everyone's surprise, spring comes early that year.

ten

―――

It is the moment I reach my door that I realize I left my house keys in my locker. It's Thursday, the day my mother goes to see her therapist and then to the gym. She won't be home until five-thirty. It's two-thirty in the afternoon in early March. The snow is gone, but it is still cold out, and it's about to rain.

I stand facing my door for a moment. I have two options. One is to stay on the porch, hope the rain doesn't blow on me, and later try to explain to my mother why I didn't take the second option.

―――――――

"I'm locked out," I say as he opens the door. Even so, a flicker of confusion passes over his face.

"Oh. Okay," Finny says. He steps aside and lets me come in. I'm wearing Doc Martens and a new pink tiara. He's wearing khakis and a sweater. He's kicked off his shoes already. His socks are green. I nearly say something. What kind of boy wears green socks?

"What time does your mom come home?" I ask.

"Four," he says. His mother has a spare key. "Where's your mom?"

"It's therapy day," I say. I follow him into the living room, where he sits down on the couch. Aunt Angelina's house is always just a little bit messy, the lived-in kind of messy where books get piled into corners, and throw pillows and shoes seem to be everywhere. Aunt Angelina has never quite finished decorating either; on the wall above Finny's head, there are three different samples of paint spread in large splotches. They've been there as long as I can remember.

"What do you want to watch?" Finny says. He picks up the remote and looks at me.

"I'm going to read," I say. I had been planning when I got home to edit a poem I started during history class, but there is no way I could take out my notebook and start writing here, in front of him.

I sit down in the armchair across the room. It's bright blue, and for years Aunt Angelina has been going to have it reupholstered, as soon as she decides on a color scheme for the room. When I hear Finny start flipping through the channels, I take my book out of my bag and glance up at him.

Finny looks like a Renaissance painting of an angel or like he could belong to some modern royal family. His hair stays blond all winter and looks like gold in the summer. He blushes a lot, partly because he is so fair, partly because he's shy and gets embarrassed easily. I know that Sylvie must have approached him first and she was definitely the one who asked him out.

42

Finny never tells anyone how he is feeling; you just have to know him well enough to understand when he is sad or scared. Today his expression does not tell me how he feels about me being over here. Either he couldn't care less, or he could be annoyed.

We see each other frequently, but we rarely are alone together. And even though we will still sometimes side together against The Mothers over an issue, we never have anything to say to each other that isn't superficial.

Years ago, Finny and I strung string and two cups across our bedroom windows so we could talk to each other at night. After we stopped talking, we never took it down, but finally the string rotted away.

Finny's cell phone rings, and he leaves the room without saying anything.

I look down at my book and begin to read. The rain has started, and I am distracted by the sound of it. Finny used to ask me to go outside with him to save the worms on the sidewalk. It bothered him to see them drying and writhing on the pavement the day after rain. He hated the idea of anyone—anything—ever being sad or hurt.

When we were eight, we heard his mother sobbing in her bedroom after a breakup, and Finny pushed tissues under the door. When we were eleven, he punched Donnie Banks in the stomach for calling me a freak. It was the only fight he ever got in, and I think Mrs. Morgansen only gave him detention because she had to. Aunt Angelina didn't even punish him.

"Autumn is already here," I hear him say in the next room. There is a pause. "She got locked out." There is a longer silence. "Okay," he says, and then, "I love you too."

This time he looks at me when he comes back in the room.

"You guys are having dinner over here tonight, so Mom says you might as well just stay."

"But my dad's supposed to be home tonight," I say. Finny shrugs. My dad cancels family dinners frequently enough that I suppose it isn't worth pointing out to me. I shrug back and look down at my book.

When I look up again, it is because I hear Aunt Angelina coming in through the back door.

"Hello?" she calls out.

"In here," Finny shouts back. He mutes the TV and his mom walks into the room.

"Hi, kids," she says. Her long patchwork skirt still swirls around her ankles even when she comes to a stop. She brings her scent of patchouli oil into the room with her.

"Hi," we say. Aunt Angelina looks at me and smiles with the left side of her mouth. It's the same crooked smile Finny has when he's feeling playful.

"Autumn, why are you wearing a Jimmy Carter campaign shirt?'" she asks.

"I dunno," I say. "Why is your son wearing green socks?"

She looks back at Finny. "Phineas, are you wearing green socks?"

He looks down at his feet. "Well, yeah."

"Where did you get green socks from?"

"They were in my sock drawer."

"I never bought you green socks."

"They were in there."

"This all sounds very suspicious to me," I say.

"Agreed. Finny, Autumn and I are going into the kitchen, and when we come back, you better have an explanation for your socks." Finny and I glance at each other in surprise. I look away and set my book down. Aunt Angelina waits for me at the door. When I reach her, she lays one hand on my shoulder as she walks with me into the kitchen.

"Honey, your mom isn't having a good day," she says quietly. "Your dad had to cancel dinner tonight, and it really upset her."

To other kids, this wouldn't sound like a big deal. But when your mom has been hospitalized twice for depression, you learn to read between the lines.

"Okay," I say.

Last time Mom was in the hospital, I was in sixth grade. I spent two weeks living with Aunt Angelina and Finny. At the time, it was fun. Everyone kept telling me that my mom was going to be okay. They told me about chemical imbalances and how it was a sickness like any other, and that Mom would get better. So I accepted it, and every night Finny snuck into the guest bedroom and we would draw pictures on each other's backs with our fingers and then try to guess what they were.

I doubted it would be like that this time. Any of it. For one thing, this time I'll ask why, if it's a chemical imbalance, Dad seems to be causing it.

"She'll be fine. We just all need to be really understanding tonight, okay?"

"I get it," I say. She's saying not to stage a teenage rebellion at the dinner table.

"Your mother loves you very, very much," she says.

"I get it," I say again. "It's okay."

"All right," she says, and she squeezes my shoulder. Despite her promise to find out more about the mysterious socks, Aunt Angelina does not follow me back into the living room. When I come back in, Finny mutes the TV and watches me sit back down.

"Everything okay?" he says.

"Yup," I say. "Isn't it always?"

He laughs, a quick exhalation through his nose, then his face becomes serious again, and he cocks his head to the side. He's asking me if I want to talk about it. I shake my head and he looks away again quickly. The sound comes back on the TV and I pick up my book again.

———————

Back in sixth grade, he had to sneak into the guest bedroom because we weren't allowed to sleep in the same bed anymore. We hardly ever broke the rules and I was nervous every time he came, but I never told him not to. The truth of the matter is, if they hadn't suggested it, it never would have occurred to me that things could be different between us just because we were older. We lay on our stomachs side by side and we only touched to draw on each other's

46

backs. I drew flowers and hearts and animals. Finny drew rocket ships and soccer balls.

On my last night there, Aunt Angelina came and stood in the doorway. She was silhouetted in the darkness by the light in the hallway. I suppose she could see us better than we could see her.

"Phineas, what are you doing in here?" she said.

"Autumn is sad," he said. It wasn't until he said it that I realized it was true. There was a long silence. Finny lay still next to me. I watched her dark form in the doorway.

"Fifteen minutes," she said, and then she left. It was Finny's turn to draw on my back. I closed my eyes and concentrated on the shapes he traced over me. It always tickled, but I never laughed.

"Two houses," I said. "And four people."

"It's our houses," he said. "And our family."

My mother skips the gym and comes straight home. Aunt Angelina orders pizza, and we eat in front of the TV, something we never do at my house. Afterward, I claim to have homework and go home. My mother stays. She says she'll be home later.

When I get home, I call Jamie to tell him everything. I cry, and I tell him that I'm scared. I tell him that I found out that they only hospitalize you if you're suicidal. I tell him it's supposed to be genetic.

Jamie tells me that he will always love me and take care of me, no matter what. He says it over and over and over and over again.

47

eleven

———

THE FIELD AT THE BOTTOM of the Steps to Nowhere floods with the spring rain. The boys walk around this impermanent lake together, threatening to push each other in or pretending they are about to jump in to make us scream.

We hear that hardly anyone ever goes to the Spring Fling, so we decide that it must be cool and that we will go.

The girls all come over to my house to get ready. The dance is casual, and we're all wearing jeans. I'm going to wear the corset I bought with Sasha last fall.

Brooke wants to do everyone's makeup, so we take turns sitting for her while the other girls watch. I go last, and it's during my turn that she says it.

"Autumn," she says, "I'm not going to spend the night tonight."

"Why?" we all chorus. Everyone's overnight stuff, including Brooke's, is all clustered together by my bed. Brooke stops putting foundation on me and takes a deep breath.

"Because Noah's parents are out of town, and I'm going to his place," she says. There is a moment of silence.

"Are you…" Angie says, her voice trailing off. Brooke looks around at all of us, and nods. We scream and Brooke covers her face with her hands.

"Guys!" she says.

"Oh my God," Sasha says.

"Why?" I say, and then wonder if it was the wrong thing to say. Brooke uncovers her face and smiles.

"Because I love him," she says, "and it just feels right."

"Awww," Angie says.

"Wow," Sasha says. "Now I'm going to be thinking about it all night." We laugh.

"We're going to walk to his house after the dance. Tell your mom I got sick and left early, okay?" Brooke says. I nod. "I'll come get my stuff tomorrow."

"You're going to tell us everything, right?" Angie says.

"Well…" she says.

"You have to!" Sasha says. We all agree that she has to.

When the boys arrive, we all file downstairs together and my mom takes our picture before we all pile into the van to go to the school. Jamie looks hot, and I tell him in his ear on the way there. He smiles and doesn't say anything, but when I squeeze his hand, he squeezes back.

Out of fifteen hundred students, about sixty show up for the Spring Fling. We have the floor to ourselves, and we dance together in the middle and shout requests at the DJ, who actually complies. Because there are so few students, nobody stops us when we start to dance on the tables. It doesn't matter how we dance because there is hardly anyone to see us, and our dance moves and requests become more and more ridiculous. We make a conga line. We do the Macarena when the "Electric Boogie" is blasting out of the speakers. We exhaust ourselves dancing, drink some punch, and then go dance again. At the first slow song, Jamie asks our principal, Mrs. Black, to dance, and she does amid cheers from all across the room.

We congratulate ourselves and agree: the Spring Fling is cool because nobody goes.

It's a long time before the DJ plays another slow song. By then my heart is pounding, and I'm so out of breath I practically collapse into Jamie. He looks so handsome that I get butterflies in my stomach looking at him. I wrap my arms around his neck and we sway to the music.

"I love you," I say, and I'm not saying it to remind myself that I do; at this moment I can feel it.

"Love you too," he says.

"Did you hear about Brooke and Noah?" I ask. Jamie rolls his eyes and sighs.

"Yeah, he was bragging about it all afternoon," he says.

"Really?" I ask. "What did he say?" He shrugs.

"He just said that they were gonna do it."

"And?"

"And what?"

"What else did he say?"

"He didn't say anything else. He just said they were gonna do it tonight."

"Well, that's not bragging"

"Yes, it is."

"Why?"

"What are you talking about?" Jamie says. "I just told you that he was bragging about it all afternoon."

"I just don't understand how he was bragging all afternoon if all he said was that they were going to do it. That's like, *one* sentence."

"Never mind," Jamie says. "I don't want to talk about it."

"Why not?"

"I just don't, okay?"

"But why—"

"Autumn, I don't want to talk about them having sex, okay?"

"Fine," I say. We finish the song in silence. Afterward, I ask Angie to go to the bathroom with me. We talk about our hair and how much fun we are having, and a little bit about Brooke, of course.

"It's kind of weird, isn't it?" she says. "I mean that Brooke won't be a virgin tomorrow. It doesn't seem real."

"Yeah, I know," I say. We go back outside. I look at Jamie from a distance and try to bring back the good feeling I had before, but I can't. I wonder if when Brooke kisses Noah, if she sometimes imagines that he's someone else. I wonder if when she touches herself, he is the only one she ever thinks about.

I tell myself relationships are hard work. No one is perfect. There's no such thing as happily ever after.

On Monday, on the Steps to Nowhere, Brooke says that afterward you don't feel any different, except you love him so much more than before.

"But you're not like, 'Oh my God, I'm not a virgin anymore.'"

"Really?" I say. I think that would be the only thought I could think afterward. I think that I would look at myself in the mirror and say it over and over again.

"Yeah," she says, "It's just like—" She doesn't finish her sentence; she just looks down at the boys standing by the water. They are seeing who can throw rocks the farthest. I watch Jamie win. I imagine it just feeling right with him.

"Did it hurt?" Angie says.

"Oh yeah," Brooke says.

twelve

"So what do you know about Sylvie?" my mother says. I take a large spoonful of ice cream into my mouth and regard her. We are sitting on the outside patio of the Train Stop Creamery, the town's only ice cream parlor. It is the first hot day of May.

"Finny's girlfriend?" I say. My mother nods. "I dunno," I say. "Why?"

"No reason," she says.

"You just started wondering about her all of a sudden?"

"Well," she says.

"What?" I say.

"Angelina and I were just talking about her the other day, and I wondered what you thought."

"She's okay," I say. "I don't really know her." We eat quietly for a while before I ask. "Does Aunt Angelina not like her?"

"Oh, she likes her, but I think she's never gotten over the disappointment that you and Finny didn't end up together." She nudges me under the table with her foot.

"Mom!" I say. I glare at her. "I have a boyfriend."

"I know, I know," she says. "We just always thought that's what was going to happen."

"Well, it didn't," I say. "We don't even hang out with the same people."

"I know," she says again. She sighs. I roll my eyes and eat my ice cream.

Whenever I wonder what it would be like if Finny and I were together, I never imagine that there is anyone else with us. I don't like to think I would have had to become a cheerleader to be Finny's friend again. In my imagination, Finny isn't in my group, and I'm not in his; it's just the two of us, like it used to be. At school, we eat lunch together and he walks me to my classes. We do our homework together. He takes me to art films in the city. At night, we lie on our backs in the grass and talk. We burn CDs for each other. We pass notes. We hold hands at the bus stop. I imagine adoring him without question. I am certain that I would if I were in love with him.

"Is Aunt Angelina out somewhere with Finny, asking what he thinks of Jamie?" I ask. My mother smiles.

"Yes, sweetie. It's a conspiracy," she says.

"Well, if you two were talking about Sylvie, why not Jamie?"

"I like Jamie," she says. She spoons her last bit of ice cream out. "I can tell he's a good kid. His parents seem like good people."

"But you guys aren't sure if Sylvie is a good kid?" I say. I'm pleased with the direction the conversation is going, but I don't want to show it.

"Is she?" my mother says.

If the rumors are true, Sylvie is not a good kid. There is a story about her and Alexis making out in a Ferris wheel while all the guys watched, and the whole group supposedly gets drunk sometimes. They are good students though, so most adults don't suspect them of anything.

It's hard for me to imagine Finny drunk, or liking a girl who makes out with another girl for entertainment. I wonder if he's still shy when he is drinking, if he blushed when he watched Sylvie kissing Alexis.

I wonder what Aunt Angelina would do if she knew about Finny's friends.

"Oh," I say, "Sylvie is a cheerleader. She's on student council and the honor roll. She's too busy being perfect to be shooting up heroin on the side."

"All right, all right," my mother says. We stand and throw away our plastic bowls and spoons and walk out to the car.

I imagine Finny loving Sylvie, but sometimes wishing she were different, the way I sometimes wish Jamie were different. I imagine him being aroused as she made out with Alexis in front of everyone and afterward asking her never to do it again. I imagine him feeling free and confident as he drinks with his friends, feeling included with them, a part of something.

In the car, I roll down the window and feel the warm night air blowing on my face. My mother is quiet next to me. I wonder where Aunt Angelina and Finny are tonight, what they are talking about.

55

I imagine Finny and I sneaking out of our houses to fool around down at the creek. I imagine leaving my blinds open for him when I change clothes. I imagine his hand moving up my thigh as we watch a movie with a blanket thrown over our laps.

I imagine that even though we were friends as children, we wouldn't have stayed children just because we were together.

thirteen

THE LAST DAY OF SCHOOL feels as if it is truly the last, as if I am being set free not for three months but thirty years. My scary finals are all over; all I have today are my English and health finals. I'm taking honors English in the fall, and the health final should be simple. Drugs and sex are bad; water-skiing is good.

There is hugging and squealing on the Steps to Nowhere. Sasha is the only one studying; the rest of us are more or less free. Jamie kisses me loudly and wraps his arm over my shoulders.

"Ugh, I cannot wait for today to be over," he says.

"Me neither," Noah says.

"You still haven't signed my yearbook yet, babe," I say. This is the third day I've asked him. He keeps saying he will do it later.

"I know, I know. Give it to me," he says. I hand it to him and he opens his book bag.

"Why don't you just sign it now?" I say.

"I don't feel like it right now. I'll give it to you at lunch," he says. He shoves my yearbook into his bag and zips it closed.

"Fine," I say. I've found it's just easier to let him have his way on all the little things that shouldn't matter.

"Hey, Mom says she can drive for our girls' day tomorrow," Angie says.

"Yay," Sasha says between flash cards.

"Yeah, well, you know that we're going to have a boys' day tomorrow too," Alex says.

"Okay," I say.

"And we're going to do boy stuff that you aren't invited to," Jamie says.

"All right, whatever that means," Brooke says. "But we're just going to the mall."

"Hey, guys, let's go to the mall," Noah says.

"No," Sasha says, "you cannot go to the mall. We are."

"We can get our nails done," Alex says.

"And our hair. I need highlights," Jamie says.

"Oh, shut up," Brooke says. "You don't even know what highlights are."

"Why is it you guys get weird every time we do something alone?" Angie says.

"Yeah, do you think we're plotting against you?" I ask.

"No," Jamie says, but for once neither he nor any of the others have a comeback. The boys start talking about going to Noah's tomorrow to play some video game.

I love you, Jamie's note says. *You are the best thing that ever happened to me. All I want from life is to marry you and have our family. Have a good summer. With me.*

I close my yearbook and stuff it back in my book bag. Jamie didn't give it to me at lunch; it's now the end of the day. He asked me not to read it in front of the others, so I told everybody I had to go to the bathroom before we walked to Jamie's house. I flush the toilet even though I didn't use it, because Brooke came to the bathroom with me. When I come out of the stall, she is staring at herself in the mirror. I wash my hands and look over at her.

"Hey, are you okay?" I say. It takes her a moment to answer.

"Yeah," she says, "Sorry, I just zoned out for a second there."

"It's cool," I say. "I can't believe that we're not freshmen anymore. Can you?"

"No, not really," she says.

At Jamie's pool, we play chicken-fight, climbing on the boys' shoulders and knocking each other down. Jamie and I win, and he parades around with me on his shoulders, then suddenly drops me to make me scream. I pout; he kisses me and then dunks me. A dunking war breaks out that the boys win even though there are more of us. They high five and we roll our eyes.

We lean up against the wall in the shallow end and the boys wrap their arms around our bare waists. The sun is warm on our heads and the water. It is summer and we are free.

The pizzas arrive, and we lay around eating by the pool until we think we'll never have to eat again. We decide to ignore the one-hour rule and jump back in. The boys begin to wrestle and we stand to the side and watch them. After a while, I get bored, and I'm thinking I'll try to get Jamie alone in his room, when I realize that Brooke and Angie have been gone for a long time. I go inside and pad barefoot across the kitchen. The bathroom door is closed. I lean my head against it. I can hear them talking on the other side. I knock.

"Hey, what's going on?" I ask. There is a pause, and then I hear their voices again. Angie opens the door a crack.

"Are you alone?" she asks.

"Yeah," I say. She opens the door enough for me to squeeze in.

Brooke is sitting on the bathtub. Her eyes are red, and she is dressed in her shorts and shirt again.

"Oh my God, what's wrong?" I ask. Brooke looks down at our feet on the tile floor.

"I cheated on Noah," she says. Angie is leaning against the sink with her arms crossed. This is not new information for her. Brooke loses herself in her tears again. I sit down next to her.

"With who?" I ask. Brooke continues to cry.

"It was her lab partner, Aiden," Angie says. "They've sort of been friends all semester."

"Aiden Harris or Aiden Schumacker?"

"Aiden Harris," Angie says.

"We just had fun together in class," Brooke says. "I didn't think it meant anything."

"What happened?" I say.

"He invited me over to study for the final," Brooke says. "He kissed me, and for a moment, I let him."

"That's all?"

"I stopped him and left, and I wasn't going to ever tell Noah," Brooke says, "but I hate keeping secrets from him." She begins to cry again. Someone knocks on the bathroom door.

"Hey, guys," Sasha says. "What's going on?"

We let her in and tell her the story.

"It was just one kiss?" Sasha asks. Brooke nods.

There is a knock on the door.

"Hey," Jamie's voice says. "What are you guys doing in there?"

"Are you plotting something?" Alex says.

Sasha opens the door and sticks her head out.

"Look, guys," she says, "we have a really serious situation in here, so cut it out."

"What do you mean?" Noah says. Next to me, Brooke's cries turn into a wail. "Hey, what's going on? Brooke?"

"Brooke, honey, do you want to talk to him?" I ask. Brooke wipes her nose and nods. Angie and I instantly stand at attention and crowd behind Sasha.

"She wants to talk to him," I say. Sasha opens the door just enough so we can file out and Noah can slide in. We shut the door behind him and turn to face the boys.

"We should go outside," Angie says.

"Yeah," I say.

"What's going on? Is Brooke okay?" Jamie asks.

"We can't tell you," I say. The back door closes behind us and we walk to the edge of the pool.

"Why not?"

"Because you're guys," Sasha says. She, Angie, and I sit down and dangle our legs in the pool.

"Noah's in there," he says.

"It involves Noah," I say.

"How does it involve Noah?" Alex asks.

"We can't tell you that," Angie says. I nod.

"This is stupid. She's my cousin," Jamie says.

"I know," I say. "But we can't tell you."

"It isn't our place," Sasha says. All three of us nod to that.

"Are they breaking up?" Alex asks.

"Maybe," Sasha says.

"Oh my God, I hope not," I say.

"They won't," Angie says.

"Okay, this really is stupid," Jamie says. He and Alex go and sit on the patio chairs. The girls and I begin to whisper. After a while, Noah comes out and asks for Angie. She comes out alone a few minutes later.

"Is she okay?" I ask. Angie nods.

"Yeah," she says. "She told Noah. They're gonna walk home and talk about it."

We swing our legs in the water and make waves, but nobody really talks. We've said everything we have to say to each other, and we still won't tell the boys. Finally, after half an hour, we gather our stuff to walk home. Alex stays behind with Jamie.

When I kiss Jamie goodbye, he does not hug me back, and he looks away afterward.

"Bye," he says.

"Bye, love you," I say. "I'll call you."

"Okay."

<hr />

That night we fight on the phone. Even though I cry, he still does not forgive me until I tell him Brooke's secret. He is instantly sweet again, and we don't talk about the fight.

At the mall the next day, Brooke tells us about her conversation with Noah while we eat in the food court. She says that Noah has forgiven her, and that Noah said he knew she was sorry and that he hated seeing her cry.

"I can't believe how much he loves me," she says. She looks down at her plate of French fries and smiles.

I start to wonder what Jamie would have said if it had been us, and I push the thought away. Nothing like that would ever happen to us.

fourteen

WE SPEND THE FOURTH OF July at the fair in the park. Angie's Hazelwood boyfriend is with us, and we are pleased to be a complete set of four couples. We wander around the scant stalls and booths and listen to the music. Every time we see someone from school we stop so that Angie can introduce Mike. Finny and Sylvie are at the fair too, but we do not stop for them. The fair is small so we pass by them frequently. I knew they would be there, but every time I see them, the image jumps out at me like pictures in a pop-up book. We eat a meal of hot dogs and funnel cakes, and the girls decide we want to go to the petting zoo.

I fall in love with a brown baby goat, and it falls in love with me; when I picked it up, it nuzzled me and laid its head on my chest. I ask Jamie if I can have a baby goat when we get married. He says no, and then says maybe, if it means he doesn't have to mow the lawn.

I sit on a bale of hay with Augusta, my goat, cradled in my lap like a human baby. She gazes up at me, and either she is mesmerized by the glitter of my tiara, or she thinks I'm her mother. I am singing Augusta a lullaby I have made up for her when I look up and see Finny smiling crookedly at me; Sylvie is crouched next to him looking at the pen of piglets. I stop singing and glare at him. His shoulders shake with silent laughter.

"Oh, Finn, look, it likes me," Sylvie says. Finny turns away from me and kneels down with her. I've matured enough in the past few months to remind myself that I don't really know her; maybe she's very nice.

Jamie and the others come to stand around me. They have gotten as much enjoyment as they can out of the fair for now, and they want to go back to Sasha's.

"But I don't want to leave Augusta," I say.

"You *named* it?" Jamie says. I nod.

"Okay, put down the goat and walk away slowly," Alex says, both hands held out in front of him.

"That joke doesn't make any sense," I say. Jamie tugs on my arm.

"Come on, I'm hot," he says. I sigh and kiss Augusta on the top of her head and put her down. When I leave, she runs to the end of her tether and bleats.

"Oh," I say. Jamie takes my hand and keeps walking, pulling me along. I look back once over my shoulder. Finny is bending over and scratching the top of Augusta's head.

We wait through the heat of the day at Sasha's, then walk back to the park just before sunset. This is where I will have to leave them. My father said he would leave the office in time to watch the fireworks with us, so Mother wants us to do it as a family. Family, of course, means Aunt Angelina and Finny too.

"Do you have to go?" Jamie says. I nod and peck his lips.

"I'll miss you," I say. He looks so handsome that even waiting to see him until tomorrow kills me.

"Call me when you get home," he says and kisses me again, for longer. I flush with pride and smile. Before I go, I wave to the others; they wave back and watch me turn away. When I glance back at them, they are all walking away together.

My mother, father, and Aunt Angelina are sitting by the lake where we always watch the fireworks.

"Hi, sweetie," my mom says. She is smiling and holding hands with my father. He stands up and hugs me.

"Had a good day, Autumn?" he asks. I nod. He steps back and looks at me quizzically. "Your hair?" he says.

"I dyed it brown again," I say. "Yesterday."

"Yesterday?" he says.

"Yeah," I say. We smile at each other. We are both pleased that he noticed the subtle difference so quickly.

"Finny told me you made friends with a goat," Aunt Angelina says.

"Yeah. I want a goat, Mom," I say, then I look at Aunt Angelina. "Finny was talking about me?" I say.

"He gave a detailed description of you rocking and crooning to a little goat," she says. Her eyes focus over my shoulder "There he is," she says. I turn around.

Finny is walking toward us, holding hands with Sylvie.

"Hey, everybody," he says. Sylvie grins and waves with her fingers. My father stands up.

"And who is this?" he says.

"Uncle Tom, this is Sylvie," Finny says. "Sylvie, Uncle Tom."

"Hi," she says and grins again.

"Nice to meet you," Dad says. "Here," he adds, stepping to the side, "I'll move so you girls can sit together."

It seems my father cannot tell the not-so-subtle difference between Sylvie and me.

I am now sitting between my father and Sylvie. Finny is on the other side of her, and The Mothers are talking together on the other side of Dad.

I stare straight ahead at the patch of sky where the fireworks will be. Finny and Sylvie are holding hands next to me. I have a choice. I can either continue to sit with them in silence, or I can try to be friendly and have one of the shallow conversations Finny and I sometimes have when we are together.

"How much longer do you think it will be?" she asks. Finny looks at his watch.

"Ten minutes," he says. She sighs.

"Have you ever noticed that time goes slower while you're waiting for fireworks?" she says.

"Well, time always goes slower whenever you're waiting for something," he says.

"I think it's even slower when you're waiting for fireworks," she says. Finny opens his mouth.

"I agree," I say. Sylvie looks at me in surprise. "I think it's because when we're not looking at our watches, we're looking at the light fading in the sky. The anticipation never escapes our perception."

"Huh," Finny says.

"I guess so," Sylvie says. She looks like she thinks that there will be a catch to agreeing with me. We've never spoken before outside of necessary pleasantries at school or the bus stop: *Excuse me. Thank you. Hey, you dropped this.*

"So, by your logic, if we look at the lake instead of the sky, time will go faster," Finny says.

"Well, only as fast as when we're waiting for something else," I say.

"Okay, well, let's look at the lake," he says. I look at the lake. Once, in that time I call Before, my father decided to take Finny and I fishing. I was bored and climbed a tree overhanging the water. Finny thought that it was thrilling and sat all afternoon, telling me not to shake the branches of the tree because it was scaring the fish. I tried to be still for him. He caught one small fish. Aunt Angelina had no idea how to clean it, so she put it in the freezer, where, after she had forgotten it, it froze completely solid. Sometimes Finny and I would take it out and examine it. We ran our fingers over the stiff scales and poked its frozen bubble eye, and talked about what it must be like to die. Months later, when his mother finally remembered to throw it out, we were sad for the loss.

"I went fishing in this lake once," Finny says to Sylvie.

"Really?" she says.

"I was just thinking about that," I say and laugh.

"Our frozen fish?" he says.

"Yeah," I say.

"I don't think time is going any faster," Sylvie says, but just then the fireworks begin.

I'm quiet for the next hour, and let them whisper to each other. Sylvie leans her head on his shoulder. I think about Jamie somewhere in the park watching these fireworks without me. I imagine leaning against him, feeling him breathe next to me, and I ache as if I had not seen him for weeks.

The fireworks leave smoky patches in the sky, and the smell of sulfur drifts down on us. Next to me, Sylvie giggles. I am wishing she were not here. It is not fair; it was supposed to be just us, family.

I want to either be alone with Jamie or be alone with Finny.

The thought startles me, and I glance over at Finny's handsome face, momentarily lit up by the lights in the sky. I never let myself think about what it is that makes me imagine us together sometimes or if it means anything. I love Jamie.

I look back at the sky.

fifteen

JAMIE AND I ARE HOLDING each other and listening to the rain. My wet hair is splayed across his bare chest and his hand is tucked inside my bikini top. The air is cool on my bare skin.

I'm glad now that it started raining.

I sigh and nuzzle his shoulder. His smell is so familiar to me, so comforting, that my muscles relax even more with every breath I take.

"You sleeping?" he mumbles.

"Not yet," I say. I'm trying to make my breath rise and fall with his. I'm feeling satisfied, which does not always happen when he and I are together. I've never told him this though; since I'm always silent when he kisses me, all I have to do is say nothing when he stops moving against me and he assumes I've finished too.

Today, though, my toes curled and my fingers dug into his back. Nearly skin to skin, it felt so real that I couldn't think of anything but the moment I was in, with him.

"I love you," Jamie says. He moves his hand over my breast as he says it.

"Do you really?" I ask.

"You know I do," he says. I think about our future together, how perfect it will be. We'll buy a house and have a family and be happy together. Jamie is perfect and his life will be perfect, so if I am a part of his life, then I will be perfect too. I trace my fingers down his chest and he flinches away. "Don't," he says. "That tickles."

"Sorry," I say. I lay my hand back on his shoulder. There is another silence. My eyes start to drift closed.

"I want you," Jamie says. I feel my eyelashes graze his skin as I open my eyes.

"I want you too," I say. "Just not yet." I feel him sigh beneath me.

"Why?" he says, even though I've already told him.

"I want it to be special," I say.

"It would be," he says.

"How?" I ask. "Here, in this room?" I look at his room with the rock posters and anime action figures lining the shelves, his dirty socks on the floor, and the view of the back patio from his window. When I daydream about my first time, I see it happening in a beautiful room with a gilt canopy bed and a view of the Eiffel Tower out the window, or in a leafy green forest on a velvet blanket with wildflowers surrounding us.

"Yes," he says. "Or your room."

I grimace and struggle for words while trying to control my panic at the very idea of my room or, worse, his.

71

"No, you don't understand," I say. "It has to be *perfect*. Absolutely perfect."

Jamie shifts underneath me, trying to sit up. I let go of him and sit back facing him.

"If it's you and me, then that's all that really matters, right?" he says.

"Yes." I draw the word out slowly, feeling the incompleteness of my reply, how much it leaves unsaid.

"And nothing in life is ever really perfect. I mean, what are you waiting for?"

"I'm just waiting for it to feel right," I say. I look down at his comforter and pick at a ball of lint.

"When will that be?" he asks. I shrug and don't look up.

"Are you mad?"

"No, I'm frustrated," Jamie says. His voice is hard and sounds as if it's coming from very far away.

"Are you going to leave me?" I ask. Swiftly, Jamie moves closer to me and pulls me into a hug.

"I will never, ever, never leave you," he says.

"I love you too," I finally say.

sixteen

SASHA AND I ARE SITTING on Brooke's floor with her, reading magazines. Angie is off with Mike. Jamie is spending a week in Chicago with his family. The other boys are off doing something dumb at Alex's place.

We're giving each other quizzes out of the magazines. The quizzes are titled things like "Are you a good FLIRT?" and "Do you know how to get what YOU want?" According to these magazines, we are all amazingly well balanced. They're multiple choice, and it's easy to know what the right answer is; one choice will have too much of the trait in question, another not enough, and one will be just right, like a teenage Goldilocks. All afternoon, we've chosen the same answers and been told that we're doing great, that we should carry on as we are and everything will be okay. It should be boring but it isn't; it's comforting.

"You aren't afraid of taking risks but you also know to back down when things get too serious," Sasha reads. "Because of this, your friends can count on you to be a good time without things getting out of hand. You can use your good judgment to help a shy wallflower break out or keep a wild child reined in. Though you may sometimes make mistakes, like the night you get pulled over for speeding or the party where you're too shy to ask your crush to dance, your common sense—and your sense of fun—will always see you through." She tosses the magazine to the side and stretches her arms over her head.

"When's Jamie coming back?" she asks. "I want to go swimming."

"Friday," Brooke and I both say. We smile at each other. We like to make jokes about being cousins-in-law.

"I miss him so much," I say, because I do and I'm enjoying it. "I can't believe we've almost been together for a year." It's early August. I have six weeks until our anniversary, and I can't wait. To me, it will legitimize us as a couple in a new way; we will be inarguably together for the long term, and our relationship will be worthy of being deferred to over less-established couples.

"Yeah, me and Alex too," Sasha says. I think back to nearly a year before when Sasha and I battled over Jamie, and how he chose me. I smile at the ceiling and feel smug.

"Noah and I will have been together for a year and a half in October," Brooke says. I feel less smug.

"You guys are so cute," Sasha says. I have to agree that they are. Brooke and Noah never seem to argue—though Brooke swears they do every once in a while—and they do anything that the other asks them to do, so they're constantly jumping up to get sodas for the other or to rub their shoulders.

"It's been forever since we've gotten to be alone," Brooke moans. I pick up a different magazine. Sasha makes a sympathetic noise in reply to Brooke and I glance over at her suspiciously. She's flipping through a new magazine, looking for the quiz at the back.

"Oh my God," she says, "Here's one for Autumn."

"What?" I ask, sitting up and leaning over. I'm curious and liking the idea of special attention.

"*Does he like you as MORE than a friend?*" she reads. I look at her blankly.

"Who?" I ask. Sasha laughs.

"Finn Smith," she says. "Remember in seventh grade how he used to stare at you during lunch?"

"No," I say. I remember waving to him across the cafeteria. I don't remember anyone staring.

"Did he?" Brooke says.

"Yeah," Sasha says. "But he wasn't as hot as he is now."

"You think he's hot?" I ask. I think so, but I'm surprised that she does as well. Finny is so preppy, and he's quiet and introverted instead of charming and outgoing like the boys in our group.

"Yes," Sasha says, rolling her eyes to the ceiling. "I mean, I wouldn't want to date him, but yeah, he's hot."

"He's pretty hot," Brooke admits.

"Okay, but we're not friends anymore, so I can't take that quiz," I say.

"Sure you can," Brooke says. "Just answer what would have been true back then."

"I can't—"

"Number one," Sasha says. "You call your best guy friend crying after a fight with your mom. The next day at school he, A, asks if you're okay. B, doesn't mention it, since he got off the phone really quickly. Or C, gives you a hug and remembers all the details of your conversation the night before."

"Well, C," I say. Suddenly the Goldilocks answers aren't so clear anymore; I don't know what the right answer is, just what the truth is.

A. He blushed when people asked if I was his girlfriend.

C. He never talked about other girls in front of me.

B. He seemed comfortable touching me.

A. He said I was his best friend.

I look over Sasha's shoulder as she adds up my score. I'm relieved to see by the numbers assigned to my answers that they aren't all to one extreme, but many of them still are. When she is finished, Sasha looks up at me triumphantly.

"Girl, are you blind?" she reads. "This guy is jonesing for you bad—"

"Okay, stop," I say. "We were twelve. We didn't even have hormones."

"You were thirteen in seventh grade," Sasha reminds me, "and you guys were still friends until Christmas."

"Did something happen at Christmas?" Brooke asks.

"No," I say. "We just grew apart during first semester."
Sasha shrugs.

"Well, apparently he was in love with you," she says.

"Oh come on, half of those questions couldn't have really applied

76

to us back when we were kids. I mean, 'How often has he ever broken curfew to spend time with you?' 'What would it take for him to run back to his car to fetch your biology book even though his homeroom is all the way across campus?'"

"But you still had answers," Sasha says, and she has me there. I did have answers.

"I was just guessing," I say. "Like it matters anyway. He's with Sylvie Whitehouse—"

"And you're with Jamie," Brooke says.

"Exactly," I say. Sasha shrugs and we go back to flipping through the magazines.

seventeen

THE FIRST DAY OF SOPHOMORE year is going to be hot and muggy; I can already tell. I'm wearing a new tiara, purchased along with the rest of my back-to-school items. This one is black with dark stones. I'm wearing a red plaid skirt and black button-up shirt. Instead of last year's book bag, I'm carrying an army green mail sack that I've covered with buttons. Everything is new.

I'm ready to be a sophomore.

The group at the bus stop is smaller this year; there are only five of us now. Two are Finny and Sylvie. One is a junior named Todd who I have never spoken to before. The last is a nervous-looking girl who looks too young to even be a freshman. I'm fairly certain she is from a private school, and is terrified.

Finny and Sylvie are holding hands. The cheerleading uniform has been redesigned. I like it better than the old one, but I have no desire to be wearing it myself.

The new girl eyes me suspiciously when I stop at my regular spot at the curb. Like always, I am hit with the memory of flying down this hill on my bike. Finny was never afraid. I always was.

"Hi," I say to the new girl and smile. She mumbles something and smiles back, a small grateful smile. "I'm Autumn," I add. I'm feeling generous today. I also have a plan.

"We're going to have so much fun in chemistry together," Sylvie says.

"I'm Katie," she says.

"Did you go to St. John's?" I ask Katie the New Girl. She nods.

"Did you?" she asks, frowning.

"Oh, no, not me," I say. For one moment, I have an urge to glance behind me at Finny. In fourth grade, my father wanted me to transfer to St. John's, and it might have happened if I hadn't cried every night at the dinner table and refused to eat. I wanted to stay at Vogt Elementary with Finny. At the time, I thought separation from him would be the worst thing that could happen to me. I lay awake at night wondering how I could survive without him. Knowing that Finny was there in the room with me made every test less scary, every taunt less painful. I would look over at him sitting at his desk and know that everything was okay. The thought of enduring every day without him took away my sense of self, of balance, of hope. It all finally ended when Aunt Angelina told my parents that Finny was just as distraught and begging to be transferred too.

I'm so distracted by the strength of the memory that it takes me a moment to realize that my plan is far exceeding my expectations.

"Yeah, he was in my class," Katie the New Girl is saying.

"Oh, really?" Todd the Junior says. "Did you know Taylor Walker too?" Katie the New Girl nods again. "That's my cousin," he says. They talk about Taylor, and then more people who they both might know. Somewhere behind me, Sylvie is talking too, but the plan has worked; it's all a jumble of voices now, and when I tune out Katie and Todd's conversation, Sylvie's voice fades to the background as well.

By the time the bus pulls up, I have not learned anything else about the fun Finny and Sylvie will be having this year.

eighteen

I HAVE HONORS ENGLISH WITH Jamie and Sasha, the only class I have with either of them. They're both taking all Honors this year; I only have the one. Finny and Sylvie and several of their other friends are in our class.

Because we're a small class, and supposedly the smart ones, our teacher lets us get away with a lot in there. It's delightful to us, this special treatment, this freedom. Jamie is frequently hilarious. I'm more proud when the others laugh at his jokes than I would be if they were my own. He's handsome and funny and mine.

The teacher, Mr. Laughegan, likes me; English teachers always do. Sometimes after this class, I worry that I talked too much, that I sounded like a know-it-all, yet the next class I can't keep my hand out of the air again.

The third week of school, I see a book on Mr. Laughegan's desk. He isn't in the room, but the bell will be ringing soon. It's *David*

Copperfield, a book I've long been meaning to read. I pick it up and begin reading. I'm absorbed by the first page. I sit down at his desk and continue reading.

"What are you doing?" Jamie says.

"Reading Mr. Laughegan's book," I say. Someone in the class laughs. Jamie snorts. It's hard to predict when Jamie will approve or disapprove of any eccentricity of mine. I'm guessing this is borderline; perhaps he wishes that he had done it first.

"She is so weird," Jack says. I feel the usual swell of pride and shame, and I am determined to stay at the desk and read.

I'm still reading the book when Mr. Laughegan comes in.

"Hello, Autumn," he says. "Do you like Dickens?" I nod. "I'll loan that to you after I finish writing my paper if you like." The surprise must show on my face, because he adds, "I'm taking night classes for my master's."

"Oh cool," I say. The bell rings, and I go to my seat without being asked.

Mr. Laughegan makes good on the loan; Jamie teases me about my new best friend the English teacher and mocks the length of the book. I make a habit of sitting in Mr. Laughegan's desk before class, reading his books, sometimes going through the drawers. He never minds. I question him about the contents of his first aid kit and his preference for blue highlighters.

I think Mr. Laughegan gets me. One day he asks me if I write. I tell him I do. He asks me if I know about the creative writing class for seniors that he teaches. I do.

My one-year anniversary with Jamie is on a Tuesday. He gives me three red roses at school. I expected him to bring me a rose; I am surprised by three. The Friday afterward, Jamie and I go out to dinner and make out on my living room couch. I clutch him tighter than ever before and for the first time I forget about everything else while he kisses me. He stops suddenly and looks at me. I'm bewildered, thinking I must have done something wrong. And I'm annoyed, wondering what it is he doesn't like this time.

"What?" I say before he can speak.

"Do you want your present now?" Jamie says. He smiles and I nod. We sit up and I run my fingers through my hair as he reaches into his pocket. Suddenly I'm nervous that I won't like what he got me. He hands me a flat white box, and I stare at it.

"Go on," he says. His voice is so eager, I promise myself that no matter what it is, he will believe that I love it. I close my eyes before opening the lid. The room is dark; when I open my eyes, I have to lean forward to see what is lying on the cotton.

A silver bracelet with two charms. I lift it up and try to see them in the weak light. One is a turtle. The other is a heart with something engraved on it. I hold it closer to my face.

"It's the day we met," Jamie says. "That starts it. And then the turtle is our first year together. And I'll get you one every year for the rest of our lives, and when special things happen, like our wedding and our kids."

My eyes and throat feel tight, like I might cry. I hug him and rest my head on his shoulder. I think about how certain he is that those years together will come. Our age doesn't matter to him. He never fears that we aren't meant to be together. He never doubts us; he never doubts anything.

"I love you, James Allen," I say. My voice cracks. The tears do not spill from my eyes, but I'm still amazed. I've never cried from happiness before.

"Are you crying?" Jamie says. I nod, even though it isn't quite true. His fingers tighten in my hair and I press my face into his shoulder. We sit together like that for a long time. I think to myself, *This is it, I really do love him.* Tonight it's easy to say, to feel.

"Why a turtle?" I say finally.

"They're slow but steady," he says. "And I like turtles." He laughs when I laugh, and we lean our foreheads together. He reaches up and brushes his fingertips under my eyes; I squeeze them closed so that a few tears dampen my lower lashes for him to wipe away.

———————

Mr. Laughegan suggests more books for me and loans me several others. I work hard on my first book report for him; I want to impress him.

At lunch, I show everyone his comments on my paper.

"Read this," I say, shoving it in Brooke's face. "'I've never noticed that before, Good Job.' I made a point that he had never thought of!"

"That's neat," she says.

"I like Mr. Laughegan too." Noah says, "He's cool."

"Oh, I just adore him," I say. Jamie rolls his eyes.

"Yeah, you're in love with him," he says.

"No, I just love him," I say, and I realize it's true. I do love Mr. Laughegan, not like a crush or like a father or a brother or anything that I can define, I just love him. I love him because he said I could stare out the window when it's raining as long as I'm still listening, and because he said Macbeth was a jerk. I love Mr. Laughegan, and it is a simple and easy thought to have; it is nothing at all to say it.

Jamie rolls his eyes again.

"You're in love with a teacher," he says under his breath. I ignore him and read through Mr. Laughegan's comments again.

"Hey, Autumn," Finny says. I stop in my tracks. His voice is low. He doesn't look directly at me when he speaks. We're standing outside the closet-sized classroom. His book bag is slung over one shoulder, and he stands to one side of the door so that he cannot be seen from inside.

"Hey," I say. I wonder if something is wrong.

"Happy birthday," he says. He still is looking down at our feet.

"Thanks," I say. I'm confused. He could have said this at the bus stop this morning. He could have waited until tonight, when we go out to dinner with The Mothers and my dad. Finny turns away and walks into the classroom. I follow him. To the others, it only appears that we arrived at the same time.

Since it's my birthday, Mr. Laughegan says I can sit at his desk for the whole class if I promise to behave. I fold my hands and sit up straight, miming perfect attention, as if I would ever give Mr. Laughegan anything less.

And yet I am distracted. His desk is to the side of the room, perpendicular to the board. From this angle, I have an unobstructed view of Finny. By looking at the board, I see him too. I see him only.

And I love him. For all of my memory, I have loved him; I do not even notice it anymore. I feel what I have always felt when I look at him, and I have never before asked myself what it is exactly. I love him in a way I cannot define, as if my love were an organ within my body that I could not live without yet could not pick out of an anatomy book.

I do not love him the way I love Jamie. It's not the way I love Sasha or my mother or Mr. Laughegan.

It's the way I love Finny.

And it's impossible to say and even harder to feel.

nineteen

WHEN THE WEATHER TURNS COLD, the War breaks out.

On a Monday in mid-November, as I enter the cafeteria, Angie rushes up to me with her eyes narrowed. "They're at our table," she says. I know who she is talking about without having to ask.

"What?" I say. I follow her through the crowd to an unfamiliar table. Jamie, Alex, Brooke, Noah, and Sasha are all already crowded around the small square. "I cannot believe this," I say as I sit down. I glance over to where Alexis, Jack, Josh, and Victoria are sitting, with ample room about them. Alexis waves to someone in the crowd. I follow her gaze to Sylvie and Finny, weaving their way toward them. Finny and Sylvie pull up chairs at the round table.

"This is not cool," Noah says. Jamie shakes his head.

"No," he says, "it is not."

The table they took was inarguably ours; no one changes tables halfway through the school year. This is an act of hostility. But it must be ignored on the surface. To actually confront them or admit that we're angry would give them the chance to roll their eyes and say, "What? You're upset about a *table*?"

"Well, they're not sitting there tomorrow," Alex says.

"I will run from chemistry," Noah says.

"I'll beat you," Jamie says. We are livid for the rest of lunch. I'm not the only one who glances over their shoulders to watch our table being defiled. They laugh and toss things at each other and act as if they have sat there every day. As if they will, every day.

The boys make good on their promise, and Tuesday the table is ours again. We foolishly think that this will be the end of it; we have staked our claim again. Surely they will back down now that they see we are not going to give in to them.

On Wednesday, we are back at the tiny square table, our knees knocking against each other.

I actually run on Thursday, but Alex is already there, his book bag on the center of the table, leaning against the side, his arms crossed over his chest as he stares out defiantly at the rest of the crowd.

"Go, Alex," I say. We high-five. I look across the room and see Alexis and Sylvie staring at us from what used to be their normal table. I smile and wave and sit down.

When we win the battle again on Friday, I think that it is over; we've surely won the War now. They cannot possibly have the gall to keep this up on Monday.

———————

They do. They do have the gall.

We reacquire the table on Tuesday, and there is celebration all through lunch. Part of me says that it *is* just a table, but if I were certain that there was no hostility, then it would be nothing more than an annoyance to sit at one of the square tables.

But it is hostility; we are halfway through the semester, every other group has claimed their table and stuck to it, just like last year. Sasha and I left them and we've carved a niche for ourselves with a new group. We are tight-knit. We get good grades. Our boys are handsome and our girls are pretty.

For a year now we have been their foil, and they have been ours.

This is about more than a table.

On Wednesday people stare as I run through the halls to get to the cafeteria. My green bag bounces against my leg; I ignore it and the people around me. I am visualizing the empty table in my mind.

My vision is nearly true. The table is empty for a moment. Then Finny steps out of the crowd and lays his bag on the table. My feet come to a stop as I watch him standing there. Across the room I see Jamie and Noah slow to a walk. Sylvie and Alexis are crossing the room too. They have also slowed to a walk, their smiles triumphant as they look at Finny. Jamie's gaze meets mine. He rolls his eyes and scowls.

For the past week I had not included Finny in my anger. I had somehow thought of him as blindly following his friends without realizing the implications of their actions, the meaning of securing the table. But there he is, claiming the table as if it has always belonged to him. Suddenly it feels as if someone has placed their hands flat on my back and pushed me forward.

I walk in a straight, steady line up to Finny, to our table. I toss my bag on the table next to his and tilt my head up to look at him.

"Are you sitting with us today?" I say. He does not answer me immediately, and for a moment I have lost my words as well. It's been a long time since I have looked directly into his face.

His blue eyes have flecks of gold in them; it's hard not to stare at the strange combination. I want to reach up and brush his blond hair away from his forehead so that I can see his eyes better. His face flushes pink, and—before I can remember that I shouldn't feel this—I am thinking he is beautiful. I know it embarrasses him when he blushes, but I can't help but think it is nice. It makes him look so innocent, as if he has never done anything wrong in his whole life.

"I, um—" Finny says. He stares back at me. I wonder what he is thinking. It feels like we have been staring at each other for a full minute, but surely it has only been a moment. I take my first breath since speaking and I am filled with his familiar smell. Part of me wants to close my eyes and focus on the scent; another part just wants to keep looking at him.

"Sylvie asked me to save us a table," he says. Her name breaks my trance. I pull out a chair and sit down.

"Oh. Well," I say, "this is where *we* usually sit."

Jamie comes up behind me and pulls up a chair. "Hey, pretty girl," he says. "How's your day going?"

"Okay," I say. Noah sits down on the other side of Jamie. They both ignore Finny. Finny picks up his bag and turns away. Sylvie is only a few feet behind him, but she does not look at him as he approaches her; she looks at me. Her eyes narrow. I only hold her gaze for a moment before turning back to Jamie.

This is just about a table, I tell myself. It isn't anything personal. It's just a table.

twenty

THE DAY AFTER THANKSGIVING, MY parents fight. I stay in my room through the day, listening, trying not to listen. Sometimes my mother screams and he shouts in return. Sometimes they whisper to each other angrily. Sometimes there are silences. Doors slam again and again.

At noon I go downstairs and steal some cheese from the refrigerator. The voices falter and fall quiet until I am safely upstairs again.

I lay on my bed in late afternoon, watching a patch of light move across the floor, my throat tight, my body still. This is the saddest part of any day, when too much time has passed to create happiness while it is still light out. It's too late. The daylight has been squandered on my immobility. The patch of light falls still; it begins to fade. It will be better when it is gone. This is only one day, I remind myself, and it is very nearly over.

The voices quiet. The border between day and evening fades. No one calls me to dinner. The sun is gone and my room is dark, but I do not move to turn on a light. I let the darkness move over me and I am still.

A crash downstairs jolts me. I spring up into a sitting position. The voices begin again downstairs. They grow. They shout. A door slams. The voices are outside now.

I move to the window. I cannot see them, only the side yard and Finny's dark window. In the weeks since the War, the line drawn between my friends and Finny's has become a wall of ice. No longer are there civil exchanges between them and us in class or when our paths cross in the halls or restrooms. We all do our best to pretend the others do not exist. Finny and I have not spoken since the day I stole the table back from him.

I lean my forehead against the cool glass and close my eyes. My parents' voices are clearer now, even though they speak more quietly.

I listen to the purr of my father's car driving away. My mother begins to cry. The gravel crunches under her feet as she walks inside. I flick the light switch on. My body reacts to the light; I am suddenly alert. I pick up my book and lie down on my bed. The house is quiet again.

It isn't long before the knock I am expecting comes. The door creaks open and my mother's head peeks in. She smiles at me as if her eyes aren't puffy.

"I'm going over to Angelina's, sweetie," she says. I want to throw my book at her. I want to ask her what's the point of pretending everything is fine, which would hurt her far worse than the book.

"Okay," I say. She disappears.

I wake up hungry. It is still dark, still quiet. I shuffle barefoot downstairs. Everything in the old house creaks under my touch. I heat up the leftover mashed potatoes and watch them spin in the microwave. I'll enjoy the meal more this time. It was an awkward Thanksgiving.

Every Thanksgiving and Christmas for as long as I can remember, my father has sat at the head of the table, The Mothers on either side of him, and Finny and I next to them, across from each other. Yesterday Finny sat in his mother's spot instead of across from me. The Mothers glanced at each other but didn't say anything in front of us. They've accepted that we aren't best friends anymore, but I could see they won't accept us not being friendly. All day, we never crossed the line between us. We only spoke when one of the parents spoke to us first, and there was nothing they could say that would make us speak to each other.

The Mothers probably would have said something eventually, but whatever had erupted between my parents today had been brewing yesterday, and it was probably all too much for them too. I felt bad for Aunt Angelina and Finny; I wondered if they would have been happier in their own home, where there are no divisions, no unspoken contention.

I take the plate out of the microwave and reach into the fridge. I take chunks of the cold white meat into my hands and drop them onto my plate. As I stand upright again, I look out the window. The kitchen light is on in the house next door. I imagine Aunt Angelina and my mother sitting across from each other at the kitchen table, mugs of tea between them.

The wind shakes the leaves and I have a sudden urge to go outside. The gray world out there looks inviting, velvety and cool. I glance at the clock. It's just after one.

There is no one at home to care what I do tonight.

I take my plate in hand and head out to the front porch. On the other side of the threshold, the air is cold and damp on my skin; the floorboards chill the soles of my feet as I sit down on the steps. I realize that I have forgotten a fork, and then decide not to care. I grab hot chunks of the potatoes and lick my fingers.

It's a silly rebellion, eating mashed potatoes with my bare hands on the front porch after midnight, but it's what I have at the moment.

I eat the cool turkey more slowly, picking through the pieces carefully, taking small bites from my fingers.

When I am finished, I lay the plate to the side and lean against the porch railing on the right. The wind is blowing through the trees again. I shiver but I do not move. I want to see how long I can stand it out here. Perhaps I'll stay all night. I shiver again and close my eyes. It is cold. I hear the sound of a car and right away my eyes are open again.

A blue car has pulled up in the street. The door opens, and the dome light comes on. I recognize the male shapes inside the car, one in particular. Finny stumbles out of the car. He laughs and says something to his friends. They shout something back, and he puts his fingers to his lips. He waves, and they drive away too quickly.

I watch him walk up the lawn. I cannot see his face, only the shape of him against the night. There is something odd about his gait tonight; his steps are too small, and he leans too far forward. He's feeling his jeans pockets as he walks. The light from the kitchen window makes him clearer as he comes closer. He stops a few feet from his porch and frowns. I lean forward to try to see him better, to see what is making him frown, and the steps creak beneath me. Finny looks up and our eyes lock. My breath catches in my throat.

"Hey," he says after a moment.

"Hey," I say. He stares at me, still frowning.

"No tiara," he says.

"What?"

"You're not wearing a tiara," he says. He sounds odd, his words slurred together as if he were very tired.

"I'm in my pajamas," I say.

"Oh." He sways slightly.

"Are you drunk?" I ask. I've never seen someone drunk before.

"Yeah, kinda," he says.

"You probably shouldn't go inside then," I say. He still has not looked away from me. Sweet, shy Finny: drunk. Even though I'd heard about it, even though I'm seeing it, it's still hard for me to believe.

"Why?" he says.

"The Mothers are in your kitchen."

"Oh." He sways again. "Can I come sit for a while?" he says.

"Sure," I say. He stumbles over to me and sits down heavily on the steps. He lets out a long breath and leans his head back against the railing. Mrs. Adams, our health teacher, made it sound like alcohol turned you into a different person. Finny is the same as always though, just a little unsteady, a little friendlier toward me than yesterday.

"I can't find my keys," he says.

"That's not good," I say. He nods in agreement, then looks at me again. I'm hunched forward, rubbing my bare arms.

"Are you cold?" he says. I nod. It's bearable though; I may still make it to morning. "Here." Finny starts to struggle with his letterman jacket.

"No, don't," I say. This must be what alcohol does to people; it makes them forget all the carefully drawn lines in the world.

"Come on, Sylvie, take the jacket," he says, holding it out to me.

"Autumn," I say.

"Huh?" He frowns.

"My name is Autumn. You just called me Sylvie," I say. His frown deepens.

"Oh. I'm sorry, Autumn. Take the jacket, Autumn," he says. He leans forward so that the jacket is practically in my lap. I sigh and take it from him. It is warm and smells of him. I slip it on and wrap it tightly around me. "There," he says. He leans back, satisfied, and regards me. "It fits you," he says.

"The jacket?" I say. I hold out my arms so he can see how the sleeves dangle far past my wrists.

"No," Finny says, "your name. Autumn Rose Davis. Except there aren't roses in autumn."

"Sure there are," I say. "At least in St. Louis there are." There isn't a clear border between summer and fall here. It starts and stops and moves backward, luring the trees to turn red while tricking the roses to bloom for just a little longer as the season swings back and forth, hot and cold. The leaves are gold and red, and there are still a few pink roses in my mother's garden, a bit wilted and a little brown on the edges, but still beautiful. I had admired them without making the connection to my name, but I have to admit now, it does fit me—pretty, but doesn't belong.

"Yeah," he says, drawing the word out. "But there aren't *supposed* to be roses in autumn."

"Things aren't always the way they're supposed to be," I say.

There is a long silence after that. I look away from Finny and out at the long, dark lawn separating us from the street, and the clouds hiding the stars from us. I pull the jacket tight around me again. Something shifts inside his pocket. I reach inside and my fingers close around an easily recognizable object. I smile. "Here," I say, and hold out his keys to him. He smiles back and takes them from me.

"Thanks," he says. "I didn't want to have to tell my father that I'd lost the key to that car." Finny's father—in another baffling gesture—gave him a car for his sixteenth birthday. I don't know what kind. It's something red and sporty, probably ridiculously expensive and Italian. I'm surprised that there is some way for Finny to tell him that he had lost the key. I had always thought the lines drawn between them only allowed one-way communication.

"So are you going to remember talking to me in the morning?" I ask. Finny frowns again.

"Yeah," he says. "I'm not that drunk."

"Well, I don't know how these things work," I say. He cocks his head to the side.

"You've never been drunk?" he says.

"No," I say. I realize too late that my tone sounds defensive. He doesn't notice.

"Huh," he says. "I thought—" He breaks off and frowns again. "Huh."

"What? You thought everybody was doing it?" I ask. He shrugs and looks away from me. I wonder what time it is, how much longer of my self-enforced sentence on the front porch is left. The sky doesn't look any lighter.

"Why are you out here anyway?" he asks.

I'm surprised that my throat tightens. "My parents had a fight," I say.

"Oh."

"My dad drove away and my mom's at your place."

"Autumn, I'm sorry."

"It's the same old, same old," I say.

"But I really am sorry," he says. "I really am." He has turned to face me on the step again.

"It's fine," I say.

"Do you want to talk about it?"

"You're drunk."

"I'm sobering up," he says.

"Will you still want to talk to me when you're sober?" There is another silence after that. I look into his face. I cannot read it. I stare at him and watch him take a deep breath.

"I'll still want to," he says, but something in his tone says no anyway.

"It's okay," I say. "Don't worry about it."

"Do you love Jamie?" My breath catches in my throat again. "I mean—is he good to you?" Finny says.

"What?" I ask. My shock shows in my voice, and this time it does look like he notices. I try to make my tone light, as if I'm laughing at him. "Don't tell me that you're going big brother on me all of a sudden."

Finny shrugs. He is not looking at me anymore. I wonder if he's blushing. He probably is.

"Yeah," I finally say. "I do love him. And he's a good guy." I try to imagine what sort of guy he thinks Jamie might be, what he would do if I confirmed his suspicions. I remember him punching Donnie Banks in fifth grade. "And anyway, I don't think Sylvie would appreciate it if you fought Jamie to defend my honor."

"Yeah," Finny says. His face is still turned away. "I'd do it anyway though."

"Are you sure you still would want to if you were sober?" I say.

Finny nods. "Yeah," he says again. "But I'm only telling you because I'm not."

I think about the things I would say to Finny if I were drunk, or at least brave enough to say them. First I would tell him that his jacket smells good. Then I would tell him that I liked sitting here talking to him, that I don't want to go inside and end the conversation.

"You remember middle school?" he asks.

"Yeah," I say. The wind blows in the trees. The sky still isn't any lighter. Perhaps no time has passed at all. Perhaps we will sit here together forever. I wouldn't mind; it might be better than facing tomorrow. I wait for him to finish his thought. He's frowning again.

"I should probably go inside before I say anything else I shouldn't," Finny says. "I think I can fake it enough to get upstairs."

"Oh, okay," I say. He stands up and looks at me.

"You're not going to stay out here, are you?" he asks. I shake my head.

"No, I guess not," I say. I stand up and start to take off his jacket. He opens his mouth and starts to put his hand out like he's holding traffic, then stops. He takes the jacket from me.

"Thanks," we say at the same time. We both smile weakly. "Good night," I say. He nods and walks off the porch.

"Hey, wait," he says. I look back at him. He is standing at the imaginary line that divides my yard from his. "It's a little past my curfew now. If Mom's mad in the morning, can I use you as an excuse?"

"Sure," I say. "Tell her I bawled my eyes out on your shoulder." He smiles again.

"She'll love that," he says. "Not you crying but, you know. G'night," he says. I turn away again and go inside.

I lie in my cold bed and look at the light coming from Finny's bedroom window. I remember how, whenever I was sad, I would signal him with my flashlight, and he would take the cup up on his side of the string strung between our windows, and we would talk until we both fell asleep. It's a long time before the light goes out.

twenty-one

JAMIE SAID THAT ONCE HE had his driver's license, we would be free to be together whenever we liked. Nothing would keep us apart except my curfew.

Mostly we just drive around. Sometimes we park behind the library and make out. It's uncomfortable with my head pressing into the door and my knees bent, but I pretend that it isn't because I like the idea of making out in his car; like a scene from a movie, the windows fog up in the cold and the radio plays our song.

I don't know much about driving. Jamie is the only other person my age I've ridden with, but I think he must be a good driver. I feel safe with him. I like to watch him drive, to study his profile, to see his eyes focused away from me. He is so remote from me, and it makes me want him more.

My mother has always said that my father will teach me to drive someday, and I'm still waiting for that day. For now, it doesn't matter; there is never a place I want to be that Jamie isn't going too.

Finny got his driver's license on his birthday. Aunt Angelina taught him to drive ages ago. She says he is a good driver, but she is still terrified of him killing himself on the road some night. It's hard for me to understand how she jumps so quickly from driving to death. Every night, people ride around in cars without dying.

I am a virgin, and I cannot drive.

I am afraid of losing my virginity in Jamie's car. I stay on guard for a fit of passion that could cause me to make this crucial mistake, but it never comes. I'm in control when I let him slide his finger inside me; I know what's happening when he takes my hand and cups it around his erection.

I never let Jamie see me when we touch each other and I never look at him. When I open my shirt and let him kiss my breasts, I watch him to make sure his eyes are closed. I want him to see me for the first time when we make love. It's part of my daydream—slowly undressing each other and seeing for the first time all of the secret parts of us we have hidden.

And it makes me less afraid.

One evening, Jamie asks me to hold the wheel for him as he reaches for a CD. I trust that if he asks me to do it, then it must mean I can do it. I nearly run us off the road. Jamie grabs the wheel and rights us again.

"Geez, Autumn," he mumbles. He doesn't say anything else until he pulls into my driveway at curfew. "Maybe you should never learn to drive," he says after he kisses me. "I can't stand the idea of you killing yourself."

I know that someday I will die, and I know that someday I will lose my virginity; these two things seem equally probable, equally impossible.

Finny's curfew is half an hour later than mine, and on the weekends I listen for his car as I lie in bed waiting for sleep. It's comforting, hearing the engine approach and stop and then the car door slam, the creak of his back door. I watch for the sudden glow of his bedroom window when he flicks on the light. He crosses the room with his shirt off. His light goes out again, and I know he is lying in his bed by the window, two panes of glass and twenty feet of air separating us.

twenty-two

I'M FEELING SICK THE LAST day of the semester, but I have to go—I have three finals that day. I stare at the clock all morning, counting the hours until I can go home and go to bed. At lunch, I start to feel nauseous and only have a bottled water. Jamie is sweet to me and strokes my hair when I lay my head on the table.

"Baby, I think you should go home," he says. I rock my head back and forth on the table to signify shaking my head no. After lunch, Jamie carries my book bag to Mr. Laughegan's class for me. I don't bother going through his drawers today; I immediately go to my own desk and slump down in the seat. With Christmas coming and two weeks of freedom just a few hours away, everyone else is in a great mood, test or no test. I listen to the sound of the other kids filing in and taking their desks and I want to die. Jamie lays one hand on my back and talks to Sasha about a movie they both want to see that I don't. The others are making plans to go to the mall, complaining about visiting relatives, talking about catching up on sleep. Sleep sounds good to me.

Mr. Laughegan's test is easy for me, even in my weakened condition. I finish first and lay the bundle of papers facedown on Mr. Laughegan's desk. He looks at me, and I know he is taking in my pale skin and blank expression. I smile weakly at him before he can ask me if I am okay. I walk to my seat and think that I should study for my geometry exam, but my stomach is feeling worse, and I go back to resting my head on my desk.

By the time nearly everyone else is done with the test, I am wondering if I'm going to throw up. My insides are churning below my rib cage, and my salivary glands are working in my mouth; I may need to make an exit. I try to gauge just how likely it is that I'm about to vomit. I don't feel like I can leave unless it is a certainty, but I cannot abide the idea of not making it to the bathroom on time. I'm across the room from the door. There is a trash can between me and the threshold, but that would be a fate worse than death.

The last student lays her test down on Mr. Laughegan's desk, and he stands.

"Okay, what did you guys think of the test?" he says. I bolt out of my seat and run for the door with my hand over my mouth. Mr. Laughegan steps to the side as I barrel past him. "Jamie, Finn, sit back down please," I hear him say as I run into the hallway.

It turns out my timing is perfect, though I couldn't have waited a second longer. I kneel on the floor of the stall with one hand holding my hair back and the other holding my tiara in place so that it doesn't fall in.

Afterward, I rinse my mouth out in the sink and look at my face in the mirror. I'm still pale, but I feel much better. I take a deep breath. There are still twenty minutes left in class. I need to go back before Mr. Laughegan sends someone to check on me.

I keep my head down and my eyes on the floor as I enter the room again. I hear Mr. Laughegan's voice softly.

"Autumn—"

"Oh my God, are you pregnant?" Alexis shouts. My knees lock and my head whips up. I stare at her.

"What? No," I say.

"Are you sure?" Victoria says. "Because you—"

"Alexis, Victoria," Mr. Laughegan says sharply. He turns back to me. "Let me write you a pass for the nurse."

"No," I say. I shake my head and sit back down at my desk. "I have another test next hour. I'll be fine."

"Are you sure?" he says. I nod and sit up straight to show how much better I am feeling. Mr. Laughegan shrugs and goes back to his closing comments for the semester. "Okay, since we didn't finish *Jane Eyre* in time for the final, I'm going to have to assign some pages for you to read over the break."

Jamie stretches his foot out so that our sneakers are pressed up against each other. I copy Mr. Laughegan's assignment into my notebook and smile at Jamie.

"Hey," he says when the bell rings. "You sure you're okay?"

"Yeah," I say. Outside of the classroom, he pulls me into a hug. He's headed across campus to gym; we won't see each other for the rest of the school day.

"Love you, sick girl," he says. "Even when your breath smells like vomit."

"Thanks," I say. He kisses my mouth and ruffles my hair.

I survive my math test and even the bus ride home. Finny and Sylvie get off just ahead of me. They walk down Elizabeth Street holding hands. I loiter at the bus stop and then follow thirty feet behind them until they come to the corner where Sylvie turns off. They kiss goodbye, and Sylvie crosses the street. Finny waves at her and starts down the sidewalk again.

"Hey, Finny, wait," I call out. From the corner of my eye, I see Sylvie turn around and look at us. I ignore her. Finny stops and turns. He waits for me to catch up with him. I'm surprised that he doesn't look surprised. "Hey," I say again when I reach him.

"Hey," he says. I start walking again toward our houses and he follows suit.

"I have a favor to ask," I say. I keep my eyes on the ground as I walk.

"Okay," Finny says.

"Could you make sure that Alexis and Taylor and Victoria and—" I stop myself from adding Sylvie. "And everybody don't go around telling people that I'm pregnant?"

"Why would they do that?" he says. This solves a mystery, and part of me is relieved. I'd always wondered how someone like Finny could be friends with girls like them; apparently he doesn't realize what kind of girls they are. I understand that. I used to not know either. And Finny always thinks the best of people; perhaps he thought that they asked if I was pregnant out of concern.

"Because—" I falter on how to say it so that I'm not insulting his friends.

"You're not, right?" he says quietly.

"Phineas!" I say. I look up for the first time to glare at him. He looks straight back at me.

"I—" he says. "I mean, they did say it was a possibility—"

"No, it's not." I say. "I've never even had sex."

"Oh," he says. His face changes to the startled expression I expected him to have when I called his name. I look back at the ground. We walk in silence for another minute. We're coming up on our houses now.

"Could you just make sure—"

"Yeah," he says. His tone is curt and I think I've offended him. It is true though; they are capable of spreading a rumor like that. For all I know, half the school already thinks I'll be a new mother in the spring.

"Thanks," I say. He doesn't answer me. I glance at his face. He's frowning. We walk up the lawn together and part ways when we get close to the porches. He does not say goodbye to me.

———————

I go straight to my room and crawl into bed. I close my eyes and try to sleep. My body is starting to relax when I remember the way Finny looked at me when I told him I was a virgin, the way he frowned.

A spike of ice impales me through the middle. I can't breathe around the spike; it's too large. The cold spreads from my stomach into my lungs and heart, but it does not numb the pain.

What does it matter to you? I ask myself. The ice melts into a puddle in the pit of my aching stomach.

My Finny.

He isn't your Finny.

I know that. But there is a difference between knowing something and feeling it. I've known that he wasn't my Finny anymore, but now he is on the other shore, separated from me by an ocean I am afraid to cross, and I can feel it.

twenty-three

I'M NOT FEELING BETTER UNTIL Christmas morning five days later. I eat the eggs my mother makes as if I haven't eaten in years. My father comes downstairs and kisses my mother for longer than normal. I ignore them and keep eating. When I'm finished, he goes into the living room to take the first load of presents over to Aunt Angelina's and I go upstairs to get dressed.

When we were small, Finny and I would camp out under whichever Christmas tree we would open presents at in the morning. We'd lie side by side, staring at the tree, adorned with either my mother's perfectly color-coordinated, store-bought glass ornaments or his mother's mismatched decorations: exotic beaded tassels from India and her own eccentric creations of clay or paper.

We would whisper together and stare at the tree until the lights became blurry. In the morning, we would wake together and then run to get our parents so we could open presents.

I put on a black skirt and a green sweater. After a moment

of deliberation, I choose a silver tiara that is so low it is nearly a headband. There were three Christmases after The Mothers decided we could not sleep together anymore that Finny and I were in such a rush to get to each other that The Mothers could not convince us to get dressed, and we opened our presents in our pajamas as if we had stayed the night together. It hasn't been like that for years, of course.

Aunt Angelina hugs and kisses me. Mom hugs Finny, and Dad shakes his hand around the last batch of presents he is carrying. Finny is wearing a button-up shirt and khakis. Our eyes flicker to each other, but we don't say anything.

By tradition, we open our presents one at a time, and we all comment and exclaim over each item. Finny is quieter than usual, but I don't think much of it. I wonder if he's still mad at me for saying his friends would spread a rumor about me.

The gift marked as from Aunt Angelina and Phineas contains a tiara made of silver snowflakes. I bound across the room to hug Aunt Angelina. My mother has accepted but never encouraged the tiaras. Sometimes I wonder if having an illegitimate child and a string of lovers has kept Aunt Angelina young. Perhaps it has. Or maybe marriage has just aged my mother.

"Thank you," I say. Aunt Angelina squeezes me back.

"Phineas picked it out," she says.

"Thanks, Finny," I say as I sit back down on the floor. He only nods, but then he smiles softly when I put the tiara on my head along with the first one.

By the time we are finished with the presents, it is after noon. The Mothers go into the kitchen to get lunch together. I go to my favorite chair by the window to start one of the books I got. I have a nice pile I am looking forward to working through in the next week we still have off. Dad and Finny watch some sports thing on the couch. I barely register it when Dad gets up and leaves the room. He often has to take important calls from the office, even on holidays.

"Hey, Autumn?" Finny says. His voice is suddenly so close and low that I start in my chair. I look up. Finny is standing by the arm of the chair looking down at me. His hands are stuffed in his pockets.

"Yeah?" I say.

"I don't think the favor you asked me is going to be a problem."

"Thanks," I say. I smile, but he doesn't.

"What are you two whispering about?" Aunt Angelina says from the doorway.

"Nothing," we both say. She cocks her head to the side and smiles at us.

"Lunch is ready," she says.

———————

"So how is Finny holding up?" my mother asks as we cross the yard back over to our house. It is evening now and I rub my arms against the cold, glad the walk isn't far.

"What are you talking about?" I say.

"The breakup," she says. I catch myself before I stop in my tracks from surprise.

"Finny and Sylvie broke up?" I say.

"I thought you would know that," my mother says. She opens the door and we take off our coats in the entryway.

"Mom, why in the world would I know that?" I say.

"Angelina said he was pretty broken up about it the night it happened, but I thought he seemed okay today," she says, ignoring my exasperation. She goes into the kitchen with a plate of leftovers for the fridge. "Of course," she calls from the kitchen, "it's always hard to tell with Finny." I follow her and stand in the doorway. I doubt that Finny would dump Sylvie because she told someone that I was pregnant, but the thought has crossed my mind anyway.

"Why did he break up with her?" I ask.

"*She* broke up with him," Mom says.

"Seriously?"

"You're surprised too?" she asks.

"It just always seemed like she was so into him," I say.

"That's what I said," Mom says. "And of course I'm biased, but he's such a handsome and sweet boy, I don't know why she wouldn't be."

"I hope he's okay," I say. Thinking of Finny with a broken heart hurts me. I want to ask Sylvie what she could possibly be thinking. Whatever her reply would be, it wouldn't matter; I'd still want to pull her ponytail for hurting him.

"Why don't you call and ask him?" my mother says. "Or go back over there?" I roll my eyes.

"Mother," I say. She sighs and shakes her head.

I go upstairs with my books. Finny's light is on, but his curtains are closed. Aunt Angelina said he seemed pretty broken up the night it happened. For someone as quiet and stoic as Phineas Smith, that says a lot. I remember the couple of times I saw Finny cry when we were kids. My throat tightens.

"Fuck you, Sylvie," I say.

twenty-four

FINNY AND SYLVIE AREN'T THE only casualty of Christmas break. Mike dumped Angie. The first day of the semester she cries in the bathroom during lunch. We crowd into the stall with her and hold her hands.

"He said I didn't do anything wrong, but it just wasn't working," she says between sobs. "What does that mean?"

"That he is an idiot," Sasha says. "That's what it means." We nod and she goes back to crying. I look at her face.

I had a boyfriend for a few months in eighth grade. His name was Josh, and we held hands in the hallways and talked on the phone every night. He broke up with me suddenly one afternoon, saying he just didn't feel the same anymore. For days, it felt like I had been punched in the stomach. It was like I couldn't breathe, like something had been ripped from my abdomen. The feeling was so distinctive; it was different from any other kind of sadness I had known before or since. Watching Angie cry reminds me of that feeling. It's like smelling the pungent flavor of a sickening food I had once eaten. I never want to feel like that again.

We hug her for a while and head back to our table. Finny and Sylvie are still sitting at the same table with the rest of their friends, but they aren't sitting next to each other anymore. I have an idea of how awkward things must be at the table. This morning at the bus stop they stood apart from each other and didn't talk once. Finny hung his head and looked at the ground. Sylvie stared coolly down the road, her head held high. I upgraded my fantasy of pulling her hair to pushing her in front of the bus.

In Honors English, their group has rearranged so that Finny and Sylvie aren't sitting next to each other anymore. I think about how complicated it would be if one of our couples broke up. It's hard for me to imagine. Brooke and Noah still adore each other; they seem safe. Sasha and Alex are usually happy.

I try to picture Jamie and me breaking up.

My first reaction is a shocking sense of relief; if Jamie and I broke up, it would mean that he wasn't the great love of my life; I wouldn't have to feel guilty anymore that I sometimes think about being with someone else, wondering if it would be better, maybe even perfect with him.

I glance across the classroom. He's looking down, doodling in his notebook and quietly talking to Jack. He's longing for someone else too, someone who isn't me. And love the way it's described in books and poems isn't real; it's immature to long for that, and it's silly to think that with the right person it would be that. Jamie takes care of me and he loves me; in the real world, it can't get better than that.

My second reaction is a feeling of fear; I love Jamie, and the idea that love could be so impermanent scares me.

"Who read the assigned pages over the break?" Mr. Laughegan asks, breaking my thoughts. I raise my hand. Most of the others do too. "Okay, what did you think about the secret Mr. Rochester had in the attic? Autumn?"

My hand wasn't up anymore, but I know my answer anyway. Mr. Laughegan usually calls on me first to get discussions started.

"I knew there was something strange going on, but I didn't expect what happened. I seriously almost dropped the book," I say. "And then I was so upset that I couldn't sleep. I kept waking up so mad at Mr. Rochester—"

"I was so upset I couldn't sleep?" Alexis says behind me. Several people, including Sylvie, laugh. Mr. Laughegan gives them a look.

"I'm not sure if I *should* still want Jane to end up with Mr. Rochester anymore," I continue, "but I do anyway."

"Why's that?" Mr. Laughegan says. I pause for a moment, struggling to put the feeling into words.

"Because everyone always says that you never get over your first love. She loved Mr. Rochester first, and she loved him so much. Even if she fell in love again, I think part of her would always be wishing she was still with him."

"And what is it Mr. Rochester did that upset Autumn so much?

Alexis?" he says. I look over my shoulder. Alexis flushes and stumbles over her answer.

Everyone always says you never get over your first love. I imagine myself with someone else and longing for Jamie, my first love. I take a deep breath and remind myself that will never happen; Jamie says he's going to marry me.

"Never leave me," I say to Jamie as we walk out of the classroom together.

"I won't," he promises.

twenty-five

IT SNOWS FOR VALENTINE'S DAY. I put on the snowflake tiara for school; it's my new favorite, and I wear it every day that there is snow on the ground. I'll have to retire it when spring comes, but like all winters, this one lasts forever.

At the bus stop, Todd the Junior gives roses to Katie the New Girl. They're dating now; I like to think I helped make that happen. Because Finny and Sylvie no longer talk, the three of us listen to them every morning instead. It isn't as bad.

Katie smiles and looks at her roses as she talks. I know that Jamie will be waiting for me at school with a similar bunch. Jamie always gives me roses, usually red. Sometimes I wish he would be more creative, but it is ridiculous to complain about roses. Lots of girls at school wish they were the ones Jamie was bringing roses to.

Jamie is taking me out to dinner tonight. His gift is at home, waiting for me to give to him. I collected for him an assortment of little things I thought he would like; a CD I burned of songs that make me think of him, the action figure of his favorite anime character's wife, some candy, a little rubber turtle, a love letter I spent forever on.

When we hear the bus rumbling down the road, I realize that Finny isn't here yet. I look down the sidewalk toward our houses. He isn't running to get to the bus stop on time; he isn't anywhere I can see. The bus begins to slow in front of us.

"Is Finn coming to school today?" Sylvie says. It takes me a second to realize she might be talking to me. I look over my shoulder. She is looking at me.

"I don't know," I say.

"Is he sick?"

"I don't know," I repeat.

"Oh."

We line up to climb onto the bus.

I slide into the seat next to Sasha. She's wearing an army jacket that she bought at a garage sale we went to last fall. I envy the jacket. I know which tiara I would wear with it, but Jamie told me he wouldn't like me in it. He said it works for Sasha because she's boyish, but he likes me feminine. I think about telling Sasha that Sylvie asked me about Finny; she would be surprised that she spoke to me, but something makes me hold off.

"I know what Jamie got you for Valentine's Day," Sasha says. I think I probably do too.

———

In the afternoon, I get off the bus thinking of my date with Jamie. We're going to a new Italian restaurant. I'm excited to give him my present. When I get home, I'm going to take a nap and then a shower. My outfit is already lying out. I wonder if I should wear a different tiara for dinner.

"Autumn?" Sylvie says. I stop and turn. She is standing behind me, looking directly at me. Still, if she hadn't said my name, I would have had a hard time believing she was talking to me again.

"Yes?" I say. I wonder if she can hear the suspicion as well as the surprise in my voice. She looks nervous.

"Could you give this to Finn for me?" Sylvie says. She holds out a square, pink envelope.

"Okay," I say. I gingerly take it from her. Our fingers do not touch.

"Thanks," she says. I look at her to see if there will be something else. She looks at me silently. After a while, I turn and walk down the sidewalk. A second later, I hear her follow behind. I do not turn my head when she crosses the street. I'll do as she asks, but she doesn't need to know that I'm curious, that I care.

Finny's car is in the driveway; his mother's is not. Even though I could just open the back door and call his name, I go to the front door and knock; something about this transaction inclines me to formality. A moment after my knock, I see the curtains rustle, and I catch a glimpse of his hand.

"Just a sec." His voice comes through the door too muffled for me to judge the tone. I wait on the other side. I hear him mumble

123

something as the door creaks open. I start at the sight of him, and the part of my mind that is still thinking hopes he doesn't notice.

Finny's chest is bare, his arms, shoulders, and stomach all smoothly exposed to me. His skin is hairless except for a patch around his navel that trails down to the band of his boxer shorts, barely showing above his jeans. His blue eyes are sleepy, circled in gray, and his blond hair is tousled every which way. His nose is red, but it's hard to judge against the blush that is spreading across his face. I realize I have been standing here silently staring at him.

"Um, Autumn?" he says. I can hear now how scratchy and stuffed up his voice sounds. I swallow and take a breath, my first one since he opened the door.

"Sorry," I say. "You just look awful." He looks beautiful.

"I feel awful," he says. He shifts his weight to his other foot. "Are you supposed to be checking on me?"

"No—well, maybe, I don't know." I reach into my back pocket and hold out the pink envelope. His expression is startled, then confused. His eyes are cautious as he takes it from me. He looks at me suspiciously. "Sylvie asked me to give this to you," I say. He is startled again.

"Sylvie?" he says. I nod. "Oh. Okay." His voice is strangely monotone. He looks at the envelope and then at me. "Did she say anything else to you?"

"Nope," I say. He frowns.

"Was she friendly?" he says. I frown too.

"I...guess," I say.

"Hmm."

We look at each other. I realize that I am tracing the lines of his shoulders and arms with my eyes. I look down and focus on his bare feet.

"Well, you're probably cold," I say. "And I have a date so…" I shrug.

"Oh, right," Finny says. "Happy Valentine's Day."

"Thanks," I say. "You too, I guess…feel better." I turn away without raising my eyes to him again. I don't hear the door close until I'm off the porch and halfway across the lawn.

My nap is foiled by my memory of the porch. I lie on my side on the bed, facing away from the window, and try to put it out of my mind.

I know that it's normal to still find other people attractive when you're in love; what bothers me is the melting, dizzy feeling that overpowered me when I saw him. It wasn't just attraction but some combination of lust and affection that had me longing to lean into his chest and smooth down his unruly hair. I could even see it: my head on his shoulder, looking up at him as my fingers reached up to caress his hair. I imagined that his skin would be hot, feverish, and I would soak up the heat as I felt every line of his body that I had admired pressing into me.

Because of course, in this fantasy, he was holding me, caressing me back.

Wanting me back.

I am horrible and ungrateful; Jamie is better than I deserve.

125

And even as I curse myself for my selfishness, another selfish thought is crowding my mind, that I'm wasting what happiness I could have.

I love Jamie and he wants to stay with me forever. He buys me presents and calls me his pretty girl. He's gorgeous and smart and funny, and I should be perfectly content, or even better than content.

But I'm not, because this preoccupation with Finny keeps me from fully immersing myself in my love for Jamie. Keeps me from being as happy as I could be. Should be.

I want to pull Finny out of my mind like a splinter so that I can adore Jamie the way he deserves to be adored.

And even more than that, because I am a selfish, bad creature, I want to feel that adoration. I want to be free of this guilt.

"Do you like it?" I ask.

"Yeah," Jamie says as if it is a stupid question. I watch him rummage through the bag and smile to myself. The restaurant is crowded and loud; I barely hear the tissue paper ripping. Jamie laughs and leans across the table to give me a kiss. "You are the best girlfriend," he says.

"I try," I say.

twenty-six

THE BOYS ARE BUILDING A scary ramp out of snow. We are at Noah's, whose backyard has the kind of hill people would drive miles to sled on if it were public property. The plan is to spend the afternoon sledding and then go to the mall. I won't be making the second event. Aunt Angelina has decided that it's time to introduce her new boyfriend to us; my mother is having them over for dinner, and my father is even going to be home. I just told everybody I had a family thing I couldn't get out of. I try to leave Finny out of our conversations as much as possible. It's too weird for them to be reminded that the boy who is supposed to be one of our enemies at school is family to me at home.

The girls sled on our side while the boys argue among themselves about how to make the ramp more dangerous. The boys test the ramp then add more snow. They test it again and then add more snow. Finally, Jamie flies three feet in the air and crashes down again, and the ramp is dubbed a success.

The boys laugh when they tumble out of the sled headfirst. They laugh when they crash into each other. They laugh when they narrowly miss hitting a tree. They laugh at us for not trying out the ramp.

"Come on," Jamie says. He scoots back in the sled to make room for me but I shake my head. He rolls his eyes and flies down again, nearly breaking his neck as he flips off the sled and onto the ground.

"That was awesome," Alex shouts. The girls shudder.

As the afternoon passes, I persuade Jamie to go down with me a few times on what he calls "the girlie side of the hill." He sits behind me and wraps his arms around my waist and I lean back into his chest as the sled races down the hill. I like how the thrill of fear makes me instinctively grab at him. Jamie laughs at me for squealing and kisses my cheek at the bottom of the hill. His lips feel warm against my skin.

"Come down the ramp with me, please," he says, drawing the last word out like a small child.

"No," I say, just as childishly. He sighs and rolls his eyes again.

Sasha is the one to betray us. Alex calls for her just once and she says, "Oh fine," and goes over to them. I stand at the bottom of the hill and watch as they balance awkwardly on the sled together. My eyes flicker to Jamie once. He is at the top, looking at them too.

Sasha screams and Alex laughs as they hit the ramp. With two of them they aren't thrown as far in the air but the sled flips sideways when they hit the ground, and they skid across the snow face-first. The boys cheer and laugh, and Alex helps Sasha up and brushes the snow from her hair.

"That was fun!" she says. Alex beams at the rest of us.

"Yeah, my girlfriend is the cool one," he says. Brooke huffs and rolls her eyes to Noah. Angie shrugs. Jamie and I look at each other. His eyes are pleading. I stomp up the hill toward him.

"You have to be in front," I say. Jamie smiles and holds the sled in place with his foot. I sit down and he jumps down in front of me. He reaches for my arms and locks them around his waist, and for a moment I feel less nervous.

"Hold on to me," he says.

Jamie shifts his weight, inches the sled forward, and we're smoothly flying. I bury my face in Jamie's jacket. Suddenly we are jolted. My eyes squeeze tighter when I lose my grip on Jamie, and I feel my body thrown into the air. The air is like ice in my throat as I gasp. Something hard and warm strikes my face just before I hit the ground. My surprise overcomes the pain for a moment, and then I realize that I am sitting up in the snow with my hands clamped over my eye. And it hurts.

"Autumn, oh fuck," Jamie says. I hear the crunch of snow as the others run down the hill toward us. I take in a shuddering breath through my locked teeth. I find tears over physical pain so embarrassing.

"I'm fine," I say without unlocking my jaw. It's a reflex, but I know I'm not dying, so it must be true enough. Mittens grab at me, trying to pull my hands away from my face. Instinctively I shy away from them, trying to protect my pain. "Don't," I say. I open my other eye to glare at the offender. Jamie and Sasha are kneeling in front of me, their faces close to mine. The others are standing behind them.

"You have to let us see," Sasha says. My annoyance at her suddenly shifts to Jamie for making me go down the stupid ramp with him. I have a moment of fury. I hate it when he convinces me to do things I don't want to, and then I remember that I'll be embarrassed later if I behave emotionally. I slowly move my hand from my face. It's an effort to fight the instinct to hide my injury. Everyone takes in a sharp breath and stares at me.

"It's not that bad," I say. No one answers me.

"Uh," Jamie says. Sasha packs a fistful of snow together and tries to press it into my eye. I flinch away again.

"Oh man, Autumn," Alex says. "You're gonna have a black eye from Jamie's *head*."

"We have ice inside," Noah says as I try to struggle away from Sasha's ministrations. "Stop trying to smash snow into her face."

"We have got to put something on it," Jamie says. "It already looks awful."

"I'm fine," I say. I stand up and they grab my arms on either side. I let Jamie and Sasha lead me up the hill—our friends trailing behind us like a parade—and inside, where they sit me at the kitchen table. Brooke seems to consider Noah's kitchen her territory; she sends him to get a washcloth while she fills a plastic bag with ice. The cloth is wrapped around the bag, and I am allowed to hide the hurt from them again as I press it to my face.

Jamie makes me get up so that he can sit in the chair and pull me into his lap.

"I'm fine," I say again.

"Okay, okay, we believe you," he says, and I'm relieved. He

kisses me and cuddles me and I enjoy that. It's starting to get dark out the window. The other boys go to bring the sleds inside, and we talk about how horrible my bruise will be tomorrow, how long it will last, if it's worth trying to cover it with makeup. I'm able to joke now, and they lighten up. By the time Jamie and I leave to drop me off at home before everyone goes to the mall, my black eye has become a humorous story instead of cause for concern. Jamie wants me to tell everyone at school that he gave it to me to see their reactions. He thinks it will be funny.

"But you did give it to me," I say. He pulls into the gravel drive-way outside my house.

"I know. That's the best part," he says and grins. I scowl and start to roll my eyes, but the movement makes me wince. I remove my ice pack to lean over and kiss him goodbye. He kisses me gently, just as he did in the kitchen in front of the others. "Sorry I hurt you, pretty girl," Jamie says. He tweaks my nose. I smile and climb out of the car. I wave as he drives off. It's dark now, and I can only see his headlights by the time he reaches the road.

The house glows warmly as I trudge across the snow toward the back door. There are voices inside, and I'm glad to have the visible bruises to explain my tardiness. I take the ice pack from my face as I open the door.

"Oh, there she—" My mother's voice cries, and then I am again surrounded by faces, just as I had been in the other kitchen. Aunt Angelina, Finny, and my mother are the closest. My father and a stranger are behind them, looking over their shoulders. Mom takes my chin in her hand and tilts it upward. "Autumn," her voice trills, "what happened?"

"We were sledding. Jamie hit me—" I say.

"What?" Finny says. He doesn't shout it. He doesn't need to. His narrowed eyes are enough to make me stumble over my words.

"—with his head when we hit a bump and fell out."

"Are you okay?" Mom asks.

"I'm fine," I say.

"But how do you know for sure?" she says. Finny suddenly pushes his way closer to me.

"Are you dizzy?" he asks. "Blurred vision? Seeing spots?" I shake my head to all. "Can you follow my finger?" He drags his index finger back and forth in front of my face. I tear my eyes from his to obey his request. He nods.

"Okay," he says, "and you're not confused? You know who everybody is?"

"Yeah," I say. "Well, except for him." I motion to the stranger over his shoulder. Aunt Angelina laughs.

"This is Kevin, my boyfriend," she says. "Kevin, this is my apparently injured goddaughter."

"Hi," I say. "Nice to meet you. Now seriously, can you guys stop freaking out? It happened over an hour ago. I'm clearly not going to die of a concussion or something." Finny turns on his heel and marches out of the room. I wonder if I've offended him.

"Let's get you an ice pack," my father says. I hold up my plastic bag for him to see.

"Got one," I say. "See? Everything is fine. I'm fine." After another few minutes of questions and speculation, the crowd backs off and moves back to the casual positions I assume they had been in before. My mother examines my eye, sighs, and then orders me to sit down and have some guacamole with everyone while she finishes dinner. The grown-ups begin their conversation again. My mouth is full when Finny walks back into the room, so at first I cannot say anything when I see what he is carrying. He opens the freezer door. I swallow.

"Finny, is that my sock?" It's yellow with dancing monkeys on it—it couldn't be anyone else's, but I still have to ask.

"Yeah," he says. His face is hidden from me behind the freezer door. I hear the sound of ice cubes rattling against each other as he scoops them out.

"I already have ice," I say.

"I know," Finny says. "I saw. I'm making you a better one."

"So, Finny," Kevin says before I can protest. He's leaning against the counter across the room looking at him. "How'd you know all the questions you asked Autumn?" I am guessing that he is glad to have something to talk to Finny about; he sounds pleased with himself.

"Soccer," he says. He closes the freezer door and crosses the room to open the drawer next to Kevin. "Whenever a guy hits his head, Coach has to check for signs of a concussion."

"Oh," Kevin says. "I never knew soccer was a violent sport. I was a football man myself. Soccer looks tame to me." I know that he's hit on a sore spot for Finny, but it does not show on his face. He lets the faux pas pass and stretches my sock over the ice pack.

"It's where I learned this too," he says. He leans across the table and hands me the cold bundle. "That should be more comfortable," he says to me. I gingerly hold it up to my face. He's right—the rounded tip is far more ergonomic and holds the cold only against the places I need it. The soft sock is nice too.

"Thanks," I say.

"You only want to leave that on for twenty minutes at a time," he says. "Then give your skin a break for half an hour. You don't want to damage the tissue."

Aunt Angelina laughs.

"You sound like a doctor, Finn," she says. "Maybe you have found your calling."

I'm surprised when Finny shrugs. The last time Finny and I talked about careers, we were twelve and he wanted to be a professional soccer player. He's good, but I suppose he must be considering something else by now. I'm still holding on to my black turtleneck and coffee shop vision from fourth grade. Of course, Jamie doesn't want to move to New York, and he wants me to figure out a day job besides writing.

———

Dinner goes well enough. I don't like Kevin as much as Craig, me and Finny's favorite boyfriend from childhood, but he doesn't give me a particular reason to dislike him either. I wonder what Finny thinks, but it's impossible to tell—he's always polite.

For the most part, the four adults talk, and Finny and I listen. Kevin has messed up our normal seating arrangement, so Finny and

I are sitting side by side. It's been so long since we have eaten next to each other that we have forgotten I have to sit on his left; I'm left-handed and our elbows constantly knock into each other. It's embarrassing and I try to ignore it, but I like feeling him so close.

After dinner, my father brings out the port, and Finny and I are excused to go watch TV. They are laughing behind us as we leave the dining room. Everyone else seems certain to like Kevin.

Finny and I settle on a sitcom and watch it in silence. Before, we would have been deciding why we hated Kevin. We disliked the boyfriends as a general rule; Craig was the only exception.

After an hour, I go into the kitchen to refill my sock with ice. As I'm filling it, I have a nagging feeling that there was something in my sock drawer that I wouldn't want Finny to see. It's odd knowing that he still feels comfortable enough to go into my room and take something of mine, but then I think I would do the same for him if he were hurt.

Finny looks over at me when I come back into the room.

"So, did it hurt?" he asks. I sit down next to him with four feet of space between us. I ignore the urge to sit closer. This is how Finny and I always sit now.

"Yeah," I say. "A lot."

"Let me guess. You didn't cry, and you didn't tell anyone how much it hurt?"

I shake my head. "Crying is embarrassing," I say.

Finn smiles. "But if that greeting-card commercial with the old lady comes on, you'll tear up," he says. I shrug and cover my face with the ice pack.

135

"That commercial is so sad," I say.

"It has a happy ending," he says. I shrug again. We fall silent. It's Finny who speaks first again, when I take the ice off my eye twenty minutes later to not damage the tissue.

"I don't think it's as bad as before," he says.

"Really?" I say. I touch my face tenderly. The swelling is down, but I don't know how it looks.

"Yeah," he says. "The ice is closing the capillaries, but the bruising will be worse tomorrow."

"Maybe you should be a doctor," I say.

Finny shrugs like he did before. "I've been thinking about it, actually," he says.

"Wow," I say. "Just tonight or…" My voice trails off as I think about it. It makes sense now. Stoic, calm Finny who hates for anyone to suffer, even worms on the sidewalk.

"I've been thinking about it for a couple of months," he says, "but I don't know. I mean, not everyone discovers what they want to be during Job Week in fourth grade." He smiles an affectionate smile and I have to look away.

"Well, I'll have to figure out something more practical than that," I say.

"Why?" he asks. "You're good."

"You haven't read anything I've written," I say. I look back up at him again. He's acting odd. I can't remember the last time he teased me or smiled at me like that.

"I read the story you wrote in sixth grade," he says. "That was good."

"That was sixth grade."

Finny shrugs to show me how little that detail matters.

"You should be a writer," he says. "You'll find a way to make it."

"It would be a lot to ask Jamie to support me so I could write," I say. "I mean we'll have kids and a house and stuff." Finny frowns. The television has all but been forgotten. I don't even know what is on the screen anymore.

"You think you're going to marry him?" he says. I don't like the way he's looking at me now, his eyes narrowed like in the kitchen. I turn my face down again and look at the couch.

"We want to," I say. "I mean, we know we're young, but we can't imagine ever breaking up." There is a silence after I speak that startles me as much as if he had shouted something in return. I look back up at him. He's staring at me. He must think I'm weird for saying I'm going to marry my high school boyfriend. I feel a flush of heat spread across my cheeks.

"You really love him like that?" he says. I nod. "Huh." He looks back at the TV but keeps talking. "So what will you do? I mean, if you're not writing?"

"I thought about teaching," I say. My voice picks up hopefully on the last word. I realize I want his approval. He frowns again but does not look at me.

"That doesn't sound like you," he says.

"Why not?" I say too quickly. "I could teach English like Mr. Laughegan." Finny is shaking his head.

"Teaching is too—" His frown deepens. "Teaching is too *normal*

137

for you, Autumn," he says. I shrug and look back at the TV too. When he speaks again, it is so quiet I'm not sure at first if he meant for me to hear it.

"Doesn't sound like you at all," he mumbles. "Teaching, a house, kids. What happened to the turtlenecks and coffee?"

"That was a dream," I say. "I have to accept reality."

Accept when things are as good as they're ever going to get, I mentally add but do not say. It doesn't matter though. We watch the television without changing the channel or speaking. When he and his mother leave with Kevin an hour later, Finny only says a quick bye over his shoulder. I don't look up to watch him go.

Later in my room, I remember what I wouldn't want Finny to see in my sock drawer—the old framed photo of us that I hid in the top drawer last year before Jamie came over for the first time. I buried it at the bottom of the drawer, and I've hardly seen it since that day. Now it's sitting on top of the dresser, centered as if on display. I look at it hesitantly. My eyes linger over our easy smiles, our arms slung over each other's shoulders.

I take the photo and bury it again. I close the drawer with both hands. I can't afford to have him as a friend.

twenty-seven

OF COURSE, MY BLACK EYE causes a stir at school on Monday. I compromise with Jamie by telling the story the way I accidentally told it in the kitchen, allowing everyone to have the wrong impression for half a second. When Alex is there for the explanation, he gives a detailed third-person narration of the accident; it almost sounds poetic the way he describes Jamie and I crashing.

"...and then as they were twirling and twisting through the air, Jamie's head snapped back just as Autumn was beginning to descend, and they collided with a sound almost like rocks crashing together." He holds his hands apart and smashes them together to demonstrate, and his audience laughs in appreciation.

By the time the bruise is beginning to fade, everyone has heard the story and no one is asking about it anymore. Now they want to tell me how much better it looks. I have a running update by the hour, yet each classmate thinks that they are the first person to tell me this, just as they all asked me on Tuesday if I picked out the dark purple tiara to match my bruise. I smile and say thanks, but by Friday I am sick of talking about my stupid black eye.

It's on Friday that I run into Sylvie in the restroom.

I'm washing my hands when I hear a stall door open behind me. I instinctively look up, and I see her standing behind me in the mirror's reflection. I keep my face blank and look down at my hands as I rinse them. It's between classes; we are the only two in here.

"Hi, Autumn," she says. I look up at her reflection warily. I'm not sure what she could want from me; Finny is at school today.

"Hi," I say. She smiles at me. I'm too surprised to return the courtesy.

"Your eye looks a lot better," she says.

"Yeah, thanks," I say. I'm confused and worried this is going to be some kind of trap. In the back of my mind, I wonder if this is how she felt when I spoke to her on the Fourth of July, except back then no one was stealing tables or trying to spread pregnancy rumors. Or hurting Finny. I turn away and pull a sheet of paper towels from the roll. She sighs behind me.

"Look," she says, "I'm trying to be friendly." My hands pause their drying for a second.

"Oh," I say. Even though at school her friends are pretty much publicly recognized as our enemies, the social conventions of the larger world stop me from saying what I really want to say: *Why?*

She seems to understand my thoughts anyway.

"Finn asked me to," she says.

140

"Okay," I say. Once again my thoughts do not match my reply; again, I want to ask her why. This time she does not answer my question.

"So..." she says. She wants me to say something. Our eyes meet in the mirror again.

"We can be friendly," I say. *If that's what Finny wants*, I think.

Sylvie smiles. I turn one corner of my mouth up for her. I'm too confused to manage much more. I leave as she turns on the faucet to wash her hands. Neither of us say goodbye.

At lunch, as we hunch protectively around our round table, I tell Jamie and everybody about Sylvie in the bathroom. We try to guess what this could mean, but they are as stumped as I am. Of course, since I didn't tell them that Finn had asked her to be nice to me, it's probably my fault that no one guessed the answer. Maybe if I had told them the whole truth, *they* would have realized what Sylvie being nice to me meant. I didn't though, and so it wasn't until I walked into Mr. Laughegan's class that it all made sense.

Finny and Sylvie are back together. She's sitting on his desk facing him, their fingers twined together as they talk. I walk to Mr. Laughegan's desk and sit down. He's reading more Dickens, *Dombey and Son*. I pick up the book and pretend to read.

Trying to be friendly, she said. That's the same word he used when I gave him her card on Valentine's Day; he asked if she had been friendly to me.

I'm surprised when my heart leaps as I realize that he doesn't like his girlfriend laughing at me or spreading rumors about me.

Sylvie laughs and I can't help looking at them from the corner of my eye. She looks happy, and I can't deny that he does too.

And then she kisses him. And I start reading.

twenty-eight

ON THE LAST DAY OF school, I worry that I will cry when I say goodbye to Mr. Laughegan. I know that if I do, no one, not my friends or Finny's, will ever let me forget it.

"I'll see you the year after next in my writing class," Mr. Laughegan says to me.

"Hopefully," I say. "I know there is a lot of competition to get in."

"You'll be in," he says quickly. I take it as a promise.

The first day of summer, I wake up and stretch in bed, feeling all my muscles and joints. It's early still, just after seven, but the sun is bright in my window. I sit up and rub my eyes. A story idea has been bouncing around in my head for the past few days; suddenly it feels like the perfect moment to write. I'm not sure where the story begins, but I know what I want to happen.

Like most of my stories, it will end tragically.

I sit down at my desk without eating or brushing my teeth. I hesitate for a moment, then type my first sentence.

The day Edward died, I dropped a vase of tulips while walking up the stairs.

I begin to describe the tulips—red—and the white porcelain vase smashed against the dark wood of the staircase. I'm not sure what the significance of the tulips is—yet. It will come to me.

By ten o'clock, I have a rough draft. Five pages. I'm pleased with myself. The narrator was the accidental murderess; her guilt has left her reeling in near madness, and I close on the first image: the bloodred flowers, the broken innocence of the white vase.

My mother is reading the newspaper in the kitchen when I skip downstairs. She looks up at me over the rim of the paper.

"In a good mood?" she says.

I nod. "It's the first day of summer and I've already killed someone off," I say.

"In a story?"

"Mmm hmm."

"Ah." She goes back to reading. The phone rings and I pick it up.

"Autumn?" Aunt Angelina's voice says after I say hello.

"Hey, I'll get Mom," I say. My mother looks up.

"No, actually, Autumn, I wanted you."

"Oh." My immediate thought is that something has happened to Finny.

"I'm going to tear down my classroom today, and my good-for-nothing son canceled on me. Do you think you can help me? I'll make it worth your while."

"Oh, sure," I say. It's been a long time since I've been inside our elementary school. I'm curious, and spending time with Aunt Angelina can be fun.

"Really? Can you be over in fifteen minutes?"

"Easy," I say. She thanks me and reiterates the promise of making it worth my while.

"What was that?" my mother asks.

"Aunt Angelina needs someone to help her tear down her classroom," I say.

"Where's Finny?"

I shrug. It is unlike Finny to cancel on his mother, but I felt odd asking. I have a fear of someone suspecting how often I wonder about Finny. I always try not to show too much interest, just in case.

Finny opens the back door when I knock. His face is blank; he doesn't look startled to see me, and even though I'm sure that I do look surprised, he does not react to my face.

"Oh. Hi," I say. "I thought you were gone."

"I'm about to be," he says. His voice is as sterile as his face. Aunt Angelina comes in the room with a bundle of portfolio books and canvas bags.

"How long will you be?" she says.

"I don't know," Finny says. "I'll come by if I can. Sorry."

"It's fine, kiddo, get going."

"Bye," Finny says. He sidesteps me and leaves out the back door. His step is quick on the stairs. I look up at Aunt Angelina. I wasn't intending to ask, but it must be plain on my face. She knows I know Finny well enough to see when something is wrong.

"He didn't say," she says, "but it's something with Sylvie."

"Oh," I say. I hope that my face and voice give no more away. Aunt Angelina hands me some of her things and we go outside. I glance at the spot where Finny parks in the driveway, even though I know he won't be there. We don't talk as we load up the trunk and pull out of the driveway. It's a short ride to the school; less than a minute later, we are only a few blocks away.

"So Finny tells me you're thinking of teaching," Aunt Angelina says to me. I shrug and then nod.

"Gotta do something practical," I say. "I think it could be fun."

"It is," she says. She pauses as she makes a left-hand turn down the side street next to the school. "But it takes a lot of dedication." I don't say anything. She parks the car and turns off the engine. "You have time to decide though," she says.

We unload the car and walk through the side door of the school where Finny and I grew up. It's an old building from the 1920s, dark brick, high ceilings, long, narrow windows on every wall. Whenever I see or hear the word "school," this building is the picture that comes to my mind.

As I cross the threshold, I think how I don't have as much time to decide as I once did. When I was a student here, anything in the world seemed possible. It hadn't seemed like a dream to move far away and write books; it had seemed like a plan. At ten, I hadn't thought wanting to be a writer was impractical; wanting to be a pirate princess was impractical, and I had put that dream aside.

But I'm older now, and I realize that a career of nothing but writing stories all day is as likely as marrying my dream pirate prince. I've done the research; getting published is nearly impossible, and of those few who make it, only a fraction can live off their work. If it was just about me, I could wait tables in the day and write all night and be happy.

But there is Jamie now, and he wants to buy a house and raise children with me. He says I'm perfect. He says I'm all he wants. I can't disappoint him.

Aunt Angelina unlocks the door to her classroom, and we step inside. I realize now why she wanted me and not my mother. The room is even more disorganized and lively than Aunt Angelina's home. There is a half-finished mural on the wall that was a quarter-finished when we graduated four years ago. Prints from both famous and obscure artists line every other wall and cover the entire ceiling. The window ledges are lined with sculptures and various three-dimensional arts. On her desk is an asymmetrically shaped vase filled with flowers made of newspaper. I know from asking years ago that the newspaper is from the day Finny was born. On the wall behind her desk is the only framed art—a drawing we did together in third grade of a landscape littered with unicorns, soccer balls, explosions, and puppies.

The soccer balls and explosions are much better drawn than the unicorns or puppies; Finny was always better at drawing than me. I loved art class anyway though. Every year, Aunt Angelina made her seating chart so that we sat together at the smallest table in the corner that was only big enough for two. Most of our other teachers thought Finny and I were too focused on each other; they wanted us to make other friends and often sat us on opposite sides of the room. It never worked.

"If you could start wrapping up the sculptures at the window," Aunt Angelina says, "I need to clean out this desk." She sighs and eyes the mounds of paper spilling over the surface. We'll be here a while.

At the window, I can see the hill I used to sit on and read while Finny played kickball or soccer with the boys. I didn't mind that he played with them for that half hour; I always wanted to read at recess, and we would be together after school anyway.

Sometimes I put down my book and watched him play, and I would try to send mental messages to him. *Look up now*, I would think, or, *That was a good kick*. I was convinced that he could hear, because sometimes he would look up at me watching him and smile. I never mentioned our secret telepathic conversations though. I knew that if we spoke about it out loud the magic would stop working.

Aunt Angelina turns on the radio. I wrap the sculptures up in tissue paper and fill the canvas bags with them. Aunt Angelina hums along with the music. I think about the story I started this morning. I'm proud of it. I'll print it off tonight and give it to Jamie tomorrow.

Only the top of the desk is cleared off by the time I'm done; the drawers are all open and files are spilling out. Without being asked, I begin to take the posters down off the wall, making a blue ball of Sticky Tack that gets larger and larger as the minutes pass. I go one wall at a time, standing on a chair when they get too high for me. Aunt Angelina sighs just as I am almost done.

"Autumn," she says, "I would have been here all day. Thank you."

"No problem," I say. "It's kind of fun being here."

"You should go see Mrs. Morgansen before we go. She still asks about you."

"Maybe," I say. I feel shy about going to see my favorite teacher. I'm not sure where the feeling comes from. I take the last poster off the wall and slide it into the portfolio book. The ball of Sticky Tack is nearly as big as my fist now. I throw it toward the ground, but instead of bouncing, it sticks to the linoleum with a thud.

"Darn," I mumble. I bend to pick it up and set it on the nearest table.

"Okay," Aunt Angelina says. She drops a stack of books and papers onto the top of the desk. Her trash can is overflowing. "If you can get the posters off the ceiling, I'll clean out the cupboards and we can start loading up the car."

"Cool," I say. I jump up on one of the tables and start plucking tacks out of the ceiling. A familiar song comes on the oldies station and we both start singing. I start to sway to the music and I grin.

"I always wanted to do this," I say.

"Do what?" Aunt Angelina says.

"Dance on these tables. Every time I was in here I imagined it."

She smiles and reaches over to turn up the music. We start to sing again, and the next song is another favorite. I dance around the table with my arms above my head as I pluck each poster from its place. I even come up with a special shimmy-move for when I need to bend down to set the posters on the table.

It isn't until the radio switches to a slow song that I hear his soft laugh behind me.

"Ah, there's my long-lost son," Aunt Angelina says.

"Sorry I'm late." Finny looks at us from the doorway, his hands in his pockets, his head cocked to the side, and the corners of his mouth twitching upward. I want to glare at him for laughing at me, but I'm too relieved that he looks happy again.

"I could hear you guys all the way down the hall," he says.

"Autumn is fulfilling a childhood dream," Aunt Angelina says.

"Yeah, I remember," Finny says. He crosses the threshold and looks from my face to hers. "What can I do?" he says.

"Put that ridiculous height of yours to use and take down the posters Autumn can't reach from the tables," she says. Finny is well over six feet now. Soccer and track kept him from becoming scrawny as he stretched out over the winter; he's as slender and lightly muscled as before. Aunt Angelina likes to complain about how much he eats.

My dancing is done now. The three of us work quietly as the

radio continues to blare. Even with his height, Finny needs a chair to reach the high ceiling. I move to another table and he gets all the posters in between. With two of us, we finish before her again.

"Done," Finny says. He drags the chair across the floor and back to its place. I stay standing on the table, not quite willing to give up the dream yet.

"Go say hi to Mrs. Morgansen," Aunt Angelina says. "I saw her car pull up a few minutes ago."

"Okay," Finny says. He looks over at me. I shrug an assent and jump off the table flat-footed. My sneakers smack against the linoleum loudly.

We walk side by side out into the hall. The radio fades behind us as we walk, and when we reach the stairs, the building suddenly is eerily quiet; all my memories of this place are much louder. The wooden banister is smooth and familiar beneath my hand; I dreamed of dancing on the art tables and sliding down these banisters and climbing to the tops of the bookshelves in the library. I loved it here, so much that I didn't even realize I loved it. Even though I looked forward to summer, I cried every last day of school. I didn't cry yesterday.

And of course the other kids thought I was weird for liking school, but that was just another quirk among many that Finny had to defend me for.

I cautiously look over at him, wondering what he's thinking, if his memories are as happy as mine. By all means, I should have felt like an outcast here, a pariah, and Finny should have been the popular boy he is now. I wasn't, because of him, and he wasn't, because of me.

Finny looks to the side and catches me staring. I face forward again. He doesn't say anything.

At the door of Mrs. Morgansen's room, he knocks and smiles softly into the window. Through the wood, I hear a startled gasp. I step to the side as Finny opens the door.

"Phineas!" I hear her familiar voice cry before I see her. "I hoped that I would see you today."

"Of course," Finny says. Her pleasure causes the faintest of blushes to spread across his cheeks. Our favorite teacher leans forward and hugs him to her through the threshold and I see her for the first time in years. She looks just a bit older, like she's moving from middle-aged to the edge of elderly. Still, I instantly recognize the brooch on her blouse and the smell of her perfume. She sees me as she pulls away. I feel something sharp in me during the half second of confusion in her eyes, then her smile widens.

"And you brought *Autumn*," she says. Her arms are quickly transferred to me, and relief washes through my body; I had feared that she would recoil from this teenaged tiara-and-ripped-jeans me, that her affection for me would be reserved for the pretty little girl I had been.

"Come and sit," she says. She leads us into her classroom, half torn down, half familiar. She pulls out a chair and motions for us to sit down. The desks and chairs feel just a tiny bit too small. "Now tell me what you've been up to," she says. Mrs. Morgansen looks at us expectantly. Finny and I glance at each other, the same way we do when we are cornered by The Mothers.

"I haven't been up to much," I say.

"You won that poetry contest," he says. I shrug.

"That wasn't much," I say.

"Of course it is," Mrs. Morgansen says. "Though I'm not that surprised."

"It was just within the school," I say. "They picked one from each grade and printed them in the yearbook. That's all."

"But she won the overall prize too," Finny says. "She beat seniors."

"It's not a big deal," I say, because it isn't. The other winners' submissions ranged from trite to clichéd; it wasn't a hard crowd to beat.

Mrs. Morgansen laughs.

"Well, you two haven't changed a bit," she says. I frown without giving my face permission to do so. She doesn't notice. "Your mother told me that you started track this spring," she says to him. Finny tells her about the team taking bronze at regionals. He does not mention that it was something they never could've dreamed of before Finny joined them. I wasn't being humble, but he is. As I listen, I let my gaze wander around. I know it's impossible that every day I spent in here was happy, but that is how I remember it.

Finny's punch to Donnie Banks's gut effectively ended any teasing from the boys' side. Eleven was the age when all the girls decided to have crushes on Finny, and they knew being snotty to me wouldn't get them far. Not that it helped them either. Finny was never interested in girls. The only girl I have ever heard of him having feelings for is Sylvie Whitehouse. I frown again, trying to see for the millionth time how Finny, who is devoted to his mother, never has a bad word for anyone, and who every winter shovels the driveway of the old lady across the street and refuses to take a dollar for it, can be in love with a girl known for her drunken antics and dirty mind.

"It's so nice seeing both of you," Mrs. Morgansen says, and my mind moves back to the moment. "And it's nice to know you're still such good friends."

Finny and I both glance over at each other and look away again quickly. His cheeks are already turning a deep pink. It's not as if we can correct her.

"Or," she asks, "are you more than just friends by now?" and I realize she has misinterpreted his blush. Finny turns red.

"No," I say. I look back at her and shake my head, "No, no, no." By her startled expression, it occurs to me that I've denied it perhaps a bit too vehemently to be polite. "I just mean I've been with my boyfriend for almost two years now, well, by the end of the summer it will be. So, no."

"Oh, I see," she says. "And what's he like?"

"He's fifth in our class," I say. Finny is third. "And he's really good to me."

"Well, I knew that," she says. "Otherwise Finny wouldn't let him near you." She smiles, and I fake a laugh. Finny doesn't say anything. "Actually, Phineas," she continues, "I think your mother did say something about you and a girlfriend last time I asked."

"Oh, yeah," Finny says. He stands up. "Speaking of Mom, we should probably go. We're supposed to help load the car."

We are hugged again. We promise to come back again sometime. Mrs. Morgansen tells me to send her some poems and, embarrassed, I try to laugh it off. Finny closes the door behind us and we head toward the staircase again. I think about Mrs. Morgansen's memories of us. Of course she would have no reason to think we'd be anything less than the closest of friends. When I let myself remember how we used to be, it is hard to believe things could change so quickly.

I think about Mrs. Morgansen saying we *hadn't* changed, and I think of the girl I used to be here, in this school. I want it to be true. I don't want to be so different from her.

"I'm going to do it," I say to Finny when we reach the stairs. We both stop.

"Do what?"

"I'm going to slide down the banister," I say. I grab the railing with both hands and throw my leg over.

"Hold on," Finny says. "Let me get to the bottom so I can catch you if you fall." I roll my eyes as he rushes down the stairs.

"You're ridiculous," I shout down to him. My voice bounces through the corridor.

"You're wearing a tiara and straddling a banister," he calls back up to me. I let him win and wait until he is poised ready at the bottom.

They must have just polished the wood; I fly down and have to

155

catch myself at the bottom so that I don't fall to the floor. Finny grabs my elbow, but I right myself quickly, and his hand drops.

"That actually looked like fun," he says.

"It was," I say. Aunt Angelina stumbles into the hallway carrying a potted tree that is clearly too heavy for her. Finny rushes to take it from her and the three of us load up the car quickly.

"Can you come to lunch with us or are you going back to Sylvie's?" Aunt Angelina says when we are done, standing by her car. Finny's face returns to the blank look from this morning.

"I need to go back," he says evenly.

"All right," she says. She reaches up on her tiptoes to kiss his cheek. "Thank you for coming to help."

"Of course," he says. "Bye." He glances at me and walks to his red car across the street.

At the diner nearby, Aunt Angelina chats with me about my plans for the summer and our visit with Mrs. Morgansen. I tell her about sliding down the banister and Finny standing at the bottom. She laughs.

"Sometimes you two are just so predictable," she says, making me think of Mrs. Morgansen's comment again. We talk of other things for the rest of lunch, and it isn't until we are walking to the car that she brings him up again.

"I don't suppose he told you what's going on with Sylvie?" Aunt Angelina says. I shake my head. "I suppose I didn't really think so," she says. She changes the subject again.

156

twenty-nine

WE ARE LYING OUT ON the grass looking up at the stars like characters in a children's book. It came about naturally though, without any intentions of being cute, so I do not mind.

It's Brooke's backyard, and the ground is level and soft with the expensive grass her father is obsessed with. With the hand that isn't holding Jamie's, I stroke the cool, lush tendrils with my fingers. The others are scattered around close by. We had been laughing at something the boys had said, but a silence has fallen over the last few minutes, the kind of silence that makes you feel closer to the people you are with. I can hear everyone's breathing, though I can't pick out any individual rhythms besides Jamie's. Someone— Brooke?—sighs happily.

"So what's the meaning of life?" Angie says.

"To be happy," Jamie says immediately.

"Really?" Noah says. "I was thinking it was to do good or something."

"And I was thinking it was to have orgasms," Alex says. There is a sound that I assume is Sasha hitting him.

"Isn't that the same as being happy?" Brooke says.

"Well, that's just one kind of happiness," Jamie says. "I'm talking about having lots of *different* kinds of happiness."

"But you don't think we're supposed to make the world better?" Noah says.

"Of course we are," Jamie says. "That's another kind of happiness."

"Huh," Angie says.

"I can see that," Sasha says.

"I think it's just to truly love somebody before we die," Brooke says.

I add up everything I deeply want out of life: writing as much as I can, reading everything, the vague impressions of motherhood I cradle in me, seeing the northern lights and the Southern Cross. And other desires that I don't let myself think on too long because I've already settled that part of my life.

I try to find the sum of these things.

"I think," I say, "I think we're supposed to experience as much beauty as we can."

"Isn't that the same as happiness too?" Jaime says. I shake my head. The grass pulls at my hair.

"No, because sometimes sad things are beautiful," I say. "Like when someone dies."

"That isn't beautiful. That just sucks," Jamie says.

"You don't understand what I mean," I say.

"Orgasms can be beautiful," Alex says.

"Yeah, they can be," I say. Even though I've never had an orgasm that can be described as beautiful, I agree with the idea. "And making the world better would be beautiful too."

"But we aren't here to suffer," Jamie says.

"I don't think that," I say.

"But you think we're here for beautiful things and you think sadness is beautiful?"

"It can be," I say.

"I didn't think this discussion would be so serious," Angie says. "I thought everybody would make jokes."

"I tried," Alex says.

———————

"Do you really not think sad things can be beautiful?" I say as Jamie drives me home. He isn't shallow; surely he has felt what I'm talking about. His favorite song was on the radio when we got in and I wasn't allowed to speak until now. I've been thinking of examples to make him understand. Jamie doesn't take his eyes off the road, doesn't look at me.

"Nope," he says. "You're just weird."

"Why does that make me weird?" I say. I momentarily forget my arguments and examples. "Just because I think something different from you doesn't make me weird."

"I bet if we took a survey, everybody would agree with me."

"That doesn't make you right," I say. "And you're supposed to be against being just like everybody else."

"It's not about being *like* everybody else. When someone dies, it's bad," Jamie says. "That's just something everybody *knows*."

"You don't understand," I say.

"I do understand," he says. He pulls the car into my driveway. "You just see things differently and that's okay, because I like you weird. You're my weird, morbid pretty girl." I let him kiss me good night. I sigh.

"Hey," he says. "What's wrong?"

"Nothing," I say.

"What?" he asks.

"What about *Romeo and Juliet*?" I say. "That's beautiful and sad."

"But that's not real life."

"So?"

"There's real life and then there are books, Autumn," Jamie says. "In real life, it would just be sad and stupid."

"How could two people dying for love be stupid?" I say. We are sitting in the dark facing each other in the seats, our seat belts off.

"Would you kill yourself if I died?" Jamie asks. I look at his face in the darkness. He stares back calmly. I think about him running down the steps with the other boys. I think about the sly grin on his face before he says something to tease me. I think about him being gone and under the ground, never to be seen again.

"No, I guess not," I say.

"See?" he says. He leans forward and kisses me again. "I wouldn't want you to either," he says. "I'd want you to be happy."

"I would be very sad though," I say. "For a long time. And I would never forget you."

"I know. Me too."

"But you wouldn't kill yourself," I say.

"No," he says.

I add up again all of the things that I want from life. There is real life and then there are books. I try to puzzle out what is real and what isn't, what I can have and what I never will.

"But you do love me," I say.

"Yes," Jamie says, "the way people love each other in real life."

I lean forward and lay my head on his shoulder.

"I guess I love you in the way people love in real life too."

He smiles and I feel his lips in my hair. I close my eyes and bury my face in him.

thirty

I'M SITTING ON THE BACK porch reading after a trip to the library this afternoon. The book is old and has that dusty, musty smell I love. The author is Irish, probably dead, and someone I've never heard of before today. The book is surely out of print by now, and I feel as if I am holding a lost treasure in my hands. I stop suddenly and close my eyes. This book *is* a treasure; I did not suspect it would be so good when I picked it up, but now I can feel the printed words seeping through my skin and into my veins, rushing to my heart and marking it forever. I want to savor this wonder, this happening of loving a book and reading it for the first time, because the first time is always the best, and I will never read this book for the first time ever again.

I sigh and look out across the backyard. Today is the longest day of the year, and the sun is only just reaching the horizon behind the trees. The air feels good in my lungs, and my muscles are relaxed and warm in the slowly fading sunshine. I will sit here for a moment longer and be happy. Though I am dying to look down again and read more, I'll sit here and love this book and know that I still have so much more left to read because that won't be true for very long.

Next door, the back door slams and two voices are talking quietly on the porch. I glance up startled.

"So that's it then," Aunt Angelina says. Her voice is calm and even.

"Yes, it is," the other says. "I'll be in touch later, but for now this is it."

"Fine then. Goodbye."

"Goodbye, Angelina."

Kevin the Football Man walks off the porch and into his car without looking back. Aunt Angelina stands on the porch and watches him as he maneuvers out of the narrow, long driveway and disappears.

After he is gone, she continues to look out over the gravel driveway into the yard and setting sun and I look at her.

"Autumn," she says. I start in my seat and stop breathing. She still stares straight ahead. "Try to marry your first love. For the rest of your life, no one will ever treat you as well."

She turns to leave then and closes the door behind her.

Suddenly it is very quiet outside, and the glitter is gone from the grass and leaves, and even though the sun is only beginning to set, I think soon it will be too dark to read. I close my book and stand up.

I'll go inside and make something for dinner and read more later. I will have to wait for the magic to come back before opening it again. I'll wait until I remember that Aunt Angelina is happy with her life and that I *will* marry my first love. It will only be the first time once.

thirty-one

SASHA AND I ARE WALKING to the drugstore, even though she could borrow her mother's car and drive us. It takes up more of the long, hot day if we walk, makes it more like an adventure than just something to do. Against the sound of the cicadas, our sandals smack on the sidewalk as we hike our way toward Main Street. We stop along the way to scratch bug bites on our ankles and make sure our bra straps aren't showing from under our tank tops. We are talking as we walk, in spite of the clouds of heat that puff down our throats with each breath.

When we get there, we will sigh in the air-conditioning and run our fingers through our hair. Perched side by side atop the layer of magazines on the bottom shelf of the massive stand, we will flip through articles about sex and hair. We will even balance the month's massive bridal book on our knees and look at the white dresses and rings with a sort of reverence. Afterward, we will stroll through the aisles and pick out lip gloss and candy, nail polish and sodas. We'll walk back to my house then, and in my room we will stretch out on my bed, our bare legs brushing, and read the magazines we bought and eat licorice.

This is the background of our day together, but the real purpose of being together is talking. Sasha and I can talk about nearly anything, and when we talk, we talk for a long time, a whole day even.

There is a sudden lull in our conversation, an unnatural pause after my story about last night's date with Jamie. I look over at her, but she stares straight ahead down the sidewalk as if there is someone waiting for her there.

"I have to tell you something," she says, still staring at the invisible person.

"What?" I ask. My mind is already tabulating all the possibilities; I'm the sort of person who tries to figure out the end of the book as she reads it and my conversations are no different.

"I think I'm going to break up with Alex," she says.

"You can't," I say, as five different threads run through my mind and I try to sort through all the thoughts and reactions: jealous that she is so brave, smug that Jamie and I lasted, worried for Alex, surprised—

"I'm going to," she says. "I've already decided really."

"But why?" I ask, the shock momentarily overshadowing all the other reactions. She shrugs and looks down at the sidewalk to frown. Up ahead, I see the corner where we will wait at the crosswalk. In our impatience with the heat, we will push the button again and again, and even though we know it will not make the green letters appear any faster, we will stare at the sign expectantly.

"I still love Alex," she says, "in a way. But I don't feel about him the way I used to. Nothing is romantic anymore. It's more like we're old friends."

"But that's what long-term relationships are like," I say. "You can't just throw him away."

"I'm not throwing him away," she says. "But I'm not in love anymore, and I need you to support me."

"I'm sorry," I say. I stop walking and we turn to each other. I hug her and she holds me back. We're both dewy and hot to the touch. "I'm just surprised. And sad."

And jealous, and smug, and worried.

We let go of each other and continue our walk and our day together.

thirty-two

THE BREAKUP HAPPENS AND THERE are days of discussion. Jamie is annoyed with Sasha, but I defend her right to end the relationship. The boys are vague in their reports on how Alex is doing. They try to tell us that they don't talk about Sasha when they hang out, but that is too ridiculous to be true.

In August, Angie gets a new boyfriend, also from Hazelwood High, but this one is, to our amusement, on the football team and rather preppy. Angie warns us about this first, swearing that he is actually very cool and knows all sorts of good music. I wonder what kind of warning he is receiving in turn about us.

We make plans to meet Angie's Dave on a triple date to the movies. Brooke and Noah ride with us to the mall, and we laugh and wonder aloud about Preppy Dave. I'm determined to like him for Angie's sake, but I worry a bit about the boys.

"This is going to be hilarious," Jamie says.

"Don't tease him too much," I say.

"I'm not going to be mean to him," Jamie says. He rolls his eyes even though he's driving and I glance at the road for him. "But we might need to do a tiny bit of hazing, you know, just to make sure this prepster is good enough for Angie. Right, Noah?"

"We can't have Angie with someone who doesn't deserve her," Noah says.

"You will both behave," Brooke says. I twist around in my seat to watch her glare at Noah. "Or you will both be in trouble." She turns the glare over at her cousin in the driver's seat, but he obviously can't see her, so she smacks the back of his head.

"Hey!" Jamie says. He reaches one hand back and grabs at her knee; the car swerves, and we all laugh and scream. Brooke squeals the loudest as Jamie pinches the soft place above her kneecap and we laugh again. Jamie rights the car again and we speed down the road, talking loudly now above the radio and laughing as we trade threats back and forth with the boys.

I feel a pang of guilt knowing that Sasha and Alex are at home while we're all out without them, but it's just the way things are now. Maybe someday they'll both be seeing other people and we could have a quintuple date.

Angie, with new pink streaks in her blond hair, is waiting for us at the food court with a tall broad-shouldered boy who has vibrant red hair. She waves enthusiastically when she sees us and tugs on his hand as she points. She is wearing the authentic poodle skirt she bought last spring, and he's wearing a polo shirt. They couldn't look more odd together if they were different species. He looks nervous as we approach, and that immediately endears him to me.

"Hey," Angie says. "Everybody, this is Dave. Dave, everybody."

The boys, in what I know is a tactic to try and throw him off, shake hands with Dave and introduce themselves formally. Noah fakes a British accent. Dave copies their formalities with a straight face but manages to convey the same mocking air as them, and I'm hopeful for him.

We have an hour until the movie starts and so we wander around the mall. When Brooke and I move next to Angie so that we can admire her new hair, the boys suddenly flank Dave. I'm worried again, but they seem to have decided to think of him as some sort of pet. Jamie tells Dave that he also owns a polo shirt. It's black and has a little man on it riding a horse. Noah, still faking his British accent, says he only wears his polo shirts when he is playing polo, but he would defend to the death the right for any man to wear polo shirts at all times. Dave laughs and tells them that he also owns a pair of ripped jeans; perhaps he can wear them next time they meet and Jamie can wear the polo. Noah thinks it's a jolly idea.

I had been curious and surprised when I first heard about Dave, but now in person I can see his appeal. He's bashful and frequently pink-cheeked under his freckles. His smile is crooked and unassuming. By the time we are buying our tickets, I am charmed.

There is something adorable about the way Dave looks with us, one lone khaki-clad sheep in a pack of rebel wolves. Even his expression is sheepish as he talks with us and holds hands with Angie. As we wait in line, she tells us in a whisper that he was worried that we wouldn't like him since he was different.

"Of course not," I say. "We aren't like that at all."

"I know, that's what I told him," she says.

thirty-three

WE ARE JUNIORS, AND SUDDENLY it is all happening too fast, except it has always been this way, we just hadn't realized it before. This year and then one more. This year and then one more, and one more and one more.

We are allowed to drive to school now, and Jamie picks me up every morning. It feels strange and wonderful to be responsible for arriving at school, knowing that Jamie could just keep driving forever and we would not be missed until the end of the day, and by then we would be far, far away. But we always go to school.

I have begun to receive mail every afternoon, piles of college brochures and form letters from university deans. Pictures of glossy students tumbled together in front of statues and fountains, playing Frisbee and reclining on blankets surrounded by books. These students walk through perfect autumns and warm summers. "It's like this every day here," their smiles say. "Really."

All of them have an English education major. If the brochure does not list a creative writing minor, I toss it out. If it does, then it joins the orderly and small but growing pile by my desk. The pile has a neat look of efficiency, though it sits and waits and accomplishes nothing.

On the Steps to Nowhere, we compare dreams that are beginning to sound like plans. Jamie says he will major in business. I imagine us living in a Victorian house in our town. He will have to drive to an office in the city every day. Looking at the future, I feel that I am looking into a snow globe at a tiny, perfect house with a little person that is me standing in the yard like a flagpole. One meticulously carved scene that represents the whole world—tiny, perfect, and enclosed.

Finny and I have one class together: the section of Honors English that neither his friends nor mine are in. Ours is the last class in the afternoon; theirs is in the morning. It is odd to think of it that way, of us and them. Them in the morning, us in the afternoon, us before the last bell rings.

My assigned seat is the very middle of the very front row, and, were I to stretch and lean forward, my fingertips would brush the edge of the teacher's desk. Finny's is the seat behind mine, and it would take even less to touch any part of him.

In this class, we are closer together than when we eat dinner with The Mothers or sit on the same couch while we wait for the evening to be over. Sometimes his knee jabs into my chair as he twists around to reply to a classmate, or sometimes we turn to look into our book bags at the same moment, and even though I do not look, I know our faces are inches apart.

We never greet each other. We take these assigned seats and pull our notebooks and pens out of our bags in silence or talking to the others around us. It is an unspoken agreement not to speak here, just like our unspoken decision to always exchange a few words in front of The Mothers, just like our unspoken apologies for the War last year.

And I'm grateful that he agrees with me that we should not speak here, because no one in this class knew us in elementary school. All they know is that he is Finn Smith, the most popular boy in our grade, and I am Autumn Davis, Jamie Allen's girlfriend who wears the tiaras, and that is how we would have to speak to each other, as if he was just another classmate and that is all there is between us. The strain of having to speak like that with him, along with all the other unsaid things, would be too much for me, and I don't know what I would say or do.

One afternoon, I overhear a girl asking Finny if he's picked out a major for college. This girl has been trying to flirt with him since the first day of school, but he somehow hasn't noticed. He seems to think that she is just generally friendly. I stare straight ahead but listen behind me. I hear a swishing sound that must be the girl flipping her hair.

"I want to go to medical school," he says, "so my bachelor's degree has to be something to lead into that. But I dunno."

"Wow. That is *so* cool," the girl says. Based on her tone of voice, I don't think there was anything Finny could have said that she wouldn't have found cool.

She doesn't know Finny well enough to understand how cool it actually is that he has found this calling. When we were small, he said that he wanted to be a professional soccer player, but he always said it with a shrug. He loved—loves—playing soccer, but he never felt a *need* to play in the same way I needed to make up stories. Finny's instincts have always led him to help people, and now he's found a way that he can help in a very direct and real way.

I envy how Finny has chosen the direction of his life without having had to commit to a destination. He doesn't know what kind of doctor he wants to be. Aunt Angelina said he's talked about pediatrics and Doctors Without Borders, but he's also mentioned an interest in psychiatry.

"I guess it's kinda cool," Finny says. "I'll just have to decide on something eventually."

"Yeah," the Flirty Girl says. I hear the swish of her hair again. "I don't know what I want at all."

I stop myself from turning around and telling her that knowing what you want can be far worse. There isn't any reason for me to be interested in Finn Smith's conversations.

thirty-four

FINNY'S FIRST SOCCER GAME IS on a Tuesday afternoon in September, the third week of school. It didn't seem like a day that would be important.

I hadn't even planned on going.

Finny and Sylvie weren't on the bus that afternoon. They stayed at school for his game and her cheerleading practice. I was the only one to get off at our stop. I am alone with the day as I walk down the street toward home. Yesterday, it had been as hot as August, but this morning we had a cool rain that left the air chilled. A few leaves on a few trees are starting to turn yellow or a little red. If the weather lasts the next few days, then more will turn, but before long it will be hot again; September is still a summer month.

The rosebush by the front door looks like a poet's overly enthusiastic description. It's literally drooping under the weight of so many full blooms and waiting buds.

I close the door against the chill air and drop my book bag on the floor.

"Mom?"

On the coffee table is a stack of mail. It's not like her to leave the mail out like this; it should already be opened and filed. Underneath the electric bill, I see a pile of glossy smiles all wearing the same burgundy sweatshirts. "Come to Springfield!" they say. I recognize one of them. All the kids in honors classes got to take a field trip to a college fair. It was just a huge room with booths and student representatives with brochures. One of the girls on this cover was there. She grinned at Jamie and I just like all the other people standing behind booths had. The girl asked me questions and wrote my answers down on a clipboard. I repeated my routine about majoring in English education and taking a minor in creative writing because I could always write in the summer, etc., etc. She said she was majoring in creative writing, and I was annoyed at myself for how it made me ache a little. Jamie was impatient to move on to another booth; he tugged on my hand and we moved on.

This brochure is about Springfield's creative writing major instead of their teaching program. The girl must have taken down my information wrong. I flip through the pages. It isn't very long.

My mother comes into the foyer, all smiles.

"Hi, honey," she says. I fold the brochure in half and kick off my shoes.

"Hi," I say.

"I thought you would stay late at school for Finny's game."

"Why would I do that?" I say.

"Angelina can't go because of a teachers' meeting. I'm going. I thought you knew."

"Do I have to go?" I ask. I want to be alone in my room right now.

"I thought you'd want to."

"It's not like he'll care if I'm there or not," I say. I look back at the brochure in my hand. The crease has cut the girl's face in half.

"Autumn," my mother says, "why do you always say things like that?" Her voice is a sigh.

I shrug. I could read the brochure at the game. And it's not like I *don't* want to see Finny. Sometimes it's nice to watch him and not have to worry about it looking like I'm staring at him.

"Fine. I'll go," I say. I stick the brochure in my back pocket.

———————

It's five minutes before the game starts, and I've read the brochure twice. Just because something seems impossible doesn't mean that you shouldn't try.

My mother and I are sitting on the top row of metal bleachers, facing the muddy soccer field. A chilly breeze ruffles my hair. The soccer teams are stretching while the referees trudge across the field.

It's not that I want to be a writer and not a teacher, because I already am a writer. What I want is to be a published author, to have a few readers, to be able to hope that somewhere out there, someone loved my book. When I tell this to adults, they tell me about how they knew someone once who wanted something like that and what that person actually ended up doing.

A whistle blows, and Finny leads the soccer team onto the field.

He plays defense. A long time ago, he explained to me that this means it's his job to protect one side of the field. He's naturally good at protecting. I fold the brochure and stick it in my back pocket. Finny has that determined look on his face that he always gets at the start of a game. It's the same face he made as a child, the same furrow in his brow that I know so well. He bounces on his heels as he stands on the field with the other starters, another familiar habit.

Finny said that teaching seemed too normal for me.

Isn't this what all the children's books and movies are always about? How even if the task seems impossible or you're too small or you don't have the right kind of whatever, you're still supposed to try? Until you get to high school and suddenly you're supposed to choose a safe path. A path that won't take you too far from home. A path that isn't too risky. A path that has health insurance and a 401(k).

Finny has the ball. Four players from the other team circle around him. They're trying to take the ball from him and failing.

I can't keep pretending that writing a few weeks out of the summer will be enough. I can't risk looking back on my life and knowing that I did not try to get published as hard as I could have tried.

One of the players surrounding Finny slips in the mud and slides into him. Finny is running too fast to stop; he trips and flips head over heels. Next to me, my mother gasps. I realize it looks like he landed on his neck.

My heart stops.

I am ten years old again, and I cannot imagine life without him.

"I'm okay," I hear Finny shout, but from this far away, his voice is quiet; if it were not a voice that I knew so well, then I wouldn't have heard it. The coaches and refs run across the field and crowd around him. I can't see him anymore, but I can imagine the race of his breathing and I can guess at the pounding of his heart under his ribs. I know the scars on his knees and the cowlick on the back of his head. I've tried to pretend I don't, but I can't pretend anymore.

I know what I am feeling. I know that it is real, and in this moment, there is nothing else in me but this knowledge.

I'm in love with Finny.

The crowd moves away, and I see Finny stand cautiously. He looks up at the bleachers, and I know when he finds my mother and me, because he raises his hand in a wave, letting us know that he is okay.

I've loved him my whole life, and somewhere along the way, that love didn't change but grew. It grew to fill the parts of me that I did not have when I was a child. It grew with every new longing in my body and desire in my heart until there was not a piece of me that did not love him. And when I look at him, there is no other feeling in me.

A whistle blows and the game continues. I take out the brochure again, but now I am only pretending to read it.

thirty-five

MY PARENTS ARE AT THEIR marriage counselor. When they come back, we will go out to dinner and they will ask me questions. We do this once a week now. It was my father's idea. He calls them Family Dinners. This confused me at first because family has always included Angelina and Finny before this.

I'm supposed to be ready to go as soon as they come, so I am waiting by the door. The sun is setting outside, but I cannot see it from the front window. The sky is gray. The leaves are falling early this year.

I am looking forward to eating out tonight. I wrote three poems today and copied them into my blank book with the fountain pen Jamie gave me. I used the violet ink, and I am feeling virtuous and giddy. My homework is done and tomorrow is Friday.

A car goes down the road, and the headlights briefly illuminate a lump further down on the lawn. It's nearly as tall as me and three times as wide. It only takes a moment to recognize, and then I wonder how I could have possibly not noticed it before.

I open the door and run down the lawn. I'm not wearing a jacket, and the air chills me. Just before I leap, I wonder if the leaves might be wet, but I make the dive anyway. The leaves are deliciously dry and crunchy. I am completely surrounded by their dusty smell, even over my head. I laugh out loud, and the scent tumbles down my throat. I burst out of the top, and the pile shifts sideways over the grass. I pick up handfuls and toss them in the air. They fall around me like snow and I throw myself onto my back and look at the fading light in the sky.

When we were small, Finny loved autumn, not because it began with our birthdays, but for the leaves. Finny built us forts by covering cardboard boxes with piles of leaves, and he would try to convince me to stay inside all night with him. I was less enthusiastic about the fallen leaves; they meant that my enemy, winter, was drawing near. The bare trees made me think of death, and back then I had every reason to fear death.

I did love jumping into the leaves though; Finny could always persuade me to do that. While I waited, he would create monster mounds of them, taller than our heads, until I was too impatient to wait any longer, and he would say to wait because there were still so many leaves in our huge yards and he could make an even bigger pile, but I would leap anyway and Finny would have to join me. Sometimes we took turns, and sometimes we held hands and jumped together. We jumped and jumped until the pile was flat again and the leaves were scattered over the yard. Then Finny would go back for the rake and say that this time he would make an even bigger pile, which I would ruin before he was finished. We would pass whole afternoons this way.

I leap out again, scattering more leaves, and run up the lawn again to take my second jump. I aim more carefully this time, hoping to land on top as queen of the hill instead of buried in the middle. I jump, and in my moment of flight I hear his voice.

"Autumn!"

The crunch of the leaves momentarily drowns out all sound. I slide sideways and am buried again. My left leg hangs out, and I draw it in toward my body, instinct telling me to hide even though I know it is silly.

"Autumn?" His voice is close now. I want to burrow deeper and wait for him to leave, but I know that that will not work. I shift upward so that I am sitting in the pile.

Finny is standing three feet in front of me, his arms crossed over his chest. He's frowning at me.

"I spent all afternoon raking both yards," he says. I look around. I've scattered half the pile onto the grass again.

"Sorry," I say. His anger both fascinates and frightens me; I see it so rarely. For a moment, I study his stance, his narrowed eyes. I carefully remember the tone of his voice when he spoke. Everything about him is important. There is a beat of silence. He rolls his eyes and sighs.

"It's fine," Finny says. One corner of his mouth turns up. "That's what I get for putting off bagging until tomorrow. I should have known an unguarded pile of leaves would be too great of a temptation for you."

I have to look away now. It hurts for him to smile at me like that, a friendly, easy smile that says nothing in particular, and therefore tells me everything I need to know about his feelings for me.

I thought that I would have spent the rest of September, the rest of my life, avoiding Finny, but I have not. Nothing has changed. I loved him the very first morning I stood at the bus stop with him and every night I sat across a dinner table from him. It does not matter that one of us now knows; it doesn't change anything.

"I'll fix it," I say. "I'll even bag them up for you."

"No," he says. "It's fine. Really." When I look up at him, I see that his brief anger has evaporated, and his face is clear of anything but amusement. "What's the thing people say?" Finny asks. His brow furrows again but in a different sort of way. "The more things change, the more they stay the same?"

I stumble up and try to brush myself off; suddenly I am itchy and cold. "I should clean up. I'm supposed to be ready to go when Mom and Dad get home."

"You have leaves in your hair," Finny says. "And in your tiara. And everywhere."

I raise my hand and run my fingers through my hair, and he does not move. The sun is gone now, and the evening shifts around us as cars' headlights throw their light at us and pass on. I see his handsome face and his half smile and the golden lock of hair hanging in his face.

I love you, Finny, I think.

"Where are you going?" he says. I cannot help my frown.

"Family Dinner," I say.

"Oh," he says. My next words surprise me, but Finny does not seem startled at all.

"My father's decided he wants us to be a regular family," I say.

"Sounds familiar," Finny says.

"Oh," I say. "I heard about that."

Finny's father invited Finny and Angelina out for dinner. It's scheduled for next month.

"It's okay, I guess," he says, and I'm glad. Okay means he isn't hurt or resentful. Okay means he isn't pinning too high of hopes on the man. A bit of the burden I've carried eases. But it won't last forever. There will always be something I cannot protect him from. Sylvie may break his heart again. The tendons in his legs could tear at his next soccer game. Someday someone he loves will die.

My parents' headlights flash across us.

"Have a good dinner," he says.

"You too," I say, and I think that he understands what I mean, because he nods. We turn away from each other without saying goodbye. I hear the crunch of the leaves under his feet fade away as I walk the long lawn toward the car.

"Were you and Finny jumping in the leaves?" Mom asks when I slide into the back seat. I look over myself to see if I'm still covered in leaves.

"No," I say. When I close the door, the lights shut off, and I see what she must have seen—back in the shadows, someone tall and lean is pulling himself up out of the leaves and dusting himself off.

thirty-six

I AM READING *WUTHERING HEIGHTS*. It was assigned for school, and I woke up this morning and decided to read the first chapter in bed. It is late afternoon and I am still there. An hour ago, I finished the novel and fell asleep. I dreamed fitfully of Heathcliff locking me away, and when I woke, I picked the book up again and started over.

I do not think Cathy is a monster.

Jamie calls to tell me that he has a present for me. He went to a movie with Sasha this afternoon, the kind with guns and explosions that I refuse to see and Sasha is always up for. After a day spent in bed reading, I have a groggy feeling of unreality, as if I am only watching everything that is happening.

"Are you okay?" Jamie says.

"Yeah," I say.

"You sound funny."

"I was reading," I say.

"Well, I'm coming over," he says, "so try to be in one piece for me."

After hanging up the phone, I stand in the middle of my room, unsure of what to do now. I stretch my arms above my head, and my mind clears enough to think that I should get ready to see him. As I brush my hair, I think with some worry of Jamie driving in the snow, until I remember that it is a sunny autumn day; it was only snowing inside my book. It was snowing, and the narrator was seeing the remains of Cathy's tragic mistake.

The sun is bright but the breeze carries the promise of a chill. Unaware that they have stayed past their season, my mother's roses sway in this breeze and scatter a few petals among the red and gold leaves. I wonder if they can feel the cold. I wait for Jamie on the back porch steps.

I love Jamie just as much as I always have.

My love for Finny is buried like a stillborn child; it is just as cherished and just as real, but nothing will ever come of it. I imagine it wrapped up in lace, tucked away in a quiet corner of my heart. It will stay there for the rest of my life, and when I die, it will die with me.

One of the rose petals blows across the yellow leaves and stops on the toe of my boot.

I stare at that rose petal until I hear Jamie's car stop in the driveway. I look up and see him smiling and closing the door.

"Hello, pretty girl," he says, and I smile back. His handsome face surprises me as if I am seeing it for the first time. He sits down next to me and nudges me with his elbow.

"You awake?" he asks. I nod. This is my life, I realize. And I haven't made any tragic mistakes yet. I've made a choice, yes, but no one suffers for it but me, and in the end, all will be well.

"How was the movie?" I ask.

"Awesome. And then we went to lunch and I got you this." He hands me a hard plastic egg, the kind that snaps together that you get for a quarter from a machine outside of cheap diners. I laugh, and Jamie grins at my response. It breaks open with a cracking sound. Inside is a poorly painted rubber dinosaur. Its eyes are wide as if it has been startled awake. I laugh again.

"I'll name it after you and keep it on my desk," I say.

"And this," Jamie says, and he hands me a pink bouncy ball. Before I can throw it against the steps, he holds his fist out again. Jamie opens his fingers and a wire ring with a plastic stone drops into my palm. The stone is purple and as big as one of my knuckles.

"I spent all my quarters," he says.

It almost sparkles in the weak light. He gave me another charm for our anniversary and he spent all his quarters for me on the afternoon we were apart. I cannot lose him.

"Thank you," I say. "I'll treasure it forever."

Jamie kisses me and I lean against his shoulder and listen to him talk about the movie. He does not notice that my mind is far away.

thirty-seven

NORMALLY OUR GROUP HAPHAZARDLY TRADES Christmas presents the last week of school, but Angie convinced us to do something special this year. On the last day of the semester, we exchange gifts at our favorite restaurant.

Each of my friends gives me a tiara. They planned it out together and assigned colors. Two weeks before, my very first tiara slipped off my head as I ran across the school parking lot, and it was run over before I could grab it. Led by Jamie, my friends found my distress amusing, and now led by him, they each try to replace the lost favorite. Jamie gives me a shoe rack he has converted into a "tiara stand," a cool rock that he found, and a burned CD of songs that have meaning to us.

My friends follow my suggestion to each wear the tiara they gave me so that I can better judge which is my new favorite. The waiters think we are celebrating a birthday.

I needed this; for the past few weeks, I've had this melancholy following me around. I'm happy today, and I think that maybe things will be better now.

I bought Alex a remote-control car that does flips, Angie two vintage paperback romance novels, Noah a set of walkie-talkies, and Brooke a yellow silk scarf with brown flowers.

For Jamie, I found a Polaroid camera at a garage sale. He says he will use it to provide proof to win arguments and record important moments in his life, such as beating Noah at chess or stealing traffic cones.

I bought Sasha a rosebush, because she told me she always wanted one when she was a little girl. It's sitting in a black plastic bucket and looks nearly dead this close to true winter. The boys laugh, but Sasha names it Judith and asks the waiter to bring another chair for it to sit in.

Sasha and Alex are real friends now, not just pretending to make things less awkward for us. Alex gives her plastic fruit, and they both laugh and will not tell us what the joke is about. Jamie vows to get it out of him later, and then to tell me.

Angie is still with Preppy Dave, and we all still like him. He's meeting us at the movies after dinner. They are happy. They look and act so different yet something about them tells everyone they're a couple, even if they're just standing next to each other.

On our last double date with Noah and Brooke, we girls decided to have a double wedding. We draw sketches of our dresses on napkins and annoy the boys by making decisions every time we are together. Tonight we have agreed to have at least five swans wandering around the ceremony site, which will hopefully be in an abandoned church at midnight.

We are laughing, and I look around and I cannot believe that only a few years ago, I did not know a single one of them.

"I propose a toast," Jamie says.

"You should stand on your chair," Noah says.

"I think that would be the last straw for the staff," Brooke says.

"Speech! Speech!" Alex says. Jamie raises his glass.

"To us," he says. And we drink to that.

thirty-eight

WINTER HITS ME HARD THIS year. There is no sky this winter and not a single leaf clinging to a single twig. The icy wind burns through my gloves and my fingers ache until they fall numb and silent.

I cannot find anything to read. I wander through the shelves of the library, and take piles of books with me, but each one disappoints after fifty pages, and I let them drop to the floor.

After school, I take naps in my bed and at dinnertime get up without fixing the sheets again. By then the sun is already setting, and there is nothing to do but eat and get through as much homework as I must before going to bed. I know that I should stop sleeping through the afternoons; I've started waking an hour or more before my alarm, and I lay awake in the dark and watch my window go from black to gray.

That's when I think about things that I never let myself think about during the day.

At school, I am exhausted from my early waking, and by last period, I have a terrible struggle to stay awake. My English teacher doesn't like me as much as I think she should. When she sees me doze off twice in class, she decides that I'm not a good student no matter what I write or say in class. I stop participating in the discussions.

When I come home in the afternoon and the cold gray hours are stretching on before me, I cannot stop myself from sliding under the covers and hiding in obliviousness.

I fight with Jamie because he doesn't understand anything I say. I hate him for not truly knowing me deep down inside, and at the end of our dates, I cling to his coat and beg him to never leave me. He says he never will.

It snows a few times, but a wet sloppy snow that collects dirt and makes puddles. It is never enough to cancel school, never enough to be beautiful.

It makes sense that Finny loves Sylvie and doesn't miss me.

At least once a week, he and Aunt Angelina come to dinner, or we go to them, and The Mothers talk while we eat, and afterward I say I have homework and I go upstairs or cross the lawn alone. I cannot sit in silence watching television with him. I cannot bear our small talk as he passes the remote to me. He is the better one of the two of us; he always was. Perhaps he is relieved to not have me holding him back anymore. He has so many friends now. He has Sylvie. It makes sense.

My father is back to his old schedule, no more Family Dinners, and I am angry with my mother for being upset. She should have expected this, she should have known better, and I hate her for making me sad for her. I have enough without having to worry about her too.

My hands are dry and red, and my lips chap. I look in the mirror and do not think I am pretty. Some days, I do not bother to wear my tiaras, until people's comments and questions make it easier to just grab any old one on my way out the door. I do not bother to see if it matches my outfit.

I cannot write anything good. I try and I fail. I realize now that it's all fake. It always was. I turn off my computer and rip up my paper.

I used to say to myself that I just have to get through winter, that I just have to wait. That things would get better then.

And I know that winter is supposed to end, but things are not always the way they are supposed to be.

thirty-nine

MY MOTHER SITS DOWN ON my bed. I am lying on my side, facing the window. If I ignore her, she might go away.

"Autumn?" she says. Her voice is low. She thinks I am sleeping. "Autumn, we need to talk." She runs her fingers through my hair and I let her; it feels good. She keeps stroking and the bristling resentment relaxes. I sigh.

"About what?"

"Can you sit up?"

"I'm tired."

"I'm worried about you." I shake her hands from my hair and sit up.

"I'm fine," I say. "I'm just having trouble sleeping at night. It will be okay when winter is over. I just have to get through winter."

"I think it's more than that, honey," she says. "I've made an appointment with Dr. Singh."

At first, the statement is so ordinary that I do not know why she is telling me. Dr. Singh is her psychiatrist. She sees him every few months. But she keeps looking at me.

"For me?" I say. She nods and tries to touch my hair again. I flinch away again.

"I'm not depressed," I say. "You are."

"I know the symptoms," she says.

"No. You're just projecting on me. Everything is fine. When it's warm again, I'll feel better. That's the only thing that's wrong."

"I'll be picking you up early on Thursday," she says, and she starts to get up.

"I don't need drugs," I say. She closes the door behind her. Her footsteps going down the stairs are the only sound. At dinner she says nothing, and the next day she lets me sleep.

The call from the office comes fifteen minutes into English class. I begin to pack my bag as soon as the intercom beeps. I want it all to be over already.

"There isn't any homework," Mrs. Stevens says. "Is there somebody you can get notes from?"

"Yes," I say. I am standing now.

"Who?" she says. This is why I do not like her. I suspect her of suspecting things of me.

"Finn," I say, and then I remember Jamie and Sasha have this class too. It wouldn't help to take it back now. Mrs. Stevens looks surprised. She likes Finny; perhaps she doesn't think he would associate with someone like me. The scattered whispers I hear tell me that a few of my classmates are surprised too.

"I can drop them by tonight," Finny says. I wonder if he is sort of defending me. I don't look at either of them when I leave.

My mother is sitting in the office in a tailored suit with leather pumps and a clutch purse in her lap. Her ankles are crossed, and the secretary is laughing with her. She rises when I open the door and smiles at me.

"Have a nice day," the secretary says to her, smiling too. I'm sure she could never imagine the rest of my mother's life, the medication and the fights with my father, her times in the hospital. Sometimes I admire my mother's ability to appear perfect; today I hate it.

My mother's shoes click evenly on the linoleum as we walk down the hall.

"What class are you missing?" she asks.

"English."

"Oh. Sorry. Too bad it couldn't have been math," she says. I shrug. "I love you," she says.

"Mom," I say. She doesn't say anything else.

The office my mother brings me to has the smallest waiting room I have ever sat inside. It reminds me of my mother's walk-in closet, the small, windowless room where Finny and I turned out the lights and told ghost stories in the middle of the day. I sit down on one of the padded plastic chairs, and my mother tells the nurse my name. I flinch at the sound; I do not belong here. Two chairs down from me, an old man is bouncing his left leg, then his right, back and forth. Every once in a while, he snaps his fingers as if someone just called bingo before him.

"Damn," he mumbles. Across the room from us, a large black woman is weeping silently. Both of her fists are stuffed with tissues. Still sobbing, she reaches in her purse and takes out a piece of gum, scattering tissues over the gray carpet.

My mother sits down next to me and crosses her ankles. "It'll be a bit," she says. "He's running a little late." She picks up a *Newsweek* and begins reading.

I look down at the table. Most of the magazines are for parents or golfers. While I'm looking, a man gets up and takes a kids' *Highlights* magazine off the table and sits back down.

"Mom?" I whisper. She looks at me and raises her eyebrows. "All these people are really weird." My mother covers her mouth and laughs silently.

"Honey," she whispers, "what did you expect? And what do you think they would say about the girl with the tiara and ripped knee socks?" I scowl at her and she goes back to reading.

"Aw, shucks," the old man mumbles.

———————

"Autumn?" a nurse in blue says. I stand up, suddenly feeling exposed in front of the others. The old man and the crying lady have been replaced by a girl my age and her cranky baby.

"I'll be waiting," my mother says. I do not look at her. The nurse leads me to a narrow hallway. A small Indian man is waiting for me.

"Autumn?" he asks. I nod. "Ah, come with me," he says with a thick accent. We walk to an office even smaller than the waiting room, and crowded with a desk, a bookshelf, a filing cabinet, and a small chair. He motions for me to sit in the small chair. I'm disappointed that it isn't a couch. He sits down at the desk and opens a file.

"So, Autumn," he says. "What brings you here today?"

"My mother."

"Mmm hmm, and why is that?"

"She says she's worried about me."

"Hmm," Dr. Singh says. I look back at him. "Why do you wear the tiara?"

"Because I like it."

"I see, and how long has this been going on?"

"I don't know. A couple of years."

"Are you frightened to be without it? Anxious or worried?"

"No." We stare at each other for another few moments. He writes something down.

"How is your appetite, Autumn?"

"Fine," I say.

"Really? What did you eat today?"

"My mother made me oatmeal for breakfast—"

"And did you eat the oatmeal your mother made you?"

"Yes."

He makes some notes on his papers. I watch him. His handwriting is too small and messy for me to read.

"Autumn," he says. He stands. "Come over here and I will check your weight." He leads me over to a small scale. The scale is covered with the name of a drug I've seen advertised on TV. I stand on the scale, and he makes some notes.

"I don't have an eating disorder," I say.

"Mmm hmm," he says and makes more notes. We sit down again.

"Why is your mother worried about you?" he says.

"She thinks I'm depressed," I say. "Like her."

"Like her?" He gives me an intent look as if I've let something slip.

"She's one of your patients," I say.

"Ah," he flips through some papers in the file. He reads something, looks at me, then reads again. Finally he closes the file.

"And so tell me about your depression, Autumn."

"I don't think I'm depressed."

He cocks his head to the side. "Are you sad?" he says.

"Well, yeah."

"What is making you sad?"

"I don't know," I say.

"You do not know?" he says. I shake my head and look at the floor. He writes something down and keeps talking. It is the longest he has looked away from me this whole time.

"How long have you been sad?"

"A few months," I say. "It's winter."

"Are you sad every day?"

"Pretty much, but that's not that weird, right? I mean, it's not that big of a deal."

"Do you have increased feelings of anger, Autumn?"

"I don't know."

"Are you finding yourself irritated more often?"

"Well, yeah," I say.

"Are you anxious or worried?"

"No."

"How are you sleeping?"

"Okay, I guess," I say. "I sleep a lot, but I've also been waking up early in the morning."

"And you cannot get back to sleep?" he says.

"No," I say.

He nods. Dr. Singh lays his pen down and looks at me. "Have you had any suicidal thoughts? Do you wish to die?

"No," I say.

"Are you sure, Autumn?"

I nod slowly. The question frightens me.

He continues, "Depression affects the sleeping patterns. Some sleep more and some sleep less. Very often, the people who wake up very early in the mornings are the ones who have suicidal thoughts."

"But I'm not depressed," I say.

"You think you deserve to be sad," he says. There is a moment of silence as we look at each other. "You think it is okay for you to be sad every day. But it is not okay. And you do not deserve it."

I look down at the floor, even though I know he has already seen the tears stinging my eyes.

"It is not shameful," he says. "It is okay."

I nod. I hear his pen scratching against the paper as he writes again.

My mother takes the prescription from me without saying anything and we drive by the drugstore before we go home. At first, she is constantly asking me if I took my medicine, then it drops off and no one says anything about it ever.

After a few weeks, I start to feel better, but whether it is because of the pills or because spring has finally come, I am not sure.

forty

THE SMELL OF BLEACH STINGS my nostrils, and Sasha is laughing in my ear as I bend over her. It is Thursday after school and we are dying her hair, first blond, then we will add blue chunks in the front. I'm trying to spread the white cream through her hair without getting any of it on her skin or mine. My fingers work intimately over her scalp, twined in her hair.

"Don't move your head," I say. My hands are sweaty inside the thin plastic gloves the kit provided. The window behind me is open. The air is still a little chilled, but the sun is warm and the smell is too strong not to leave it open.

"When are you going to dye your hair again?" Sasha says. Her head is tilted back, and her eyes follow my face as my hands move through her hair.

"Never," I say. "It's too much trouble."

"Is it because you don't think Jamie would like it?"

"No," I say. "Jamie says he would think I was beautiful no matter what."

"You guys are so cute. Sometimes I'm jealous." Sasha is the only single one in the group now. Alex has taken up with a freshman girl with a fake diamond in her nose. We don't like her. We think she is presumptuous and kinda slutty looking. Jamie calls her "Alex's bitch" when they aren't around.

I peel the gloves off my hands and set the timer for twenty minutes, then slump down on the edge of the tub.

"I wish you would get back with Alex," I say.

"I've been thinking about that lately," Sasha says. I sit up and grip the ledge of the claw-foot tub.

"Really?" I say.

"I miss him," Sasha says. "But he's with that Trina girl now."

"If you took her place, you would be doing us all a favor."

"Yeah, I know." We make faces of disgust at each other. I jump up.

"We need to get to work on this immediately—I'm going to call Jamie." I dash out the door and down the hall to my room, where my cell phone sits on my dresser.

Jamie picks up on the first ring.

"Hey," he says.

"We're going to break up Alex and Trina," I say.

"Awesome," he says. "How?"

"We're going to get Alex and Sasha back together."

"Oh. Can we break them up without doing that?"

"No, Sasha wants to get back with him. And this will make the group all neat again." I twirl around and cross my room.

"She does?"

"You sound surprised." I begin to make my way back toward the bathroom. I can hear the ticking of the timer again.

"I dunno if I liked them as a couple," he says.

"What?" I stop in my tracks outside the bathroom door. "Why not?"

"I don't know. Never mind. We need to get rid of Alex's bitch."

"Exactly," I say. I open the door, and the smell of bleach hits me again. "Why don't you come over after I'm done dying Sasha's hair and we can plot?"

"What color are you dying it?"

"Blue."

"Cool."

"I know. She wanted green, but I changed her mind. I'll call you okay?"

"Okay. Love you."

"Love you more." Sasha makes a gagging noise and I swat at her arm. Jamie hangs up. "He's in," I say. Sasha laughs. I look at the timer. There are still ten minutes left. I sit down again. "You're going to love your hair."

At school the next day, we complain to Alex that we never see him anymore. We make up private jokes that he missed because he was hanging out with Trina. The next night, we go to a movie, and Angie brings Preppy Dave, but we do not tell Alex to invite Trina. Sasha sits next to Alex in the theater, and they share a bucket of popcorn.

Alex spends the night at Jamie's. Jamie tells Alex that he doesn't like Trina. That nobody likes Trina. That everybody likes Sasha. That Sasha misses him.

It isn't until the following Monday, after Alex has broken up with Trina and is holding Sasha's hand on the Steps to Nowhere, that I see anything frightening in what we have done. I had not known that my friends and I held such power over each other, that we could change Alex's heart as easily as I had dyed Sasha's hair. We have created among ourselves something that is more powerful than any of us could hold separately. Over, around, and through us, we are a force, woven, tied, and bundled together. If in the future we separate, it will look so simple on the outside, a falling away, a slipping of ties. And on the inside, we will be ripped and shredded, torn as the bonds that hold us are pulled away.

We grew apart, we will say. It was an accident.

I sit on the Steps to Nowhere with my friends, and we laugh. It is spring and a breeze is ruffling our hair like loving fingers. We sit so close together that we constantly brush against each other. We touch each other with the casualness that love allows. Noah and Alex thumb-wrestle. Angie pokes me and asks what I'm doing after school. Brooke reaches out to admire Sasha's new hair. We have sat like this for a hundred days and we think we will for another hundred and one.

This is friendship, and it is love, but I already know what they have not learned yet; how dangerous friendship is, how damaging love can be.

forty-one

I AM ASLEEP IN MY bed, dreaming something that I will not remember in a few moments, because my cell phone is ringing. The glow of the screen in the dark night wakes me as much as the chirping song. I fumble instinctively for it on my nightstand, and somewhere in my mind, I am registering the late time on my clock, somehow trying to sort through the dream I am losing. My fingers wrap around the phone and hold it close to my face for reading.

Finny.

My dream is gone, and all that is left is the reality of Finny's name glowing at me in the dark. I sit up in bed. The phone chirps again.

"Hello?" I say.

"Dude, it's a girl." I do not know the voice or the laughter in the background.

"Hello?" I say. My sleepy logic thinks that if I say my correct lines, the other side will follow.

"Hey, what are you—" There is a shout and some shuffling, and the noise stops. I look down at my phone, which dutifully tells me that the conversation lasted fifteen seconds. I blink down at it, and the phone rings again. Finny. I press the button. I hold it to my ear.

"Hello?"

"Autumn? I'm sorry."

"Finny?"

"Yeah, it's me." I fall back on my pillows and close my eyes. I feel relieved, but I'm too tired to try to sort out why. It's just that it's him, so it's okay.

"What was that?"

"Some guys got ahold of my phone—I'm at a party—I guess they called you because you're first in my phone—"

"I'm first in your phone?" I feel the corners of my mouth turn up and hope he cannot hear my surprised pleasure.

"Well, yeah. Alphabetical order. You know." His voice trails off at the end.

"Oh, right." I rub my eyes and sigh. "I'm still half asleep."

"I'm sorry," Finny says.

"It's okay," I say. "Really."

"They're drunk and being stupid. It won't happen again."

"Are you drunk?"

"No, I'm driving."

"That's good," I say. I don't know what I mean by that, but it feels true, so it's what I say.

"Hey, hold on," he says. And then quietly, not to me, "Is she

207

sick again?" Another voice, female, answers him. "Okay," he says. "Hey, Autumn?"

"Yeah?"

"I'm gonna let you get back to sleep, okay? Sorry about before."

"It's fine. Good night."

"Good night."

I wait for him to hang up first. I can hear the noise of the party in the background. I count to three slowly, and I can still hear him breathing.

He hangs up.

The phone drops to the floor, and I roll over and bury my face in my pillow. The ache in my chest pounds and hums with my heart. When was the last time his voice was in this room with me, in the dark? A deluge of memories hits me. Us, such small children, sleeping curled together like baby rabbits. Older, we whisper secrets to each other at night. We place fingers over each other's lips to stifle our giggles. Our despair when The Mothers said we were too old to sleep in the same bed. Finny signaling me with a flashlight from his window, and me taking the cup and string to my ear, "Can you hear me?"

The love I've tried to hold back breaks its dam and flows over me, curling my toes and making fists of my hands as I breathe his name into my pillow.

"Finny," I say to the lonely dark. "Finny. My Finny." My breath shudders and my eyelids close against the pain of loving him. Finny. My Finny.

forty-two

ON THE LAST DAY OF school, Jamie and I make out in his pool after the others have gone. The concrete rim digs into my back when he presses into me. My hand is down the back of his trunks and I can feel his muscles clenching. I want to bite his shoulder but he wouldn't like it. Instead, I draw my lips back to his and he slides his tongue inside. His groan vibrates in my mouth.

"Jamie, I love you," I say.

"How much?" he says. He presses into me again.

"So much," I say. The urge comes over me again and I kiss his shoulder instead.

"Please?" he says, and as he presses, my skin scrapes against the concrete.

"Ow," I say.

"Do you want to go inside?"

"Yeah."

We pad barefoot across the patio and inside. It feels as if my heart is beating between my legs. The scrape on my back aches as my skins tightens with goose bumps. Chilled from the walk through the air-conditioning, I start to crawl under his covers when we reach his room.

"Don't," he says. "You'll get my sheets wet."

"I'm cold."

"Then take off your swimsuit."

"Yeah, right," I say. He slides in next to me, holding my eyes in his. We lie on our sides facing each other.

"Autumn," he says. He has the look in his eye that tells me what he is going to say before he says it.

"Jamie, I—"

"This is ridiculous," he says. "Look at us."

"Can't you just kiss me?"

"I want to make love to you," Jamie says.

I cannot say anything in reply. I cannot say that I want to make love to him. I cannot say that I do not want to make love to him. He says nothing. I wonder what he thinks I'm thinking about as we gaze at each other. Perhaps he thinks that I am considering the idea, deciding if I'm ready or not.

He could have just asked me if I wanted to go on the roof and try to fly. He could have suggested that we drive to the airport, right now, and buy two tickets to Paris. It's not that I don't like the idea; it's just not possible.

"We can't just have sex," I say.

"Why not?"

"Because," I say, but I cannot find the words to explain what is so obvious to me.

"What can I do to make it right for you?" Jamie says.

"I need—" I don't know what I need, so I hazard a guess. "I need time."

"How much time?"

We look at each other. His gaze is intent, calculating. He studies my face.

"A year," I say.

"Okay," he says.

"Okay?"

"After graduation."

"Okay."

Jamie kisses me.

Perhaps in a year, I will have found out what it is I really need. Perhaps if I can't find it in a year, then I will never find it. Perhaps it will be better then to just give in.

Jamie kisses me. I close my eyes and lose myself in the pure physical sensation of it, the warmth and the skin and our breath. We're barely clothed, in bed, and in love, and this is almost sex. And it's almost right.

forty-three

MY MOTHER MAY HAVE TO go back to the hospital. Aunt Angelina is on the phone with the doctors. My mother is crying in the kitchen. I'm sitting on the stairs. My father is at work, but he'll come home as soon as possible.

I'm not allowed in the kitchen. I'm not supposed to know. But really, I'm always the first to know. My laundry starts to appear outside my door in a basket instead of already folded in my drawers. There are frozen prechopped vegetables in the freezer instead of whole heads of fresh cauliflower and bright yellow peppers and squash. She leaves a few dishes in the sink overnight. She isn't wearing makeup when I come home in the afternoon.

And I've learned that if I try to warn anyone, they laugh. They don't see that her tension and perfection are the only things holding her together. Even Aunt Angelina will frown and say that if my mother is learning to cut a few corners, it'll be good for her, that perhaps she is learning to relax a little.

Aunt Angelina hangs up. I hear the chair scrape against the floor. Her voice is low as she talks with my mother. My mother's voice answers shrilly, then quiets.

Finny and I loved to hear the story of how they met because it was never the same. Aunt Angelina told us my mother had rescued her from a blizzard or that they had been trapped at the top of a Ferris wheel together and had to climb down the spokes. They saved each other from drowning, met backstage at a Rolling Stones concert, and got shoved into the same locker on the first day of high school and were friends by the time they were rescued by the janitor.

My mother said they sat next to each other in math class in eighth grade. Once, she said it was seventh grade.

My mother's sobs are softer now. Even though I've never seen them in one of my mother's crises, I can imagine it clearly enough. My mother has her head in her arms on the table. Aunt Angelina strokes her hair.

They've loved each other nearly their whole lives, yet are not in love. They are passionate and devoted. They are bound to and balanced by each other—the outer chaos of Angelina's life and my mother's inner darkness, Angelina's strength and my mother's will.

I imagine Angelina's fingers twine in her hair and rest there.

"I love you," she says. She always will.

———————

My father comes in the front door. He has his briefcase in one hand. He's here sooner than I expected. He started dating my mother their freshman year in high school, just like me and Jamie. I don't know what binds them together.

"Hi, Autumn," he says.

"Hi, Dad," I say.

"Rough day, huh?" he says. I'm not sure if he's referring to me, Mom, or all of us.

"She's in the kitchen," I say. He nods. He looks at me.

"You okay?"

"I'm fine," I say. I always am. Comparatively.

I cannot imagine not wanting to live. I cannot imagine not believing that it will be better someday. I cannot imagine that there is nothing left to see, that there is nothing to tie me to Earth. As long as I want to live, then I must be fine.

My father goes in. Aunt Angelina comes out.

"Hey, kiddo," she says. I don't say anything.

"Everything is going to be fine," she says. I know that. Everything is fine already. It's always fine. Everything is fine, fine, fine.

I nod.

"Do you want me to call Finny?" she says. I might flinch; I'm not sure. Her face changes in reaction to me though, so I must have done something. "Okay," she says.

"It's not what you think," I say. I do want him. I want him here, and I want Jamie and I want Sasha and Angie and Noah and Brooke and my grandmother who died all those years ago. I want Mom. I want Mom to be okay, really okay. What other people mean when they say okay.

Aunt Angelina nods. One corner of her mouth twitches up, just for a moment.

"Love is complex," she says.

I nod again. And then I lay my head on my knees and I do not cry.

forty-four

In front of me sits a glass of rum and Coke. It has three ice cubes in it. Brooke is pouring Coke into Noah's glass. Jamie is sitting next to me at my mother's kitchen table. He already took a sip from his, until we protested and said we all had to take the first drink at the same time.

My mother is still in the hospital, and my father is on a business trip. This is the first time I've ever been left alone for days. Every evening, I have to check in with Aunt Angelina. She wants to know how I'm feeling and if I'll come have dinner with them. I'm fine, and I always have plans, like tonight.

Jamie and the others parked around the corner so that Aunt Angelina wouldn't see all the cars in the driveway. Brooke's older sister bought us the alcohol. None of us have had any since that New Year's night. We decided it was time we gave it a try again.

"Okay," Brooke says. We all raise our glasses. The ice in our glasses clinks all at once like a melody that has lost its way.

"To us," I say, remembering Jamie's Christmas toast. And I mean it. I look at each of their faces. We lower our glasses again. At first it tastes the same, as if there is only Coke in my glass, but when I swallow, my throat burns and my stomach is warm. Angie makes a face. Alex coughs. Jamie takes another drink.

"This is okay," Noah says. I take another sip.

———————————

Alex is trying to put up Sasha's hair. He has a brush and a handful of my bobby pins and a rubber band.

"You're going to look fabulous, darling, simply fabulous," he says to her. We're sitting on the living room floor, watching them and the television and laughing. My head feels heavy and light at the same time. I'm happy. I love my friends.

"Ouch," Sasha says.

"No pain, no gain, darling," Alex says. We laugh again. I hold up my glass and Brooke leans over to fill it. Some of the rum splashes onto my arm, and Jamie leans over and licks it off.

"Gross," I say. I rub his saliva off my arm and glare at him. He grins at me. Brooke fills up the rest of my glass with Coke, and I bring it to my lips. The ice in our glasses melted a while ago, but no one cares. On the television, a car flips over and catches on fire.

"Oh no," I say.

"What?" Jamie says.

"He died," I say.

"No, that's the Russian spy's car."

"Oh."

Jamie leans over and licks my arm again.

"Don't," I say. I push him away. Everybody else laughs. I try to stand up and have to steady myself on the arm of the couch. They laugh again. "I'm going to wash my arm," I say.

"What?" Jamie says.

"You licked my arm twice. I have to wash it."

"No, you don't."

"I'm going to go wash my arm now," I say. I let go of the couch and step my way across the floor. My feet aren't quite going the way I tell them to; they step to the side and fling me forward before I'm ready.

"Bring me some more hair thingies, darling," Alex says.

"You're not done yet?" Sasha asks. I grab at the door frame as I go into the hall, and I don't hear what Alex says in reply. Ever since my second drink, I have had a warm and happy, free feeling, like I'm in a nice hot bath and invincible. I've had four drinks now, and something is bubbling up in me like a laugh caught in my chest, tickling me nicely as it struggles to break out.

I go to the upstairs bathroom, my favorite because of the claw-foot tub. The year I was ten, I could lay on my back with my feet at one end and my head grazing the other perfectly. I have to bend my knees now. I step inside and wiggle around until I'm comfortable. Then I have to wiggle again to get my cell phone out of my pocket.

I shift around, trying to find the comfortable spot again as the phone rings. When he answers, I stop moving.

"Autumn?"

"Finny, hi," I whisper.

"What's wrong?"

"Nothing," I say. "I'm drunk."

"Oh," he says. And then, "Oh."

I feel a swell of pride in my chest; I surprised Finny. And I've been drunk now, just like him. I laugh, then remember that I'm trying to be quiet. "Now I know why you do this," I whisper. I cover my mouth with one hand to stifle my giggle.

"Where are you?" he says.

"In the bathtub," I say.

"Whose?"

"Mine. With the feet. I'm hiding from my friends."

"Why?"

"So I can call you, silly." He laughs, one short bark that turns to a sigh. I frown and shift again. The porcelain sides are digging into my elbows. "Was that mean to say?" I ask.

"No, it's not mean. Just true."

"But I still have to tell you why I called you."

"Why'd you call me?"

"When we go to visit Mom tomorrow night, will you come too?"

"You want me to come?"

"Yes."

"I'll come, but you have to promise me two things."

"Fine," I say.

"Number one, when we hang up, I want you to go downstairs and drink a big glass of water. And before you go to bed, have another one."

"Why?"

"You won't be as sick tomorrow, hopefully."

"Okay."

"Number two is very important, Autumn."

"Okay."

"Don't have sex with Jamie while you're drunk," Finny says. I close my eyes. I know what I want to say, but I am silent. My words can't find their way through the fog of my mind and out of my mouth. There is something here, something significant, if I could just find it. "Autumn?" he says.

"I wasn't going to," I say. The words fall from me like stones dropping into water—one, two, three, four.

"Okay," he says. We're both quiet now. There is a thump downstairs, and laughter. "I was going to come on Thursday anyway," he says.

"Jamie and I are going to have sex after graduation," I say. There is a pause. I can hear him breathing.

"Why then?"

"I dunno." I want him to tell me that it's okay, that it's the right thing to do.

"How many drinks have you had?" he asks.

"Three," I say, "and I have one waiting for me downstairs."

"I think you should stop after that."

"You're always so bossy," I say.

"Promise me," Finny says.

"I promise," I say.

"Okay then."

"I'm supposed to be washing my arm. I should go."

"Why are you washing your arm?"

"Jamie licked it. Twice."

"Is that something he normally does?"

"No. He's drunk too."

"Don't forget to drink your water."

"I won't. Bye."

"Bye."

Downstairs, the good spy is flying off on a helicopter with the girl. I've forgotten to get any "hair thingies" for Alex, but Sasha's head is on his shoulder now and he doesn't notice. My arm is red and itchy where I rubbed it with hot water, proof that I was washing it upstairs. I sit down next to the other boy I'm in love with.

"What's that?" he says.

"A glass of water," I say. "You want some?"

"Sure," he says. I hand him my glass. He takes two gulps and passes it back to me. I finish it and cuddle up next to him. He leans his head against mine. The spy kisses the girl and the music swells. The screen fades to black.

Tonight I will sleep all night with Jamie in my bed but we will not have sex. In the morning, he will kiss me and breathe his hot breath on my neck and I'll bury my head in his shoulder. Angie will be vomiting in the bathroom down the hall. Alex will be sick too. Jamie and I won't be sick. Those of us who can eat will fry eggs, and with glazed eyes we will all watch the morning news on the couch.

No one will talk much. I won't tell them that I'm visiting my mother later. When they are gone, I will be relieved, and I will go back to sleep.

That evening, I will put on a skirt and go next door. I will decline when Finny offers me the front seat. Aunt Angelina will turn the station to oldies and no one will sing along. I will watch the back of Finny's head as the car turns into the hospital parking lot because he is there, right there, and he was going to be anyway.

forty-five

I THINK I HAVE READ every book at the library. Every novel, that is. Every novel that I want to read. Or might be willing to give a try. If someone had told me that this was possible ten years ago, I wouldn't have believed it. Books are unlimited.

I spin the rack with the sign NEW ACQUISITIONS in bold letters. The air-conditioning is too cool, and I have goose bumps. My mother is home again. My father is at work. The Fourth of July is tomorrow.

The rack is not new; it creaks as it spins. In two days, we are going to visit a university, all of us—Mother, Aunt Angelina, Finny, and I. I have to find something to read or I won't be able to sit next to him for four hours with his scent and his profile looking out the window.

I reach out and take a book that I've already looked at twice. Maybe there is something here, something that I can hold on to, that can take me away for a little while.

I had another appointment with Dr. Singh yesterday. He nodded at everything I said and refilled my prescription. I think of my fantasy home where the furniture—tables, chairs, and bed frames— are all piles of books. I wonder if he would nod thoughtfully at that too. Perhaps he would ask me what books mean to me. I would tell him that it means living another life; that I am in love with both my lost best friend and my boyfriend and I need to believe in another life. He would write something down after that.

On the ride back from his office, I asked my mother if she ever thought I would need to go to the hospital, and she started crying. She didn't pull over or even slow down. She just stared down the road and cried.

"Sorry," I said.

"I'm sorry," she said. She wasn't apologizing for crying, but for something bigger, something she had given to me, done to me, withheld from me.

"It's okay," I said. It wasn't her fault.

At the bottom of the rack is a small collection of Japanese haiku. Poetry collections might be good. Poems can be read over again and studied.

Jamie comes up behind me. His chest brushes my back.

"Are you done yet?" he asks.

"No," I say.

"Okay," he says, and I can feel my love for him, a small warm place wedged between my stomach and lungs; it flutters and settles again.

"Soon though," I say. I haven't turned to look at him yet.

"We have time," he says. We're going to a movie. We'll eat

hamburgers in the mall's food court and Jamie will make fun of me for the way I eat my fries.

Jamie is going to apply to different schools from me. He isn't even considering the school we're going to the day after tomorrow. This school is the only one I can afford that has a creative writing program. Jamie has faith that it doesn't matter at all; he'll marry me as soon as college is over. We've picked out a house a few blocks from mine. It has a yellow front door; that's why I like it. He likes it because I like it.

I pick up *The Bell Jar*. I've been too afraid to read it, and partly too annoyed by the cliché to overcome that fear.

"I'm done," I say.

"Cool," Jamie says. I turn around. He's smiling at me. His dark hair is hanging in his green eyes. I remember seeing him on the steps the first time, how I stared at him as if I couldn't believe that his face could exist.

"What?" I say.

"You're pretty today," he says.

"I wish you would consider going to Springfield," I say.

"We'll make it," Jamie says. "I'll call you every night before I go to sleep."

"I'll miss you," I say.

"Good, then you won't leave me for a poet."

Outside, the hot air surrounds us like a membrane, so thick it seems palpable. My goose bumps vanish.

"And you know, you don't have to go there," Jamie says.

225

"No, I have to," I say. Jamie still wants me to teach. He wants me to at least get a minor in education. He does not say anything. The car is stifling inside, and Jamie rolls down the windows before starting the engine. Jamie can't understand my need to major in writing. Or even my need to write. Acceptance is what he has given me, and I know I'm lucky to have that. And I think that's enough.

forty-six

─────────

THERE WAS A MOMENT, AFTER the campus tour, when Finny and I were alone, standing by the fountain. The sun was bleaching every-thing around us a painful, bright white. When the wind blew, the spray of the fountain cooled us, so we stayed where we were, waiting for The Mothers to stop taking pictures and head back to the hotel. I was looking around at everything, anything that wasn't him, when he spoke.

"So what do you think?" he said. I shrugged.

"I like it, but I'm not sure if I would be happy here."

"You would be," he said. I looked up at him. He was looking at me.

"Why?" I said. He shrugged.

"There are lots of trees," he said.

─────────

We're heading home now. Finny is driving. It surprised me—though it shouldn't have—when Aunt Angelina shook the keys and asked him if he wanted to take a turn. She offered me the front seat too, so I could stretch my legs out. In the back seat, The Mothers are feeling sentimental. They want to talk about the Christmas the power went out or Finny's fifth-grade soccer team or the poem about dead fairies I wrote when I was ten.

"Do you guys remember your first day of school?" my mother says.

"No," I say.

"I do," Finny says.

"You ran off without Finny," Aunt Angelina says. "He was still clinging to my skirts in the door and you shot across the kindergarten to the monkey bars."

"And then you hung upside down and scared me to death," my mother says.

I don't just *not* remember it; I don't *believe* it either. I was terrified of being away from Finny, and he was at home wherever we went.

"You guys must have that backward," I say.

"You were wearing a skirt and everyone could see your underwear," Mom says.

"You were always the brave one," Aunt Angelina says.

"It was you," Finny says. His eyes don't leave the road. He does not see me glance over.

I don't remember always being the brave one. I remember being afraid that he would leave me someday. I never would have left him.

"What about you?" I had asked him. We were sitting on the edge of the fountain now. The Mothers were still wandering with the camera. I watched them as they walked this way and that.

"I like it too," he said.

"Really?"

"Yeah," he said, "and it's not too far from home." He paused then, and I looked back up at him. He wasn't looking at me. "I think maybe I'll go to New York for med school though." Finny in New York instead of me. By then, I'll be married to Jamie and be back here. It's funny how things don't turn out the way you thought they would.

"Will you wear black turtlenecks and drink coffee for me?" I said.

"I don't like coffee," he says. I laugh.

"You know what? Me neither," I said. We both laughed. The Mothers took a picture of us but we didn't know. They were far away and we are small, sitting together on the corner of the fountain. I'm looking at the ground; he is looking at me. We look as if we sit there every day, together.

On the way home, I look out the window and watch the trees fly by like road markers telling us how far we have come from where we were.

forty-seven

On August 8, nothing happens.

Lightning does not strike the Earth. No old woman shows up at the door with a warning. Finny doesn't see a black dog staring at him as he gets out of his red car. No one says anything prophetic or ironic. I do not awake in darkness to hear the clock strike thirteen.

Did Finny feel something? Was there something nameless that shifted within him? Did that last year feel to him like late afternoon, the sunlight creeping across the floorboards of his room, slowly fading until there is but a thin veil of gray between day and night?

Did I feel something? Did I know?

Like all things that have become history, I now feel as if I always knew it, as if all through this story, it had been lurking in the shadows. The story underneath the story.

forty-eight

On the first day of school, Jamie and I drive past my old bus stop, and the freshmen look like children. A girl with black hair and combat boots shuffles her feet and glares at the ground. I wish her well.

"We're seniors!" the girls squeal to each other. The boys mimic our squeals and roll their eyes. It's deathly hot on the Steps to Nowhere, but we will have to sit there before class and during lunch so that all the freshmen know it's off limits to them. We sit together before the first bell rings and talk about realizing that, in a way, this was our last summer. Next summer, we won't be children in any sense of the word. We're almost there, that finish line that has stood before us all our lives. We are almost adults; our lives are about to begin.

I'm in Mr. Laughegan's creative writing class.

"I told you I'd see you in here again," he says when I walk into his janitor's closet classroom. He tells us to write a page on what kind of fruit or vegetable we would be. I would be a kiwi, obviously.

I also have a college credit literature class, two English classes, and no math class. It's almost more than I can bear.

I do have gym though, a themed class called lifetime sports. It's supposed to be sports that you'll be able to play your whole life, like bowling or walking or something. I signed up for it because it sounded easy.

I'm not sure why Finny signed up for it. He's good at all sports; I can't imagine why he would want a class with so little activity. I'm already sitting on the bleachers when he comes in the gym. The teacher takes his name and he sits down in front of me. I'm not sure if he saw me.

While Ms. Scope goes over the expectations of the class, what we'll be doing, and when we'll do it, I look at the back of Finny's head. His mother probably thinks he needs a haircut, but I like it when it gets a little long. At the end of her speech, Ms. Scope says we must choose a partner for the semester, someone to play shuffleboard with and keep score in pool. Everyone looks around and whispers, pairing off as quickly as possible so as not to be left behind. Finny turns around and looks me in the eye.

"You want to?" he says.

"Sure," I say. I think about standing at the bus stop with him that first day of freshman year, too awkward to even say hello back to him. We couldn't have been partners that year, or maybe even last year. He's still the most popular boy in our school, and I'm still the girlfriend of the misfits' leader, but since we're the only seniors in the class, we can be gym partners; it won't look like it means anything.

Ms. Scope writes down every pair and tells us we are free for the rest of the period to shoot baskets or sit on the bleachers. Everyone else gets up or climbs higher to gossip in the corners. Finny and I stay sitting. He turns to me again. I'm not allowed to wear a tiara in gym, and I feel strangely exposed to him.

"So we're seniors," he says.

"Yeah," I say.

forty-nine

ANGIE AND PREPPY DAVE HAD sex the second weekend after school started.

"Where did you do it?" Sasha asks her. It's lunchtime and the boys are flinging themselves around in the field, punching shoulders and calling names. The concrete step is warm through my jeans. I remember sitting exactly like this and listening to Brooke tell her story.

"We were in his car," Angie says. "We didn't plan on it," she tells us. "It just kinda happened." She doesn't look upset though; she looks beautiful. There is a flush in her pale cheeks, and her eyes are bright.

"Really?" I say. I don't understand how sex can happen by accident. After Jamie and I have been kissing for a long time, I tell him that we should stop, because that's what the girl is supposed to say at some point. But I've never said that we should stop because I thought we actually needed to. I've never forgotten that we're in his car, that the moment isn't right.

"It hurt like hell, right?" Brooke says.

"Actually," Angie says, "I threw up."

"Oh my God," I say. She looks at my face and laughs.

"Was he...you know, done?" Brooke says.

"Yeah," Angie says. "But it *was*, like, right afterward."

"You threw up in his car?" Sasha says. Angie shakes her head.

"No," she says. "I rolled over onto my stomach, opened the door, and threw up in the driveway."

"Oh," I say. I can't think of anything to say to this, but Sasha can.

"Wait, if you weren't planning on it, did you use anything?"

"Well, no," Angie says. "But it was just the once, and next time we'll get some condoms, or, I don't know, something."

"It only takes once," Brooke says.

"Mmm hmm," Sasha says. "And you guys need to sit down and *talk* about birth-control options before there can be a next time."

"Guys," Angie says. She sighs. "Don't ruin this for me."

I frown again. If being in the back seat of a car and vomiting in the driveway didn't already ruin it, I'm not sure what we could do that would. I don't understand how Angie could be happy with such a clichéd place to lose her virginity. I don't understand why Dave didn't come to his senses when he remembered that there was no birth control. Brooke puts her arm around Angie.

"Sorry," she says. "We're happy for you, really."

"Yeah," Sasha says.

"Good," Angie says, "'cause I can't stop smiling and—" She sighs again. "I love him so much that every time I think of him holding me afterward, I just want to cry."

I would want to cry too if I were Angie, but for different reasons. I don't understand how something like this happens.

On the way home from school, I tell Jamie Angie's story. He listens quietly and stares straight at the road.

"I mean, I guess I'm happy for her if she's happy," I say. "But doesn't that sound horrible?"

"I dunno," Jamie says. "I think it'd be cute if you threw up."

"What?" Jamie looks calm.

He shrugs and smiles. "I'd hold your hair back for you and take care of you."

"I won't throw up," I say.

"And you won't do it in a car. I know, don't worry." Jamie pulls into my driveway.

"Well, not the first time," I say.

"We'll get a hotel room," Jamie says. He glances over at me now. "A really nice one. And we'll dress up and have an expensive meal first."

"That sounds…" I pause. "Nice." I unbuckle my seat belt and turn toward him. Jamie kisses me, and I realize that, during that dinner, he will give me a charm for my bracelet, something subtle that only he and I will understand. It's romantic, and I wish I hadn't already thought of it so that it could be a surprise. I try my hardest to forget.

fifty

WE'RE PLAYING BADMINTON, AND I just flinched when the plastic feather thingy flew at me. Even though it's sitting right next to my sneaker, Finny walks over to pick it up. He backs up a few paces and holds up his racket. There are too many pairs of us to be able to use the nets, so we're scattered in random intervals throughout the gym.

"Try again," he says. "I'm hitting it to you slowly. It can't hurt you." I dutifully raise the racket. With exaggerated movements, Finny tosses it into the air and hits it gently toward me. I bat defensively at it and it bounces off my racket and arches toward the floor. Finny dives, but my poor return is too much for even him. He plucks the white thing off the shiny yellow boards of the gym and looks at me again.

"Okay," he says. "That was better. This time, try to hit it upward." He gets into position again, then pauses. "But not straight up," he adds.

This time when I hit the birdie, it veers off to the left. Finny dashes to the side, and suddenly it's flying back at me.

"Whoa," I cry. I swing at it but miss and it falls to the floor. "Sorry," I say. I bend over and pick it up. It's kind of like a bouncy ball, I think. I like bouncy balls. If it didn't have so many plastic feathers sticking out of it, I might like the game better. But then it would be harder to see. I try to imagine seeing the little ball flying in the air. Maybe if it was brightly colored.

"Autumn?" Finny says. I look up at him again. I realize that I've just been standing staring at the ball.

"Sorry," I say for the second time in two minutes. "I zoned out there for a sec."

"I saw," Finny says. "So do you want to serve?"

"Sure," I say. I carefully toss the birdie in the air and watch it fall. I hit it, and it flies up and out. Finny lopes forward and hits it toward me, graceful, high, and slow. It comes straight to me, and without having to take a step, I whack it up again. We manage to pass it back and forth five times before I finally miss it again.

"That was good," Finny says. Ms. Scope blows her whistle and we walk to her to place our rackets in a pile at her feet. Finny and I walk together, but not side by side. I lag a bit behind him and keep some distance between us.

"Oh," I say, "Mom said to ask you what you want for your birthday."

"I don't care," he says. "Whatever."

"I have to have something to tell her," I say.

"Um, I could use some new sneakers?" Finny says.

"I'll tell her to get you an ant farm," I say as we turn around to walk toward the locker room. Finny shrugs.

"Okay," he says. "You want one too?"

"Yeah," I say, though the thought hadn't occurred to me. I could put it on my desk and watch it when I have writer's block. We're nearing the doors now. After I change clothes, I'll go to my literature class and not talk to Finny again until tomorrow, even if I see him from a distance here or at home. "What are you doing for your birthday?" I ask.

"Just the same thing as always, having everybody over on Friday and we'll eat and watch a movie," he says.

"Sounds like fun," I say.

"Do you want to come?" Finny asks. I stop short. Finny turns to me. We're standing in front of the locker room doors. Our classmates walk around us to get inside.

"I don't really—" I stumble on my words and have to look away from his face. "I mean, that wouldn't really work, would it?" I say.

Finny shrugs, but he doesn't smile. "I just thought I would ask anyway."

"I mean, I would ask you too, but, you know."

"Yeah, I know," Finny says.

"But on our actual birthdays, we'll have dinner with The Mothers, so—" I shrug, unsure of how to finish the thought.

"So it's fine, we're good," he finishes for me.

"Yeah," I say. "We're good."

"Finn, Autumn," Ms. Scope yells at us. "Do you want to be late?" I realize we're the last two in the gym. We turn away from each other and go through our separate doors.

fifty-one

"THE ROSEBUSH YOU GAVE ME for Christmas is still blooming," Sasha says. She sits down on the steps next to me and lays her book bag between her knees.

"They do that," I say. It's the first week of October. I have a new charm on Jamie's bracelet and an ant farm on my desk. The weather is cooling off but still warm, and a few trees have started to turn. The novelty of being seniors has worn off a bit. It's a matter of course now that we're the oldest and the coolest. All the other students are so young and awkward; how could we not be?

"We should have a party for Halloween this year," Brooke says. "I mean like actually invite people besides us. My sister could get us some more to drink—"

"Could we wear costumes?" Alex says.

"No," Sasha and I say. Somewhere in the back of my head, I think of how a few years ago I couldn't imagine Halloween without a costume.

"Why not?" Brooke asks.

"I'm not wearing a costume," Jamie says.

"I'm not," I say. "But my parents are going to some marriage camp therapy retreat thing that weekend so—"

"I'm pregnant," Angie says. All of our heads swivel together. She's standing at the top of the steps, just arrived. She wears her book bag on both shoulders, like a child. The pink streaks in her hair have faded and grown out. She stares back at us as if we had just asked her a question.

"Already?" Sasha says.

"I took a test yesterday."

The bell rings and we stand. We walk in a group toward the doors, but the boys trail behind us. The girls ask questions: What are her symptoms? How is Dave handling it?

"I'm tired and my boobs hurt," she says. "But that's all besides being late." She says Dave seemed pretty freaked out, but he also seemed excited. "It's almost like he's kinda proud of himself," she says in the same strange monotone. She laughs then, and it sounds strangely happy.

fifty-two

"WE'RE HAVING A HALLOWEEN PARTY the weekend my parents will be gone," I say to Finny. He bounces the Ping-Pong ball against the table and hits it slowly.

"Yeah, I heard about that," he says. The ball bounces and sails past me.

"You did?"

"Yes. You know you were supposed to hit that back to me, right?"

"Sorry." I bend to retrieve the ball and hit it toward him. "The thing is, I have a favor to ask."

"What?"

"Well, you know I *did* tell Mom and Dad that I wanted to have a little party for Halloween—"

"Mmm hmm." Finny taps the ball smoothly toward me and I dart over to whack it back.

"But, you know, it's gonna be more than just a little party. And I was worried about your mom." In spite of my clumsy dashing, we have a steady rhythm going now. Tap puck, tap puck.

"So?"

"So, I figured that if you were there, your mom would assume it couldn't be all that bad, you know? That she'd let it slide a bit."

Finny catches the ball in one hand and raises his eyebrows. "You want me to come," he says.

"Yeah," I say. I shrug my shoulders without meaning to. "I mean, of course you can bring Sylvie and everybody else too."

"You know, my mom isn't as clueless as your mom."

Ms. Scope blows her whistle, and Finny and I lay our paddles on the table and go to sit on the bleachers. The other half of the class gathers around the six tables.

"Yeah, but that's because she's cooler than my mom," I say. We sit with a foot of space between us on the bottom row.

"That's true," he says.

"Will you come?"

Finny shrugs. "Your friends won't mind?"

"We already discussed it," I say. It's an accurate way to describe the argument this proposition caused on the steps this morning, but he doesn't need to know that.

"Look, you guys," I said, "I'm not having all these people over unless I know Aunt Angelina won't say anything."

"And you think having Alexis and Sylvie over will make the party seem tame?" Sasha said.

"Having Finny over will," I say.

"I don't see what the big deal is anyway," Noah says. "I figured he'd be coming. He lives next door."

"If he comes, they'll all come," Jamie says. "They never do anything alone."

"Neither do we," Brooke says.

"I do not want to hang out with them," Jamie says.

"Me neither," says Sasha.

"How about this," Alex says. "If they try to come near you, I'll pelt them with candy corn."

"You don't have to," I say. "I doubt they want to hang out with us either."

"But you think they'll come if you ask them?" Jamie asks.

"If I ask Finny, yeah," I say. "And I'm going to."

Finny bends down and ties his shoe.

"Okay," he says, "we'll come."

"Awesome," I say. "But I didn't think it would be hard to convince a big partier like you."

"I'm not really. Mostly I just stand there. And I'm almost always driving Sylvie home, so I can't drink."

"Sounds like fun. So why do you go?"

Finny looks away and shrugs. "Sylvie needs someone to look after her," he says.

"Oh," I say. It's as if someone has opened a window and a cold breeze is fluttering around us. And suddenly it's unbelievable again that I could invite Finny—and Sylvie!—to the Halloween party with all my friends. Finny and Sylvie were Homecoming King and Queen this year. Up on stage, Finny looked miserable and blushed while they crowned him, and Sylvie beamed at the crowd. They held hands. I can't have them in my house.

"Well, thanks for the favor. You don't have to stay the whole time if you want," I say.

"It's fine," Finny says, and I know he can feel it too. We sit in silence for the rest of class.

fifty-three

I open my notebook and turn to a fresh page.

"Okay, remember the rules, no crossing words out, no stopping. Ready?" Mr. Laughegan says. We look at him expectantly. "Your strongest memory. Go!" I bend over my desk and my hand flies across the page.

The night Finny kissed me I—

My hand recoils from the page as if burned. This isn't the right answer. That isn't my strongest memory. That's the memory I've tried so hard not to have. I can't possibly remember it well enough to write it down.

"It's a stream of consciousness, Autumn. Don't stop."

I can't disobey Mr. Laughegan.

The night Finny kissed me I didn't know what to do.

We'd hardly spoken for weeks. All autumn we had drifted and drifted away from each other, and I never knew what to say to him anymore. That last week of school before break in eighth grade, we had even stopped walking to the bus stop together. My mother asked me if we had had a fight.

But then it was Christmas Eve. My mother and I came over, and I sat down next to him on the couch, and there weren't the other popular girls or our different classes or the way the kids at school thought our friendship was strange. There was only our family together and the tree and our presents, and we watched *It's a Wonderful Life* together while The Mothers made dinner.

We didn't talk about how things had been different, because suddenly everything was the same again. On Christmas morning, we laughed and threw balled-up wrapping paper at each other. It was unseasonably warm that afternoon; we went into the backyard and for the hundredth time he tried to teach me to play soccer. The next day, he came over and we made a fort in the attic. We lay on our backs and looked at the sunlight bleeding through the ripped quilt above our heads, and I told Finny the plot of the novel I was going to write, about a kidnapped princess whose ship sinks and she has to start a new life among the natives of the island she washes up on.

For a week, we were us again, and I forgot to call Alexis back, and Finny shone his flashlight in my window at night. We made popcorn and watched movies. We took silly pictures of each other with his mother's camera. I made paper snowflakes and he hung them in the windows.

It had been like rushing down a swift river. I had been swept away from Finny and into popularity without the chance to come up for air. But now I was breathing again, and I thought we could find a way to stay friends. I don't know what he thought.

We had one week. And then it was New Year's Eve. My parents were going out, and I was going to stay with Finny and Aunt Angelina until they came home. After dinner, Finny and I baked a cake with his mother, and while it was in the oven, we sat at the kitchen table and made increasingly silly lists of resolutions, that we would befriend ducks and build jet packs, meet five dead celebrities, and eat an uncut pizza starting from the middle.

"Here's a real one," Finny said. "Let's build a tree house this summer."

"Okay," I said. "Can I paint it?"

"Sure."

"Any color I want?"

"Yeah."

"Even if it's pink?"

"If that's what you want." Finny added it on the bottom of the list, drew a dash, and added a notation on color schemes. "I missed you," he said, his head still down. My throat tightened. He looked up. We stared. I don't know what my face looked like. His cheeks were pink, and I remember thinking that his eyes looked different, darker somehow. And something else. Something had changed in the weeks we had been apart, but I couldn't place it.

"Finny, Autumn, it's almost time," Aunt Angelina called. Finny broke our gaze first, and went to grab wooden spoons and pots for us to bang.

When the moment came, we ran down the lawn together, and the neighbors were setting off fireworks, and we stood on the sidewalk and whooped and banged and watched. Finny was louder than I had ever seen him be before. He yelled and his voice cracked; he raised the pot above his head and it clanged like a gong. It unsettled me slightly, like his eyes. He didn't seem the same anymore.

"Okay, come on, guys," Aunt Angelina said. We turned and, still breathing hard, began to trudge up the lawn behind her. She had almost reached the porch when Finny grabbed my arm.

"Wait," Finny said. I stopped and looked at him. He swallowed and stared at me.

"What?" I said. I saw him lean in, but I thought I must be confused. He couldn't be about to kiss me. Then he turned his face to the side, his nose brushed along my cheek, and Finny's lips were on mine. Warm. His lips moved gently against mine once; there was only enough time for my eyelids to instinctively flutter closed and open again. He pulled away slowly, his eyes never leaving my face. His hand was still on my arm, his fingers clenched around me. My stomach had tied itself into a knot.

"What are you doing?" I said, even though Finny wasn't doing anything now. He was just looking at me with an expression I'd never seen before. His fingers dug deeper into my arm. We took a breath.

"Kids?" Aunt Angelina called from the doorway. "Come on. Cake's done."

249

I gently tugged my arm and his hand dropped. I took a step away from him. Our eyes never wavered.

"Kids?"

I turned and ran up the lawn. He followed me, and I imagined him grabbing me and pinning me to the ground.

Finny, my Finny, kissed me. It was horrible. It was strange and wonderful. It felt like I was watching a meteor shower and did not know if it meant the stars were falling and the sky was breaking apart.

When I got back home, I closed my blinds and buried my face in my pillow. My tears were hot in my eyes, and it was hard to breathe.

"What are you doing?" I said. "What are you doing?" I whispered it to him again and again until I had cried myself to sleep.

The next morning while The Mothers made our New Year's brunch, Finny and I sat on the couch with three feet between us and did not talk. We stared straight ahead.

There were four round bruises on my arm where his hand had clasped me. He had never hurt me before.

And we weren't friends anymore.

———————

It's not fair I wasn't ready It's not my fault. Did you kiss me because you wanted to kiss a girl or did you kiss me because What was I supposed to do I wasn't ready I wasn't ready I didn't know

"Time," Mr. Laughegan says. I drop my pen, and it rolls off my desk and onto the floor. "All right. Now read over what you wrote. Is there a story there?"

fifty-four

I AM DRINKING WHITE WINE out of a blue mug. The party is crowded and hot, a success. Some people are dressed as pirates or hobos; I am dressed as myself in a blue T-shirt, a black skirt, neon tights, and a silver tiara. I watch the party alone, leaning against the doorway of the living room. Brooke and Noah are in the kitchen making drinks. I don't know where Alex and Sasha have gone. Angie and Preppy Dave are snuggling on the couch, drinking Coke and whispering. Jamie is standing on the coffee table, telling a story to his captive audience. He spreads his arms wide and shrugs, and everyone laughs.

"So I went back to the car *again*," he says. One laugh stands out this time, and I glance around him to the other side of the room. Sylvie sits cross-legged on the floor next to the couch, a beer in hand and her eyes shining. I know that look. Sylvie has been charmed by Jamie. It happens easily enough and to nearly everyone.

Jamie throws back his head to laugh at his own joke, and Sylvie grins. My mouth eases into its own smile, and I watch Jamie jump off the coffee table and take a bow. Sylvie may like him now, even want him maybe, but he is sauntering across the room to me. Jamie lays his hands on my hips and leans close.

"Hey," he says.

"That was a very entertaining story."

"I know," he says. Now that his epic tale is done, the room is beginning to fill again with other voices, a low humming around us. He is so close that all I can see is his laughing, mocking eyes staring into mine.

"I really want—" I say.

"Want what?" he says.

"To be alone with you," I say. The skin crinkles around his eyes as he grins.

"Let's go," he says. I shake my head.

"If everybody sees us go together, they might duck under the rope too," I say. Before everyone came, I strung a piece of twine across the stairway to keep the party downstairs, the madness and mess contained.

"I'll go now," Jamie says, "and you follow in a minute with drinks."

"Okay," I say. He kisses me hard, pressing me against the door frame, the way he never does in front of others usually. He leaves me breathless and flushed; I tip the mug back and finish the wine in one swallow.

I walk over to the couch and sink down next to Angie. I cup my hands around my mouth and lean into Angie's ear.

"Whisper, whisper, whisper," I say. She shoves me gently and laughs. "What are you guys plotting over here?" I say.

"We're gonna get married," Preppy Dave says.

"In December, maybe," Angie says. "We're going to tell our parents soon."

"Wow," I say, "that's really—" Out of the corner of my eye, I see Finny enter the room. "Big," I say. They both nod, and Dave's arm tightens around her shoulders. I stumble up and stand with one hand on the couch. "I'll leave you two kids now," I say. "I have an appointment to keep in my bedroom."

"Be safe," Preppy Dave says.

"Yeah," Angie says. I laugh and take my hand away from the couch as I turn away, and I stumble into Finny's chest.

"Oh!"

"Sorry," he says, even though it is clearly my fault. His drink spilled down his front when I ran into him. He wipes at his chest with one hand while I look around for something to blot his shirt with.

"Oh, baby," Sylvie says. She touches his chest and clucks like a mother hen.

"I'm so sorry," I say.

"It's fine," Finny says.

"You're going to reek of alcohol, baby," Sylvie says.

"Let's go in the kitchen and get a towel," I say. "And you can have a drink from our stash." He steps around the table with me and we walk to the kitchen.

"You don't have to do that," Finny says.

"It only fair," I say.

"That's very nice of you, Autumn," Sylvie says. Finny and I don't say anything in reply.

In the kitchen, Brooke and Noah are trying to make a martini shaker by fitting a plastic cup over a glass tumbler. Drops of vodka fly across the room with every shake.

"I don't think it's working," Noah says.

"No," Brooke says. She lays the makeshift shaker down sadly.

"Hey," I say, "make something for Finny from our stash."

"Would you like a custom hand-shaken martini?" Noah says. I open a drawer and take out a tea towel.

"Say no," I advise.

"Um," Finny says, "perhaps something that won't make a mess in Aunt Claire's kitchen."

"Who?" Brooke says.

"My mom," I say. I hand Finny the towel and he blots his chest, but his shirt is only damp now and it doesn't do much good. While Brooke and Noah make a rum concoction for Finny, I fill my mug and a plastic cup with wine.

"Here you are, my good man," Noah says.

"Thanks," Finny says. The three of us—me and Finny and Sylvie—walk back to the living room. The hallway is empty. I duck under the rope and look over my shoulder to make sure no one saw.

Finny is standing at the bottom of the stairs, his drink untouched in his hand. Sylvie is gone. I hear her laughter in the next room.

"Hey?" he says.

"Yeah?"

"Don't forget what you promised me, okay?"

I try to flip through all of my memories of us, trying to find a promise that hasn't been broken yet. There were a lot of promises; there isn't much left.

"Not while you're drunk," he says. My grip on the wine tightens, and I feel myself start to nod and then shrug.

"You don't need to worry about me, Phineas," I say. "Okay?"

He looks at me, not blinking, not moving. He does not blush. From the next room, Sylvie calls his name. He doesn't seem to hear. I swallow, trying to push my heart back out of my throat.

"Fine," I say, "I'm not—we aren't going to, okay?"

"Okay," he says, and turns on his heels.

"Finn?" Sylvie calls.

fifty-five

"So, did you hear about Thanksgiving?" Finny says. He's lining up his pool cue with the white ball. He shoots and breaks the triangle in the center of the table. Balls roll in every direction. One falls into the left pocket.

"Does that one count?" I say. Finny shrugs and motions for me to shoot. "We might as well count it since you're going to win anyway."

"You don't know that," he says.

"Yeah, I do." I lean over and try to position myself the way he did.

"Don't hold it so high in the back," he says. "Don't hunch, either." I shoot anyway and hit the ball on the side. It bounces off the rim and hits the floor. Finny grabs it and places it back on the table. He opens his mouth to explain to me what I did wrong.

"What were you saying about Thanksgiving?" I say. He looks down and begins to line up for his next shot.

"My father wants me to come over to his place and meet his wife and daughter." He shoots and the white ball hits the one I think he was aiming for, but it doesn't go in the hole.

"You have a sister?" I say. My chest feels hot and my stomach sinks. Finny shrugs, and anyone else would think that he could care less. I know he cares. And it's another connection to rival mine. First Sylvie and now this sister.

"What's her name?"

"Elizabeth."

"How old is she?"

"She's four," he says. I relax a little bit.

"How long have you known about her? Why didn't you tell me?" He looks up at me again. We're standing across from each other, on different sides of the table, pool sticks in hand. Around us, other conversations buzz, and balls clack against each other. I know why he didn't tell me, because we were hardly speaking to each other when she was born. He doesn't bother reminding me though.

"Your turn," he says.

"So, you won't be with us on Thanksgiving?" I say. I shoot, and the white ball hits the orange number six, which clacks uselessly against the wall and rolls to a stop.

"No, I will," he says. "I'm supposed to come over later in the evening, for cocktails and leftovers."

"Oh," I say. He shoots, and another ball rolls into the pocket.

"You look relieved," he says. He smiles.

"Would you want to be alone with them all day?"

Finny shrugs. I lean over and try to aim.

"Stop," he says. "I can't take it."

"What?"

He doesn't answer, but walks around the table and stands behind me. He lays his hands over mine. They are dry and warm. His hip presses against mine.

"Like this," he says. He adjusts my hands. I close my eyes. We are still. His hands press against mine. I take a breath. I hear the clack of the balls.

"Oops," Finny says. I open my eyes. The ball we were aiming for bounces off the side and rolls slowly to a stop. We straighten and step away from each other.

"I guess I'm too big of a screwup even for you to fix," I say. He doesn't answer me or move to take his aim. "Finny?" I say. He blinks.

"That wasn't your fault," he says. "It was mine." He hands me the cue again.

fifty-six

WE ARE IN THE COURTHOUSE downtown. I'm holding my new digital camera, a gift from my birthday. Angie's dress is short and white, with blue tights. She has a large white flower pinned in her hair. Her back is to me now, but when she turns in profile, I will see the barely discernible swell in her middle. Preppy Dave is in a gray suit. His hair is wetted down and combed so that the lines show. His mother is crying. I'm not sure if they're happy tears or not. I raise my camera and take another shot. Jamie leans over and looks at the screen. He nods in approval. All of us are sitting in one row on the left. On the other side, three of Preppy Dave's teammates sit. They are the only other young people here; the rest are parents and grandparents, a few aunts and uncles. There is one baby in the crowd and every few minutes, it mews and is shushed again.

I reach over and take Jamie's hand again.

"We're next," I whisper. He smiles briefly and squeezes back.

Preppy Dave and Angie turn to face each other, and I let go of his hand and raise my camera again. Her smile sends a knifepoint into my stomach; my hands shake and the picture is blurry. I delete it before Jamie sees.

Someday I'll be happy like that, I tell myself.

Angie's hands squeeze Dave's and I think about his hand over mine as we aimed the pool cue. I squeeze Jamie's hand.

fifty-seven

ALL DAY, THE MOTHERS MADE a big deal about this being our last Christmas before we leave for college, and Finny and I had to not roll our eyes or laugh when they got sentimental. Sometimes our eyes would meet, and we gave each other silent warnings not to give in and snort or sigh in reply to them. We didn't see how things could be so different next year, and they were ridiculous and maudlin in our eyes.

My parents gave me a laptop. Good for schoolwork, they said. Good for writing, I thought. I've started something new, something secret, and now I can carry that secret thing with me wherever I go, bouncing against my hip in my messenger bag.

Finny got a sound system for the little red car from his father. He was never that much into music, but he shrugged and kind of smiled.

We're sitting on the couch watching TV with the lights off. Christmas is at Aunt Angelina's this year. The pine tree by the window sometimes blinks randomly in one section or another, but never all at once or to any rhythm. Finny had tried to find the problem and fix it, but then Aunt Angelina decided she liked it. Because of the tree, the light in the room dances across the ceiling and makes the windows darken and flash again. Finny has the remote. He flips through the channels until he finds *It's a Wonderful Life*. He sets the remote down on the coffee table, leans back against the cushions, and stretches his long legs out in front of him.

At Thanksgiving, when he got up in the evening to leave us for his new other family, our eyes met briefly but we did not say anything. Without him, I sat in the corner with a book and went upstairs early. Nothing about his evening came to me through The Mothers, and he did not say anything about it in gym class. All I know is that he isn't leaving us tonight.

The Mothers laugh in the kitchen, and Jimmy Stewart falls in the swimming pool. We both smile, and the movie fades into a commercial break. I stand up.

"Do you want a Coke?" I say.

"Sure," he says.

I kick his foot. "You're blocking traffic with those things," I say, and he folds his legs back and stretches them out again after me like a toll booth.

Those legs took our school to state soccer finals this fall. I went to their last game with The Mothers and got to watch him running for an hour and a half. The muscles in his legs, the way he lifted his shirt to wipe the sweat from his face, the concentration in his eyes as he ran—it made my chest constrict. I felt as if I would never see him play again, and I somehow knew they wouldn't win the game, that they wouldn't make it to championships, and this would be Finny's last game ever. Finny's last game in high school, I amended in my mind, but my chest still hurt when the whistle blew and he trudged across the field in defeat.

In the kitchen, my mother is checking on the lamb, and Aunt Angelina is pouring a glass of wine.

"Twenty more minutes," Mom says.

"I'm just here for Cokes," I say. Aunt Angelina reaches on top of the fridge and gets them down for me. I take a warm can in each hand. Finny and I like to drink our sodas out of unrefrigerated cans; sometime around third grade, we got the idea that there was something wild and rebellious about drinking soda straight from the can, and for years we refused to drink it any other way. It's habit now. Jamie thinks it's odd, probably because I have never given him an explanation, not that the real one would help. He still offers the opinion, whenever it comes up, that my relationship with Finny is weird.

"Throw it," Finny says when I come back. He holds out his hands.

"Do you have a death wish or something?" I say. I cross the room and place the can in his hands.

"Nah. Even if you hit my head, you couldn't throw it hard enough to do any real damage." I sit down on my side of the couch and open my can. He's probably right. I'm taking my first sip when he speaks, and he's too quiet for me to hear.

"What was that?"

Finny clears his throat. "I'm going to miss gym class with you," he says.

"You mean you're going to miss laughing at me in gym class?"

"No. I mean I'm going to miss hanging out with you."

A lump forms in my throat. I shrug, smile, and try to speak around it. "We see each other all the time. We have dinner with The Mothers, like, twice a week."

"I know," Finny says. He looks down at his can. "But I dunno. We should hang out sometime when we don't have to. Go see a movie or something."

"Um," I say. I'm looking away again now. I feel warm and fluttery inside. I cannot say anything. Perhaps it is possible for us to have come full circle, from as close as two people can be to awkward strangers to nearly friends to—

To what?

What could we, would we, be now? It's possible to love two people at once, but could it be possible to stay loyal to one?

I look up at his face, his flushed cheeks and nervous blue eyes, and I want to say "Sure." I want it too much.

"I'm not sure, Finny," I say. Even allowing myself to say his name hurts. "I don't know if Jamie would like it. It might be kinda weird."

"But I thought Jamie and Sasha hung out all the time?"

"Yeah, they do," I say. "But they're friends—"

I flinch, and I can't speak anymore. I stare straight ahead and try to breathe without trembling.

"I see," Finny says. I hear my mother's cell phone ring in the kitchen. I take a deep breath and stand up.

"It's probably almost time for dinner," I say. Finny watches the TV and says nothing. I step around the coffee table and walk as quickly as I can out of the room.

In the bathroom, I sit on the edge of the tub and press the heels of my hands into my eyes until I see strange shapes in the darkness. My fingers tremble in my hair.

"Don't cry, don't cry, don't cry, don't," I whisper.

"Finny! Autumn!" Aunt Angelina calls.

Finny and I meet in the hall and say nothing. We walk into the dining room together and stop at the threshold. An hour ago, Finny and I set the table for five. Aunt Angelina is taking off the china and silverware from one seat. She carries them into the kitchen. My mother sets the rack of lamb on the table and sits down with her hands in her lap.

"Mom?" I ask. "Where'd Dad go?"

"I don't know, honey," she says. "But he just called to say he won't be coming back tonight."

"Oh," I say.

Aunt Angelina comes back into the room and puts her hand on my mother's shoulder.

"Come on and sit down, kids," she says. Her voice and face plead with us. Finny takes a step forward but I don't. He turns and looks at me. Our eyes meet. He reaches out and lays his hand on my arm.

"Come on, Autumn," he says. He squeezes gently and kind of smiles.

"Okay," I say.

Aunt Angelina and Finny talk for us while we eat. Afterward, The Mothers close themselves in the kitchen, and Finny and I watch TV until midnight. We don't say anything else to each other.

fifty-eight

JAMIE ANSWERS ON THE LAST ring, just before his funny and clever voice mail message would have played. His voice is blurry with sleep. It's eight o'clock in the morning, the first Saturday since we started school again. It's the year we graduate now, the year we're supposed to be grown up.

"Jamie?"

"What? I was sleeping."

"Jamie, my parents are getting a divorce." There is a silence. I imagine him sitting up, rubbing his face with one hand.

"God, pretty girl, I'm sorry."

"I'm not even sure why I'm upset," I say. I'm in my room curled in my desk chair. It's raining outside, dark and cold. I have a quilt over my shoulders and my cheek resting on my knee. "Hardly anything is going to change. Apparently Dad moved into an apartment downtown a week ago and I didn't even notice."

"When did you find out?"

"They told me last night, over dinner. And they said all that bullshit about how it wasn't my fault and they both still loved me, etc., etc., like I was six or something."

"Why didn't you call me?"

"I did. You didn't answer."

"Oh shit. I remember. I was at the movie with Sasha—"

"I know. It's fine."

"I meant to call you back."

"It's fine," I say. My words sound harsh in my ears but Jamie does not say anything about it. I swallow. "Do you think you could come over?"

"Yeah," Jamie says. "Just let me shower first—hey, want me to take you out to breakfast?"

"I don't think I can eat."

"Are you sure?"

"Yeah," I say. I pull the quilt tighter around me. "Just come over and hold me."

"Will do, pretty girl. I'll see you in a minute."

"Wait! Jamie?"

"What?"

"Will you ever leave me?"

"Nope."

"Promise?"

"Yup."

"Okay. Bye."

"Bye. Love you."

"I love you too, Jamie."

I lay my phone on the desk and watch the rain outside my window.

fifty-nine

AT SCHOOL, ANGIE LETS ME feel her stomach. It's still not very big, but it's taut like a drum. Everyone at school knows about her now, and all my friends know about my parents. At lunch one day, Alex asks if it means that my mother and Aunt Angelina are finally getting together. Sasha punches his shoulder and calls him an idiot.

"Seriously, dude?" Jamie says, "Did you really just say that?"

"You were all wondering it too!" Alex says. He rubs the shoulder Sasha punched with one hand.

"Yeah, but we weren't going to ask," Noah says.

"Noah!" Brooke hisses.

"Look, everybody, I knew you were thinking it. I don't care. And no, they're not."

"Autumn, you want to feel my belly again?" Angie says. She knows it cheers me up.

"Sure," I say.

There isn't much else to cheer me up. I hate winter. Dr. Singh raises the dosage on my medicine. Last semester, I told Mr. Laughegan that I was starting a novel. I don't feel like working much and I don't want to disappoint him.

"Maybe you should get one of those sun lamps to sit under," Jamie says. He's driving me home from school. It's snowing but not sticking, melting against the windshield and running off in thin streams of water.

"This isn't just about the weather, Jamie. My parents are getting divorced."

"Yeah, but you're also depressed every winter, so maybe—"

"Are you sick of taking care of me?" I turn sideways in my seat to face him.

"No. Jeez, Autumn, I was just saying maybe it would help."

"Sorry. I love you."

"I love you too." He turns on the windshield wipers, and we don't talk the rest of the way home.

——————

Angie and Preppy Dave show us their apartment in his parents' basement. They have a bed and a kitchen table. We aren't allowed to stay for very long. Dave's parents say they are giving them a place to live, not a place to hang out. At school, the other kids alternate between thinking it's cool she's married and looking at her with contempt. Angie seems oblivious to both, and every time her hand is on her stomach, she is smiling.

At the end of March, Sasha breaks up with Alex. She says it's for good this time, and I believe her. They agree to go to prom together in April anyway, for old times' sake. And then Brooke and Noah tell us, casually, that they don't plan to stay together when they leave for college. They aren't going to the same university, and they say they don't want to ruin what they have by trying to make it work. None of us, except Sasha and Jamie, are going to the same school.

Sometimes when we're all together, we talk about how high school is almost over. And how we will always be friends.

We're eating dinner with Aunt Angelina and Finny nearly every night now. Afterward, my mother stays late over there and doesn't come home until I've gone to bed. I hate being in the house by myself, so sometimes I bring my homework over and work at their kitchen table. Finny joins me and we do our homework together like we used to, except we don't talk as much. Every evening, Sylvie calls him and he takes his phone into the other room for half an hour, then comes back and shoves it in his pocket before sitting back down. I heard at school that she isn't going to college in the fall. She's going to go to Europe for the summer, then take a year off to find herself or something like that. I want to ask Finny if they are planning on staying together, but I can't.

I'm supposed to spend one evening a week with my dad, but it doesn't always work out. When it does, he takes me out to restaurants in the city and asks me about school and Jamie. He's always liked Jamie. His apartment overlooks the river and the Arch. It has a second bedroom that he says I can use anytime I want. I'm not sure what I would use it for.

A few green shoots begin to appear in the beginning of April. It's still cold out, but things are getting a little better.

But only a little.

sixty

―――――

"ARE YOU GOING TO VOTE for Finn?" Sasha asks.

"For what?" I say. We're at Goodwill, looking through a rack of old wedding dresses. It's Sasha's idea for her prom dress. Mom is making me buy a dress from a department store; she says that, right now, she needs something like buying me a real prom dress. I didn't put up as much of a fight as I might have in the past. Brooke bought a dress from a department store too. She says that there are a lot of sequined nightmares at the mall, but it won't be as hard as I think to find something cool.

Angie is making her dress out of blue crepe. It's hard for her to find clothes now. Her mother-in-law buys her maternity shirts that look like something Sylvie would wear if she ever got fat. Mostly Angie wears giant T-shirts from bands that broke up in the nineties.

Angie holds up a mock Victorian dress with a high collar for me to see.

"If you want to tell Alex to keep his hands to himself, that will do it," I say. I go back to searching the rack.

"Well, since I'm about to be the last virgin of our friends, I might as well look the part," she says. I look up again. Sasha has the dress flung over one arm.

"Jamie told you about that?" I say.

She nods. "Yeah, why didn't you?"

I shrug. "I dunno," I say, and I honestly don't. "It doesn't seem real, I guess."

"Well, you've got two months and one week until it will be all the way real."

"Yeah, I guess so," I say. I finger the yellowed lace on the nearest dress. "What were you saying about Finny?"

"Oh, are you going to vote for him for Prom King?" I feel my face scrunch into a grimace.

"He's going to run for Prom King?" I say.

"He and Sylvie together. I thought you would know." I'm not surprised that I didn't know though. When Finny and I do talk, he never mentions Sylvie. Ever since Christmas, he usually only asks how I'm doing and I say fine and then we watch TV or go finish our homework. Sometimes we talk about school or the weather.

"I guess that was Sylvie's idea," I say. "No wait, I know it was. He hates being the center of attention."

"But he's so popular," Sasha says. I shrug.

"That's not his fault," I say. "He's likable."

"I guess," Sasha says. "And he is so hot." I shrug again. She looks down at the dress in her hands. "I'm going to look so cool," she says.

My mother and I go shopping on the first day that it actually feels like spring. Mom's face is thinner and there are always circles under her eyes, but today she is excited.

"Now," she says, as we glide up the escalator toward evening apparel, "is all pink entirely banned?"

"Not if it's like a sassy pink," I say. "But if it's a sweet, girly pink, yes. Maybe some shade of sarcastic pink if it isn't too abrasive."

"I'll keep that in mind," she says.

I try on all kinds of pink, for her. I wear blues and greens because Dad is leaving her, and we consider oranges and reds because the whole world is open to us now. In the mirror, I see the girl I could have been if I'd tried out for cheerleading. I see what I would have looked like if I was the sort of girl who could turn a cartwheel and have more friends than favorite books. Every dress is another girl who is not me.

And then there is one. Beige satin, nearly the color of my skin, with one, just one, layer of black tulle over the skirt and bodice. A corset top and a black ribbon for my mother to tie in the back. We watch me in the mirror.

"Okay," my mother says. "So."

"Please," I say.

"Oh yes," she says. I smile and then I laugh. I try to hold my hair with my hands but it falls between my fingers.

sixty-one

WHAT'S WITH SASHA'S DRESS?" JAMIE whispers in my ear. I glance to the side where she and Alex are posing for a picture. The girls all got ready at my house, and all the parents came to take photos of them picking us up. The parents are misty-eyed; we're excited and trying to be cynical. It isn't cool to think prom is a big deal.

"It's an old wedding dress," I tell him. The dress, while a cool idea in theory, is not as great as we thought it would be. She looks pretty, but also like she is going to a Halloween party. Sasha thinks she looks terrific, and I haven't told her otherwise. Angie looks amazing, and we've all told her so, in a sort of awe. With her supple pregnancy encased in blue and her blond hair curled in to soft ringlets, she looks like a Renaissance painting of the Madonna. Dave has not taken his eyes or his hands off her.

"I like your dress," Jamie says.

"Do I look pretty?"

"Of course you do."

"Smile!" my mother says. We grin and press cheek to cheek.

"Can we go yet?" Brooke calls out. She's wearing the sarcastic pink that I had tried to explain to my mother, with a flared short skirt and black lace gloves. Her hair is in a bun like a ballerina. Noah is wearing a matching pink tux with a black shirt and tie.

In his tuxedo, Jamie is handsome like a playboy from the 1950s; he looks suave and sharp, and if I had just met him, I wouldn't trust him not to break my heart.

"One more picture with everybody together," Sasha's mother says. We press together and wrap our arms around each other's waists.

"Ow," Brooke says. "You stepped on my toe."

"Smile!" my mother says.

We don't have a limo. Kids who rent limos are pretentious and are taking prom way too seriously. I ride in the passenger seat of Jamie's car with Sasha and Alex in the back. We park in the back of the hotel and weave between limos and girls with dresses big enough to house families until we meet up with the others by the doors.

"Hey," Noah says, "I think there's food inside."

"Of course there's food," Sasha says.

"What kind of food?" Alex says.

"It said in the invitations there would be a buffet," I say.

"I am so hungry," Angie says.

"Of course you are," Dave says.

"Oh, be quiet." He kisses her with his hands on her hips and I look away.

"Where's your tiara?" Sylvie says. We all turn and look at her. She and Finny are standing by us. In the distance, I see Alexis and Victoria getting out of a limo.

"Tiaras are for every day," I say. "This is a special night."

"Oh," she says. The boys snicker. Finny glances at them and tugs on her hand.

"Let's go in," he says.

"See you inside," I say. Finny nods and they stroll away.

"Well, since this is a special night, we should go eat some of that special food," Alex says.

"There's magic in the air. I can feel it," Jamie says.

"Shut up, guys," I say. "She thought you were laughing at her."

"That's not our problem," Sasha says.

"For the record, we were definitely laughing at you," Noah says.

"Even I thought it was funny," Preppy Dave says. Everyone laughs and we follow the crowd inside. There are silver stars hanging from the ceiling, and blue and white glitter on the tables.

We eat cheese cubes and make fun of most of the music. The boys take off their jackets and throw them over their chairs. We slow dance and change partners. I dance with Noah and Alex; Dave will not leave Angie's side.

I see Finny twice, once as Jamie and I sway to a love song, and again when he and Sylvie are crowned King and Queen. His face is as red as an apple, and I laugh as I clap for him, and our eyes meet briefly. Then he is gone again, and the night moves on.

At the last slow song, I am hot and tired, and Jamie and I move together with our hips and cheeks pressed together. I lean my weight against him, just a little, and he holds me.

"I love you," I say, and in that moment, it feels like a revelation. I wish I could explain to him that I really mean it right now. His fingers press into my back.

"I will never hurt you," he says, and he lets me press closer.

It was one of our best moments.

sixty-two

JAMIE IS DRIVING ME HOME from school when I bring it up. It's a gorgeous day; the sky is clear and the wind is blowing in the trees. I want to roll my window down, but Jamie doesn't like it when I do that, and I would have to beg. My book bag is on the floor, and my knees are drawn up to my chest. We pull out of the school's parking lot.

"I was thinking we should talk about it," I say.

"About what?"

"About—" It hadn't occurred to me that he wouldn't know exactly what I meant, and now I find myself unable to say it. "About what we agreed would happen after graduation."

"Oh," he says. He drives in silence. He stares straight ahead. He offers me nothing.

"I'm still not on the pill," I say. "I could get on it."

"No," he says, "you don't need to do that."

"Well, you'll need to buy condoms then, and maybe, practice—"

"Autumn, I can't even think about that right now. I'm so stressed out about finals and—and everything else. Let's just not talk about it right now."

"Okay," I say. I'm proud that unlike other boys, he isn't so focused on sex that he can't think of other things.

"I love you," I say as I kiss him and get out of the car.

"Me too," he says.

sixty-three

ALL THROUGH THE CEREMONY, I stare at Shawn O'Brian's tangled mullet, and I think, *Someday this will be the only thing I remember about my graduation.* Adults march on stage and give speeches that are full of advice for us. I try to feel as if I have accomplished something, but all I feel is that I lived through a few years of my life; getting through high school was just what I did on the side.

"Autumn R. Davis," a teacher says, and I'm moving forward to take the diploma. I remember I'm supposed to smile. Adults shake my hand and say congratulations, and I'm surprised that they look so sincere. A photographer takes my picture when I shake hands with Mrs. Black. I see spots for a moment, and then I am walking back to my seat, but it feels more like wandering.

Afterward, when we've taken off our robes and the teachers set us free to go find our families, the lobby is too crowded to move around and find them. I see Angie with Dave and her family and I hug her before the crowd pushes me away. I see Brooke and Noah in a corner, holding hands and talking quietly. I wonder if they are talking about their plan to break up in the fall—I still don't understand.

I feel my cell phone ring in my pocket.

"Mom?" I have to nearly shout to hear myself.

"Honey, we're over by the display case. Can you see us?" She's shouting too. I look around and stand up on my toes.

"No." I see Jamie, Sasha, and Alex. They see me and I wave them over. They start pushing their ways toward me.

"Where are you? We can send Finny to come find you."

"No, I'll find you," I say. Jamie stops in front of me, with Sasha next to him and Alex standing behind them. "I'll be there in a sec," I say. I hang up.

"Hey," Jamie says, "we're going to go eat. Wanna come? I'll give you a ride home."

"I have to go eat with my family," I say.

"Oh," Jamie says. "Can I come over tomorrow then? We need to talk." I feel my cheeks heat up.

"Yeah, I know," I say. I lean forward and Jamie kisses me quickly.

"I saw Finn and your mom over there," Sasha says.

"Thanks." I hug her and Alex quickly and push my way in the direction she pointed.

When The Mothers see me, they begin to wave excitedly, and Finny watches them and laughs. Dad is in Japan. He called me this morning.

"Picture, picture," my Mom says. Finny and I stand next to each other and smile. The crowd is beginning to thin, and The Mothers try to find enough space to get full-length shots of us.

"So, congratulations," Finny says. We're still looking straight ahead at the cameras, fake smiles in place.

"For what?" I say.

"I don't really know," he says. I hear him laugh next to me.

"I don't either. Congratulations for surviving maybe?"

"Maybe. But come on, it wasn't that bad was it?" I look up at him.

"Nah, I guess not," I say. He smiles, and out of the corner of my eyes, I see The Mothers' cameras flash.

That was the picture they framed.

sixty-four

JAMIE CALLS ME EARLY THE next morning. I'm surprised; he never usually wakes up before ten o'clock if he can help it.

"Hey," he says, "is it too early to come over?"

"No," I say. "I've been up for an hour."

"Oh. Okay, cool." His voice sounds strange and my stomach turns over on itself. After we hang up, I go into the bathroom to put on makeup. I remember his strange voice, and an odd, queasy excitement flutters in me.

I wait for him on the back steps. It isn't too warm out yet, but the sun is bright and it's drying the dew on the grass and warming the steps. I hear a car coming and I sit up straighter, but it is only Finny. He sees me sitting on the back steps.

"Hey," he says.

"Hey," I say.

"Whattaya doing?"

"Waiting for Jamie."

"Oh," Finny says.

Just then, Jamie's car pulls into the driveway. He gets out slowly and looks at Finny.

"Hey, man," he says.

"Hey," Finny says. He turns and goes in to the house. Jamie walks over and stands in front of me. I weakly smile at him.

"Hi," I say.

"Hi," he says, but he doesn't smile. I know it for sure then, and my chest aches exactly as if he had punched me. I close my mouth and swallow.

So this is it after all, I think. How easy and obvious it seems now. How silly and trite, how terrible and real. I want to laugh at myself and him, but all that happens is that the corners of my mouth twitch once.

I scoot over and make room for him on the step.

"Why don't you sit down?" I say.

"I thought we could take a walk," he says.

"Here is fine," I say. He shrugs and looks away. He doesn't see that I already know. He sits down heavily, with six inches of space between us, and looks at his hands between his knees. I look away, and focus on Finny's car while I wait. The queasy excitement that I felt before begins to ebb away, and I am filled with a cold dread.

"Autumn?" he says.

"Yes, Jamie," I say.

"I can't do this anymore."

"Do what?" I say, just to be cruel.

"This relationship." I see his head turn toward me to gauge my reaction, expecting to see surprise there. I try to make my face blank, but I can feel my eyes burning.

"Why?" I say. He takes a deep breath.

"I can't be who you need me to be," he says. His tone is that of someone reciting a memorized lesson, a catechism. "You need me a lot, and it's more than I can handle. You're depressed all the time—"

"I am not depressed all the time."

"Yeah, you are."

"No, I'm not."

"You're depressed a lot."

"My parents are getting divorced."

"You've always been like this. I can't do it anymore."

My arms are wrapped around my stomach now, and I'm leaning forward as if I need to hold my internal organs in place. Finny's car is blurry.

"How long have you felt this way?" I ask.

"A couple of weeks."

"A couple of weeks? You want to throw away what we've had for four years after a couple of weeks? That's stupid."

Jamie sighs, and for the first time, I do not hear pity in his voice.

"I knew you were going to say that," he says.

"Look, all your reasons are really stupid," I say. "People in relationships need each other like I need you. I know it's exhausting taking care of me, and I'm sorry. I can try to give you a break, and we can use this summer to get back on track. I really think this is just a rough patch."

Jamie shakes his head. I finally turn and look at him. He's looking at his hands again.

"So that's it? You're not even going to try? After all this time together?"

"I can't do it anymore, Autumn."

"You said you would love me forever." I'm not going to let him off easy.

"I do love you, just not that way anymore," Jamie says.

"You still love me," I say. "You just can't feel it right now. Sometimes that happens to me, and I just wait and it always comes back. I don't break up with you. I just give it time."

He shakes his head again. He sighs. I wait.

"There is something else," he says. My veins fill with ice water, and I feel like I am looking at him from very far away.

"What?" I hear myself say, and I think how silly it is that I'm asking when I already know.

"Sasha and I have discovered that we have feelings for each other."

Finally, the laughter that has been building up in my chest bubbles out. My head drops between my knees and my shoulders shake.

"Discovered?" I say. My laughter begins to sound strange to me and I swallow in an attempt to hold it back again. I laugh once more and shake my head. "'Discovered'? How very fucking special that must have been for you both."

Jamie puts a hand on my shoulder.

"We both still love you so much," he says, "and we've been so worried about you. Sasha really wants to talk to you—" I shrug his hand off.

"No, no, no," I say. "Just stop. Give me a minute."

I take a few deep breaths. Jamie watches me respectfully, his whole aura radiating sympathy. I sit up straight again and take one last deep breath.

"Okay," I say. Jamie leans forward expectantly. "Did you sleep with her?" I ask.

Jamie draws back as if I pinched him. He says nothing.

I blink. "Really?" I say. "When?"

"We never planned on any of this," Jamie says. "We feel really awful about how this has all turned out and—"

"Tell me when!" I say.

His face hardens like it did when he said he knew what I would say. "A couple of days before prom. After she went with me to order your corsage. It was an accident. We felt awful about it and we swore that it wouldn't happen again. But last week, we both admitted that we can't pretend anymore. We care about each other, but we didn't want to ruin graduation for you."

"And you guys want a damn medal?" I say. I go over every memory of the six weeks since prom. It's only in the past two weeks that I can see anything being different. I thought we were all stressed about the end of school. I trusted that Jamie would always want me. I never thought I could be free of his love for me.

"We're sorry that we've hurt you, Autumn," Jamie is saying. "But we still really care about you, and—"

"Do you want to know something funny?" I say, "I always thought you loved me more than I loved you. I always thought I would be the one to end it if it ever happened."

"For a long time, I believed that too," he says. For a moment my confession and his agreement give me a small feeling of camaraderie; together we're looking over our relationship and seeing the same thing. Then the feeling is gone, and I am alone. A strange calm has come over me. I focus on Finny's car again.

"You can go now," I say. My voice is even and quiet. I'm ready to go to my room and be done with this.

"What?" Jamie says.

"You should go now. There isn't anything else to say. You guys are assholes and that's it."

"I know you're angry and you have a right to be, but we didn't plan any of this—"

"I don't really want to hear anymore, okay? Let's just be done."

"Okay." Jamie stands. His face is hard again. At the bottom of the steps, he turns and looks at me. "Sasha wants you to know that she's sorry. She wants to talk to you, but she's going to wait for you to call her."

"I'm not going to call her. You can go ahead and tell her that." I stand and start toward the door.

"We really hope someday we can all be friends again," Jamie says. "We care about you so much. I think you should—" I open the door and turn to face him.

"Jamie," I say, "since you're the one breaking up with me, I think

I should get to have the last word. And I want you to know that I will never, ever be your friend again."

I slam the door and go to my room and cry where no one can hear me.

sixty-five

ON DAY THREE, MY MOTHER comes and sits on the edge of the bed. It's midafternoon but I'm still in my pajamas. I've worn them for two days now. I'm wearing my glasses, and my hair is greasy. I know staying in bed for most of the day isn't helping my argument that I just need to be left alone, but I can't summon the resolve to do anything else. As long as I can sleep, I feel numb, and numb is good; numb doesn't hurt.

"Autumn," my mother says.

"I already know what you're going to say, so can we just skip it?"

"Why don't you call one of your friends?" Mom says. "Why hasn't Sasha been by?"

"The Sasha who slept with Jamie right before prom?" I feel her body tense. I curl up in a ball and pull the blankets over my head.

"I'm so sorry," Mom says. I don't answer her, even though she waits. She clears her throat. "What about Brooke?"

"Jamie's cousin? I'm sure she really wants to hear all about what a bastard he is."

"Angie—"

"Is gonna go into labor pretty soon now, Mom."

She is quiet and still, and I hope that she is giving up and leaving.

"I don't suppose—one of the boys?" she says.

"Mom! Just go, please?"

I feel the mattress shift and hear her walk across the floor. She closes the door behind her. I shut my eyes and try to sleep again.

———————

When I open my eyes again, it is late afternoon, and Mom is standing at my door.

"You need to get up," she says.

"No."

"Finny's coming over."

"What?" I sit up as if a bolt of electricity has shot through me. Mom goes to the closet and seemingly reaches in at random, pulling out a blue tank top.

"Why is he coming over?" I say. Mom lays the tank top down on the bed next to me and crosses over to the dresser.

"He's coming to see you. Do you have a strapless bra clean?" She opens the top drawer of my dresser.

"I haven't even showered! And I don't want to see Finny!" I say. Mom ignores me and opens another drawer.

"Jeans or a skirt? You haven't shaved your legs, have you?

Here." She tries to hand a pair of jeans to me, but I swat them away.

"He'll be here in ten minutes, so you better hurry." She turns away from me and walks out.

"Mom!" I shout at her retreating back. She ignores me. I jump out of bed and run to the bathroom.

When I hear him on the stairs, I am dressed, but my hair is still wet, and I'm not wearing any makeup. I grab a hair band and hastily pull my hair into a ponytail. He knocks. I look around my room. I've been eating here for the past three days, and I realize that, while I was showering, Mom came in and cleared out all the empty wrappers and dirty plates. I sit down on my bed. It's been made.

"Come in," I say. The door opens a crack, and Finny's face glances around the corner and looks at me, then he opens the door the rest of the way and stands in the threshold.

"Hey," he says. He's already blushing a little.

"Hi," I say. He looks at me like he's waiting for me to do something. "Are you going to come in or lurk in the doorway like a vampire?"

"I'll come in," he says. He crosses the room and pulls out the chair from my desk. He sits facing me with one elbow on the desk. I pull my knees up to my chest and lean against the headboard.

"I'm sorry they made you do this," I say.

"Who?" Finny says.

"The Mothers." He shakes his head.

"They didn't," he says. "It was my idea." He's looking down at his lap. He doesn't move. He just sits there with me. I look at his shoulders and his hands. His hair is even more golden from the summer sun. Something stirs in me, and I push it down again. I'd rather feel nothing.

"You should know though," Finny says, "they're really worried about you."

"I know," I say. He raises his head and looks at me.

"They're talking about calling that doctor again." I sit up straight and let my feet fall to the floor.

"Singh?" Finny nods. "Oh God, he's the last person I want to see."

"Why? What's wrong with him?"

"I dunno." I shake my head. "He's writes down everything I say in this file. And every time I see him, he makes me stand on his scale."

Finny frowns. "Why?"

"He thinks I'm anorexic," I say. The corners of Finny's mouth twitch up. "It's not funny," I say. Finny grins and shakes his head.

"It's kinda funny," he says. I can't help but smile a little when he looks at me like that.

"Okay," I say, "maybe it's a little funny. But I do not want to talk about Jamie with him." When I say his name, a knife stabs my guts, and my smile fades.

"I'll take care of it," Finny says.

297

"You'll convince them not to call him?"

"Under one condition."

"What's that?" I ask.

Finny stands up. "Come get some ice cream with me," he says. I sigh and pull my knees up to my chest again.

"Finny, I really don't want to go anywhere today," I say. Finny grabs my arm and pulls me up. "Hey!" I say.

"Where are your shoes?" he asks. He sees some flip-flops in the corner and drags me over. "Put these on."

"These don't match my outfit," I say. "And I'm not wearing a tiara."

"What does that have to do with anything?" he says. "Come on." I slide my feet into the shoes, and Finny walks me downstairs, still holding my arm. The Mothers are down in the kitchen drinking iced tea. Both of their faces light up when they see us.

"We're going to get ice cream," Finny says.

"I'm being kidnapped," I say.

"Good job, Phineas," my mom says.

"Have fun, kids," Aunt Angelina says.

He doesn't let me go until we reach his car. He pushes the button on the automatic locks and opens the door for me. I sigh and sit down. This is only the third time I've ever been in the little red car; it smells of leather and of Finny. He walks around the car and slides in next to me. Without saying anything, he pulls out of the driveway and turns on the radio. He's driving to the Train Stop, where a lot of kids from school hang out or work.

"Do I have to come in?" I say when Finny pulls into the parking lot. It's nearly full. I recognize most of the cars.

"Why?" he says.

"I don't want to see all the kids from school." Finny pulls the car into a spot and turns off the engine. He turns to me in his seat.

"Do you not want to be seen with me?" he asks.

"What? No!" I say. I'm so surprised that my words come out stuttered. "I—I don't want to have to answer any questions about Jamie."

"Oh," he says. "Sorry." He gets out of the car. I watch his back as he crosses the parking lot and try to figure out why he thought I wouldn't want to be seen with him.

Finny comes back a few minutes later carrying two cones. He taps on the window with one finger, and I open the door for him. He hands both cones to me.

"Here," he says.

"Thanks," I say. He remembered that mint chocolate chip is my favorite. He got plain vanilla like always. I used to tease him about it. He turns out of the parking lot in the other direction from home. "Where are we going?" I ask.

"To the park," he says. "The longer we're gone, the better they'll feel."

When we get out of the car, I hand his cone to him and we walk on the path circling the lake. We eat in silence for a few minutes. I try to eat neatly so that I don't get any green sticky on my face.

"So," I say after a while, "what's Sylvie doing today?"

"She left for her tour of Europe. I think she's in London now."

"Oh, I forgot. When's she coming back?"

"August."

"Wow." Finny doesn't say anything. I look up at him. He's staring straight ahead. "Are you guys going to stay together in the fall?"

"I guess so," he says.

"You haven't talked about it?"

"No."

We walk in silence for a while. I eat the last bit of my cone and stray off the path to throw away my napkins. We stand by the trash can while Finny finishes his and tosses the remains in too.

"Sasha and Jamie are both going to Rochester," I say. The path winds closer to the lake and out from under the shade of the trees.

"Huh," Finny says.

"So I guess they'll be staying together."

"Maybe they'll break up by then," Finny says.

"Ha," I say. "But I doubt it."

"Well, they deserve each other," he says.

"It's not the healthiest way to start a relationship either," I say. "I can't see how this could be good for them."

"No," Finny says. "It won't be."

"And do you know what Jamie said? He said I 'needed him too much.'" I draw quotes in the air with my fingers. Finny makes a face.

"What does that mean?"

"I dunno. But do you see what I mean? What kind of relationship is it going to be if he has that attitude?"

Finny stops and picks up a piece of gravel and pitches it at the

300

lake. The rock skips four times, then drops into the water. I sit down in the shade and watch him search for another flat rock.

"You're better off without them. You know that, right?" he says.

"I know," I say. I wrap my arms around my stomach. "But I can't help wishing things could go back to the way they used to be." Finny glances at me and turns back to the lake. The rock jumps only once and falls. He bends down again and picks through the gravel. "Do you think that's stupid?" I ask.

"No," he says.

"I do," I say. "I feel like an idiot. I should be glad it's over. I should be relieved."

"You should," Finny says. He tosses the rock and it leaps across the water again and again. "But I don't think you're an idiot."

"There were so many times I wanted to break up with him," I say. "But I didn't, because I thought, 'He loves me so much. I can't do that to him.' Isn't that stupid?"

"No," he says.

"I thought if I broke up with him, no one else would ever love me like that."

"Well, that part is stupid," Finny says. He turns away from the lake and sits down next to me on the grass. He rests his elbows on his knees and looks at me.

"Are you going to give me a lecture about how I'll find love again?" I ask.

"No," he says, "I was going to ask—" He blushes and looks back at the lake. "He didn't sleep with you and then—"

"No," I say. And then, "He isn't that bad."

Finny shrugs.

We watch the lake for a little while. The sun is starting to set and turn the water warm colors. A breeze picks up and ruffles my ponytail. I hug myself again. I wonder if Jamie and Sasha are together right now, what they are doing. If they are talking about me, pitying me. I scratch my arm.

"Do you think we've been gone long enough?" I ask.

"Probably."

"I'm getting eaten by bugs."

"Okay." Finny stands and offers me his hand. He helps me up, and I pretend to dust off my jeans so I get rid of the feeling of his hand on mine.

He rolls down the windows on the drive home. I hold my hand out the window and feel the air rushing through my fingers. I take my hair out of the ponytail and it whips around my face. I don't feel numb anymore, and it's not a good thing. My stomach hurts and my chest has a familiar ache. We don't say anything until after he parks the car and shuts off the engine.

"What are you doing tomorrow?" Finny asks. I shrug. "Let me take you to breakfast and then you can spend the rest of your day lying in bed or whatever you want."

"Okay."

"See you tomorrow, then." We open our doors and get out.

We go into our separate houses, and I go straight upstairs. I cry myself to sleep again but not just for Jamie this time.

sixty-six

WHEN I COME DOWNSTAIRS, MOM is at the table drinking coffee and reading the paper. She raises her eyebrows at me but doesn't comment. I have makeup on today, and my hair is clean and dry. I picked up a tiara and almost set it on my head, but then sat it back down.

I go to the refrigerator and pour myself a glass of apple juice.

"Thank you," I say to her while my back is still turned.

"For what?"

"Not saying anything."

"You're welcome." I sit down across from her and pick up the cartoons. "What are you doing today?" she asks. She takes another sip and does not look away from the paper.

"Finny and I are going to breakfast." Mom looks up and smiles. "Try not to look so thrilled," I say.

"Sorry," she says. She looks down at the newspaper again.

Finny sent me a text an hour ago, asking me what time I wanted to leave. It woke me up. I thought for a horrible moment that it would be Jamie, and then I remembered everything. If my plans had been with anyone else but Finny, I wouldn't have been able to drag myself out of bed.

I hear his knock on the back door and I look up. He opens the door himself and comes into the kitchen.

"Hi," he says.

"Good morning, Finny," Mom says.

"Just a sec," I say. I gulp down the rest of my juice and stand.

"What time will you be home?" Mom asks.

"I dunno," I say. "It's just breakfast."

"Call if you'll be later than midnight."

"You're hilarious, Mom."

Finny opens the door for me and we go outside.

"Mine was ecstatic too," he says.

He doesn't laugh at me for ordering a hamburger and fries for breakfast. The waitress doesn't frown either, and I file it away as further evidence that I'm not the only one. Finny orders bacon, eggs, and hash browns, just like you're supposed to.

"Has your mom told you yet that we don't have curfews anymore?" Finny says after the waitress takes our menus.

"No. Are you sure it's both of us?"

"That's what she said. And she said the same thing about calling later than midnight."

"Huh."

Finny's phone rings. He pulls it out of his pocket, looks at it, and frowns. "Sorry," he says to me, and then into the phone, "Hey." I take a crayon from the jar on the table and start to draw on the paper tablecloth. "Are you still jet-lagged?" he says. I draw a flower and then a heart. I scratch out the heart. "Yeah, I'm about to eat breakfast. Really? That's cool." He listens for a long time then. I draw a house with a sun in the sky, and two stick figures in the yard playing with a red ball. I pause and make them a blond girl and a brunette boy. I give them a dog. I always wanted a dog. "Uh-huh. I do. I miss you too." My eyes are glued to the table. I will not look up. The waitress comes with our food and covers up my drawing. While Finny listens to the phone, I pick at my French fries and stir the ketchup in swirls.

"Okay. Have fun. And, Sylvie?" Even though I knew it was her, the name jolts me and I look up at him. He glances at me and looks away. "Uh, just be safe, okay? Don't do anything—you know." He pauses and listens. "I know. I know. Love you too. Bye." He puts his phone back in his pocket. I look down at my food again. "Sorry," he says.

"It's fine," I say.

"With the time difference and all the running around she's doing, she can't call that often. I couldn't tell her to call back."

"No, really, it's fine. How is she?"

"She's fine. Really excited."

"That's nice," I say. I finally pick up my hamburger and take a bite.

"So…Angie had her baby yet?" I chew slowly and watch him cut up his eggs.

"No," I say. "I haven't actually talked to her since graduation though. I know I should call her, but—" I shrug and take another bite.

"I bet she understands," he says. We eat in silence for a few minutes. Finny eats all his eggs, then all his hash browns, and when there is nothing else left, he starts on the bacon.

"Jamie said he hoped we could all be friends," I say. Finny looks up at me.

"Friends with him and Sasha?" he says.

"Yeah," I say.

Finny shakes his head. "He's unreal," he says.

"Is it bad that I want everyone else to take my side against them?" I ask.

"No," Finny says, "but you shouldn't expect them to, either. It may not happen."

"I know," I say. Finny breaks his bacon in half and offers me a piece. I shake my head.

"I'm on your side," he says. He wipes his hands on his napkin.

"You don't count," I say.

"Thanks."

"You know what I mean."

"I know."

———————

He drives with the windows rolled down again, this time because I ask him to. It's nearly noon now, and the rest of the day is stretching out blankly. I sigh and look out the window.

"Are you going to go back to lying in bed today?" Finny says. I shrug as he pulls into the driveway. "Well, what are you gonna do?"

"I dunno," I say. He parks the car and doesn't say anything else. I run my fingers through my hair again and again and stare straight ahead. I feel the lump coming up in my throat and I try to push it down again.

"Hey, Finny?" I whisper.

"What?" he says.

"I'm scared that I'm going to call him."

"Why?" he says. From the corner of my eye, I see him turn and look at me.

"Just to yell at him."

He shakes his head. "That's not a good idea."

"I know. But I'm used to being able to call him. I'm used to telling him that I'm angry or sad or whatever." I swallow and take a breath. "It's like I need him to help me get over him."

"You don't need him," Finny says. I don't say anything. My vision is going blurry, and I am concentrating on not crying in front of him. "Autumn? Hey," he says.

"What?"

"Why don't you hang out in my room today? I was just going to play a video game. You can read or whatever. I won't let you call him."

"Okay," I say.

"What?"

"Okay," I say louder.

"All right. Come on." He walks around the car and opens the door for me, and I follow him.

307

sixty-seven

WE DO THAT EVERY DAY for the next five days. We go out for a late breakfast and then I curl up on Finny's bed and read while he plays his video game next to me. In the evening, The Mothers have dinner with us. Afterward, we watch a movie, and then I excuse myself and go upstairs.

When it's finally dark out, I turn out the lights in my bedroom and spy on Finny's window. He plays video games or surfs the Internet. At eleven o'clock every night, his cell phone rings. I think it's Sylvie. They talk for half an hour or a little more, and after he hangs up he leaves the room. He comes back in his boxer shorts and gets into bed. He reads for a little while from the book I've seen on his nightstand, some bestselling thriller, then he turns out the lights.

Watching Finny keeps me from thinking about Jamie. Somehow, I don't think Finny would mind if he knew. If I'm wondering what he's saying to Sylvie, then I'm not wondering what Jamie might be saying to Sasha. I watch Finny scratch his arm or yawn, and my mind isn't anywhere but in the moment, with him; I'm safe from hurting myself.

On the sixth morning, Finny looks nervous when he comes to the back door to get me.

"Hi!" I say.

"Hi," he says. His mouth is tight and his hands are shoved in his pockets.

I close the door behind me. Finny walks with me to the car. I wait until he has slid into the seat next to me.

"What's wrong?" I say. He starts the car and backs us out of the driveway.

"Jack called last night—"

"Oh!" I say. I had wondered who the earlier phone call had been from. Finny gives me a strange look and continues.

"Everybody is talking about getting together today. We haven't seen each other since graduation."

"Oh," I say again, in a different way.

"Will you be okay on your own?"

"Yeah," I say. "I mean, I don't want you to feel obligated to babysit me or something."

"I don't," Finny says. He glances away from the road to look at me again.

"You should go have fun with your friends," I say. "It's been a week, and I feel better."

"You do?"

"Not all the way better, but yeah, better."

"Good," Finny says. He drives in silence for a while, and then our conversation resumes normally, like on the other mornings. We make fun of The Mothers and talk about the movie we watched last night.

After breakfast, Finny drops me off, and I turn and wave to him from the back porch as he drives away again. The house is empty; Mom and Dad and all the lawyers are meeting downtown today. I go to my room and lay down on my bed. I look out the window and watch the wind in the trees. I nod off after a little while. When I open my eyes again, it's early afternoon and my room is warm. The cicadas are singing, and the wind is still rustling the trees. I stretch and turn over, and my eyes fall on my laptop.

It's been a long time since I have written. I started something before Christmas, but it got lost in the muddle of winter and the excitement of spring, and now I can't remember if what I wrote was any good.

I walk across the floor, my bare feet feeling the sun-warmed wood under me, and I sit down.

It is good, but I take out large chunks and move paragraphs. I have a new vision, a new structure for the story. I'm ready to write something honest. Soon, the only sound is the clacking of my keyboard, and then that is gone too, and all I can hear are the voices in my head.

After Mom comes home, she orders a pizza, and we eat with Aunt Angelina. Finny is still gone. As soon as we're done eating, I leave, and they do not protest; I know Mom wants to talk to Angelina about my dad.

I write again, and I do not notice the sun moving across the floorboards, the light beginning to dim. When I come out of my trance, it is dark out, and I hear the sports car in the driveway. The lights in my room are already out. I close the laptop so that the room is fully dark, and I lay down on my bed, facing the window.

He comes into the room and looks around as if he expected something to be there. He crosses the room and looks out the window, and for a moment I think he can see me. Then he turns away and sits down on his bed. He takes out his phone and puts it to his ear.

My cell phone rings. I look at it vibrating on my nightstand and then out the window, at Finny stretching out on his bed.

"Hello?"

"Hey," he says.

"Hi."

"What are you doing?"

"Nothing," I say, and then, to make it believable, "just reading."

"How was your day?"

"Okay. You?"

"It was okay."

We're quiet then, but it isn't an awkward silence; it is as if we were sitting quietly together in the same room. I watch him stretch, and I hear him yawn.

"It's too bad we didn't have cell phones back then," I say. "Then we wouldn't have needed the cups and string."

"Yeah," he says, and then, "wait, are you in your room?"

"Yeah," I say, and then I remember I was supposed to be reading, and my window is dark. "I just came in."

"Can you see me?" He waves. I laugh.

"Yeah," I say. "I'm waving back."

"Hi," he says.

"Hi," I say.

sixty-eight

LATER THAT NIGHT, HOURS AFTER Finny and I have hung up and gone to bed, my phone trills again. I lift my head up and look at it glowing on the nightstand. It's a text message from Preppy Dave:

> Guinevere Angela 3:46 am 7 lbs 2 oz visiting hours tomorrow 1-6

I smile and lay my head back down on my pillow. I imagine Angie tired, happy, and crying. Before I can fall asleep, my phone cries for me again. I see Jamie's name, and my heart drops down into my stomach.

> Angie had the baby. It's a girl. We can visit her tomorrow after 1. Do you want a ride?

I throw the phone across the room and hear it crash against the wall. It might be broken. I don't care. I sleep fitfully.

When Finny knocks on my back door, I'm sitting in the kitchen waiting for him, reading a book and eating a Popsicle. When I look up, he lets himself in.

"Hey," he says, "you look—"

"Furious?" I say.

"Uh, no." Finny looks at me warily. "I was going to say tired."

"Yeah, well, I'm that too," I say. I close my book and toss it on the table. "Jamie sent me a text last night."

"What did it say?"

I sigh and lay the empty Popsicle stick on the table. "Preppy Dave sent everybody a text."

"Who?" Finny sits down on the chair across from me.

"Preppy Dave, Angie's boyfri—I mean, husband. It said Angie had the baby and it's a girl and she weighs something or other and when we can visit and all that. And then not even five minutes later, Jamie sends me one that says—" I clear my throat and try to imitate Jamie's voice. "Angie had the baby. It's a girl. We can visit her tomorrow. Do you need a ride?"

"He didn't think you'd be one of the people Preppy Dan would text?" Finny says.

"Yes!" I say, and then, "It's Preppy Dave, but yes! And that is so Jamie! Him thinking he's being so generous by letting me know and offering a ride. Assuming that I need him for those things."

"Well," Finny says, "to be fair, you do need a ride."

"No, I don't," I say. "I have you." Finny smiles.

314

"I like how you take it for granted that I'll drive you"

"You will, won't you?" I say.

"Of course I will. That's not my point." He's still smiling. I don't feel angry anymore.

We get lost on the way to the hospital and don't get there until one thirty. It's weird being at a place like this without an adult. I remind myself that I am an adult now too, but I still think the nurses are staring at us. Finny is perfectly at ease, as if he walks through maternity wards all the time.

When we come to the open door of Angie's room, I know that Jamie is inside, almost as if I could smell him. I stop and look up at Finny. He gives me a look, one that because I know him I can read, but to the rest of the world would just be a soft smile. It'll be fine.

Angie is sitting on the bed, and the others surround her as if we were on the Steps to Nowhere again. My throat constricts.

"Hey, you made it," Jamie says.

"Autumn!" Angie cries. She grins and holds out her arms to me but grimaces from the movement. I forget everything for a moment and rush to her.

"Sorry I'm late," I say as I squeeze her. "We got lost."

"You brought Finn!" she says. "Hi, Finn."

"Hi," he says. He stands in the doorway looking like the way I felt when we were walking down the hall.

"Where's your tiara?" Brooke says. I shrug.

"I'm over tiaras, I think," I say.

"Really?" Sasha says.

"Do you want to hold her?" Angie says to me.

"Yeah," I say. I look around the room, avoiding Jamie and Sasha sitting together in the corner, and finally see that Preppy Dave has a small bundle in his arms, so small that I didn't notice it before. He crosses the room and holds it out to me.

"Wow," I say as the little weight of her is transferred to me. "Wow."

She is so tiny, her face is scrunched up, and her eyes are closed as if she were trying to block out the world. "Wow," I say again. This is a person who didn't exist before. "Finny," I say, my voice still low, my mind still spinning. "Come look." I feel him come stand behind me, look over my shoulder. For a moment we are quiet.

"Her fingernails," he says.

"I know," Angie says. I like holding Guinevere, I realize. I can look at her and forget that Jamie and Sasha are sitting close together as if it were right.

"So where did you get lost?" Jamie says. I try not to grimace at the baby.

"We just missed the exit off I-70 and got lost turning around," Finny says.

"Yeah, we got a little lost too," Jamie says. "But we left early."

"We had lunch first," Finny says.

"I wish we had," Brooke says. "I'm hungry."

"Let's all go out later," Alex says.

"Yeah," Jamie says.

316

"What about you guys?" Sasha says. It takes me a second to realize that she is talking to Finny and me.

"Uh, no, we have plans," I say. What I want to say is, "Hell no," but somehow I can't bring myself to do it. I sit down on the bed facing away from her.

"What are you two doing?" Angie says. She winks at me so that Jamie and Sasha cannot see. I feel my cheeks burn, and I look at Finny.

"We're going to a movie," he says, even though we have never discussed it. His self-assurance has returned to him. He sits down next to me on the bed.

"What movie?" Sasha says.

"Finny, you hold her," I say.

"Oh no," he says. I laugh at him, and he holds up his hands defensively.

"Come on," I say, and push her toward him. I force him to take her, and when she is in his arms, he looks at me as if I am supposed to explain to him the next step. I laugh again and lean over her. "Look at her frowny face," I say. I realize that my head is nearly resting on his shoulder, and that I cannot bring myself to move it. Finny looks down at the baby. For a moment, it feels as if we three are the only ones in the room.

"Is there anything sexier than a guy holding a baby?" Angie says, and even this does not bring me to my senses.

"Nope," I say, and I flinch. I move an inch away from Finny, and I can actually feel the loss of his body heat.

"All right, my turn," Brooke says. "Stop torturing the poor guy."

She walks around the room and takes the baby from Finny. I avoid looking at him.

For the next hour, we talk about normal things and watch TV. I don't look at Finny and I am careful to not brush against him as I shift my weight on the bed. Jamie talks the most, orchestrating the conversation so that it exhibits his charm and humor. It isn't any different than before, but it feels different. Jamie and Sasha do not hold hands or kiss, but they sit close together.

During the theme song of the next show, Guinevere begins to cry.

"She's hungry," Angie says. She says it with a certain authority that intrigues me. She's only known her daughter for less than half a day.

"We should probably go," I say. Finny and I stand up together. Angie looks at us, but her gaze is distracted.

"Thanks for coming," she says, and looks down at the baby again. I walk quickly toward the door.

"Bye, everybody," I say.

"Goodbye," Finny says.

"We should get going too," I hear Jamie say, but I do not look back or slow down. Finny and I walk side by side. The others are all behind us, Jamie, Sasha, Alex, Brooke, and Noah. They are talking about what they will do next. We walk as if we do not know each other. Finny presses the button at the elevator, and the doors open immediately. We step inside, and Finny press the first-floor button as the others round the corner. I look at them, and they look at me. The doors close. Finny turns to me.

"You okay?" he says.

"Yeah," I say.

"You really want to go see that movie?" he says.

"Yeah," I say, "and we'll see whatever you want. Thanks for coming."

"No big deal," he says. Finny grins at me, and I finally realize that I never, never felt this way about Jamie, even at the best of times.

sixty-nine

WE ARE ON HIS BED. I am curled up near the headboard with my laptop on my knees; Finny is stretched out on his stomach, finishing off a boss in his video game.

I just finished a chapter and my head feels light. I watch his character throwing bombs at the dragon. It's just past noon, but I'm not hungry; we stay out late now and sleep past breakfast time. We spend most of the time driving around with the windows down. We go to drive-thrus after midnight and wander the aisles of twenty-four-hour grocery stores. Last night we sat on the hood of his red car and ate sugary candies with neon food coloring and artificial flavors. Finny left the radio on and we leaned back against the windshield, but the streetlights were too bright to see stars.

I close my laptop, and Finny must hear the click because he says, "You done?" Another bomb explodes on the screen, and his controller buzzes.

"For now," I say. I lay my computer next to me and stretch my arms above my head. I watch him win the fight and save his game.

"So when do I get to read it?" Finny says.

"Never," I say without thinking. "Sorry," I add.

"Why not?" He sounds surprised. He isn't looking at me; he's playing his game again.

"Because it's private," I say, "and it isn't very good yet."

"Can I read it when it's good?"

I shrug even though he can't see. "Probably not."

"Why are you writing it if nobody can read it?"

"I didn't say nobody could read it."

Finny looks at me over his shoulder. "So it's me then?" he says. On the screen, his character runs in a circle and hits a tree repeatedly.

"No," I say. I scoot forward on the bed and stretch out on my stomach next to him. "It's—it's that I know you. And if you read it you might think 'Oh, this character is that person' or 'she's talking about that time here,' but it's not really like that."

"What if I promise not to read into it? No analysis at all. I swear on my mother's grave."

"I'm going to tell her you said that."

"Come on, please?"

I shrug and roll my eyes. "Maybe."

"Ha." Finny turns away and looks back at the TV. He holds up his controller and begins pushing buttons. "That means yes."

"It does not!"

"Does too."

"Does not!" I punch him in the shoulder and he laughs.

"So what do you want to do now?" he says. I shrug again, but I'm smiling.

"This," I say.

seventy

FINNY ANSWERS HIS PHONE AFTER one ring.

"Hello?"

"Hey, I'm home."

"You still outside?"

"Yeah," I say.

"Stay there," he says. "I'll be down in a minute."

When he comes out the back door, I am sitting on the hood of his car. It's almost midnight. The crickets are chirping and the air is still warm.

"So how was it?" he says.

"It was okay," I say. "I think she was acting as a representative of everyone else." I just got back from seeing a movie with Brooke. During the half-hour car ride home, she told me that everyone understood that I was mad at Jamie and Sasha, but that everyone still wanted to be my friend, that I was still part of the group.

"She said that nobody wants to take sides," I say.

"I figured it would be something like that," Finny says, "You hungry?"

"Yeah."

On our way to the all-night drive-thru, I take off my sandals and hang my feet out the window. Finny doesn't mind.

"Do you feel any better?" he asks. I shrug.

"Kinda. I mean, it's nice that I can still be friends with the rest of them, but—" I shrug again and sigh. "I dunno. How can we still be a group after this? And we're all going to different schools..." My voice trails off. A minute passes in silence. We pull up to the bright lights of the fast-food restaurant.

"Is it that easy for you to drop friends?" Finny says.

"No," I say. I pull my feet inside and lay my cheek on my knee. "I really did think we would be friends forever," I say.

"Are you talking about us or them?" Finny says. He is looking out the window.

"Can I take your order?" The box squeals at us.

"Hold on," Finny says, and then turning to me, "do you know what you want?"

My heart is still beating fast from his other question. We haven't spoken about being friends again. The Mothers are beside themselves, but they know better than to mention it. Just before Brooke dropped me off, she asked me if I was with Finny now. I said that he was still with Sylvie and got out of the car.

"Just get me a number one. With a Coke," I say. He orders for us and pays. After he pulls forward and we are waiting on our food, I say, "Them, just then. But I thought that about you too." He doesn't answer me. He hands me the bag and pulls the car around. When we're back on the road, he says, "Sylvie's in Italy now."

"Oh?" I say.

"She was in and out of art museums all week."

"I can't really imagine Sylvie in an art museum," I say. Finny glances at me. He frowns at the road.

"You know, you wouldn't think she was so bad if you gave her a chance."

"Who said I thought she was 'so bad'?" I say. "I just don't see her as an art museum kinda person."

"From you, that is a bad thing," he says. "And you don't really know her,"

"Okay. So I don't really know her," I say. "She doesn't really know me either, and God knows what she thinks about me."

"Mostly she's scared of you," Finny says.

"Scared of me?"

"You intimidate her."

"Whatever."

"I'm serious," he says.

"Okay. You're serious," I say. We sit in silence the rest of the drive home. After Finny pulls into the driveway, he turns off the engine and we stare straight ahead.

"Are you mad at me?" I ask.

"No, I'm not," he says. I can't think of anything else to say, at least not anything I should say, so I don't. I take out the food and hand Finny's to him. "Thanks," he says. His profile is handsome in the dashboard light. I want so much to lean over and lay my head on his shoulder. When we were kids, I could have.

"I don't hate Sylvie," I say finally. "I don't know her, you're right. But that means I don't know if she'd like museums." Finny shrugs, but it isn't a dismissive shrug. "I bet if she knew me she'd see what a dork I am and wouldn't be scared of me," I offer. "Does she know that I got dumped by Jamie?"

"I told her," he says. He looks over at me. "I didn't give her any details though," he adds quickly.

"Does she know about us?" I ask. Finny shakes his head and looks out the window again. "What are you going to tell her when she comes home?" I ask.

"I don't know," he says, and then, "you're not a dork." I eat my burger before it gets cold. Finny eats all of his fries first, then starts on the burger. I leave half of mine behind and wrap it in the foil before dropping it back in the bag. Curled up in my seat facing Finny, I watch him eat in the half-light. The radio is playing quietly. It would be kinda romantic if we were together.

"So," Finny says, "what are we doing tomorrow?"

seventy-one

WE ARE SITTING TOGETHER BY the lake. The sky is slowly darkening, and the fireworks will start soon. Mom and Aunt Angelina are nearby, but they are not sitting with us. They leave us alone these days, and I pretend not to know why, and Finny doesn't seem to notice at all.

"They should start now," I say. "It's dark enough."

"They will soon," he says, and then we hear a pop, and the sky lights up.

I lean back, so that when I look up I can watch him and pretend to look at the sky. His chin is tilted up, a smile curling the corners of his mouth gently up. He reaches up and brushes a lock of his hair out of his eyes.

At moments like this, it amazes me that the words don't come tumbling out of me. I can feel them in my mouth like three smooth pebbles. I can feel them there when I swallow and when I breathe.

His eyebrows raise slightly, and I wonder what it was in the sky that surprised him, but I cannot look away.

Is it possible that the last six years were real, and not a dream as they feel to me now? I think that if I concentrated, I could make those memories vanish. I could close my eyes and believe that we have never been apart. I could invent a new past to remember.

I see myself sitting on the bleachers at Finny's soccer game. He looks up at me and I wave. We are fifteen.

"Autumn?" I open my eyes and he is looking at me. "What's wrong?"

"Nothing," I say. "I'm just tired."

"Do you want to go?"

"No, no." I smile at him. "Don't worry about me." I rip my eyes from him and look at the sky.

seventy-two

WHEN FINNY'S CAR PULLS UP, I am sitting on the front steps waiting. They are early. Finny honks and I stand up. It is night, and it is warm. I run down the long lawn to him.

When I get there, Jack is getting out of the front seat and moving to the back.

"Oh no," I say. "I can sit in the back."

"No," he says, "ladies up front." It's our longest exchange ever. I sit down and close the door.

"Jack likes to pretend that he's a gentleman," Finny says. "But don't be fooled."

"Finn, how am I supposed to make a good impression on your friend if you talk about me like that?"

"I didn't say you had to like each other," he says. What he did say—to me at least—was it bothered him that his two best friends hardly knew each other. He just wanted us to go to one movie together, just one. I had been ready to protest, but when he called me his best friend, I was too pleased. I'm not sure if Jack was hard to convince.

"Let's get along just to spite him," I say. Jack laughs. This might be okay.

I don't want to see the spy movie or the comedy with crude humor, so the boys convince me to agree to the horror flick. In the first fifteen minutes, the girl opens a closet door and a dressmaker's dummy falls out. I scream and cover my eyes. Jack and Finny both laugh, but Finny also asks if I'm going to be okay. I nod and hunch down in my seat.

An hour later, we are at the climax. The girl opens another door and sees her boyfriend hanging from the rafters. She screams and the camera zooms in for a close-up of his face. I flinch and turn my head to the side. My forehead nudges into Finny's shoulder. More screams, and I flinch again.

"You okay?" Finny whispers. I nod, and my forehead rubs against him. He pulls away from me. Mortified, I quickly lift my head and look back at the screen.

And I feel Finny put his arm around my shoulders.

Kind of. Mostly it's just on the back of my seat and sort of touching me, just barely. But his fingers are definitely on my shoulder and at the next scary part he gently presses them into me.

"I'm okay," I whisper. Jack looks over at us.

Afterward, as Finny is starting the car, Jack says, "Hey, do you guys want to get drunk tonight?"

"Yes," I say. Finny shrugs.

"If you guys want to," he says.

"Where would we get it from though?" I ask.

"My brother works at the liquor store on Rock Road," Jack says.

"Are you serious?" I look at Finny. "Is that where you always got your stuff?"

"Yeah," Jack says. Finny shrugs again.

We sit in the parked car with the windows down and get drunk behind our mothers' houses. The boys got a liter of Coke, poured a third out, and filled the rest up with whiskey. They are sitting in the front passing it back and forth. I'm stretched out in the back seat with a six-pack of something pink with tropical flowers on it. Finny picked it out for me. He said I would like it. I wonder if it's what Sylvie drinks.

"You're going to have to stay at my place tonight," Finny says. "I'm not going to be able to drive you home." Jack takes a long swig and passes the bottle.

"You sure won't," he says. I giggle and watch Finny take a huge gulp. He wipes his mouth with the back of his hand and somehow makes the gesture masculine and elegant.

"So, Autumn," Jack says. He turns around in his seat to face me. "Why did you break up with Jamie? 'Cause everybody thought you two were gonna get married and stuff."

"Yeah, so did I," I say. "But he cheated on me with Sasha, so that's not happening."

"Seriously?" Jack says. He makes a face and holds his hands up. "She's not even—um—"

"Half as pretty as me? Yeah, I know."

Jack laughs out loud. "Well, you're modest."

"But it's true."

"Yeah, but you're not supposed to know that."

"Why?" I say. I sit up and lean forward so my head is between their seats. "Why should I have to pretend that I don't know I'm pretty when everybody's telling me all the time?"

"You're just not supposed to know."

"While you two argue, I'm gonna go to the bathroom," Finny says. He gets out and closes the door. Jack watches him go.

"I mean, it's not like I think I'm a better person or something," I say. "It's not even an accomplishment. It's just the way I look." I hear the screen door close behind Finny.

"Listen," Jack says. He looks back at me. "Can you honestly tell me you're not just screwing with his head?"

"What?" I say.

"I'm serious. Finn's my friend, you know?"

"I don't know what you are talking about."

"I was there back in middle school," Jack says.

"Okay," I say. "So was I."

Jack sighs. "If you're not serious about this, then don't mess with his head. He and Sylvie aren't always good together, but it's better than him obsessing over you again."

"He—what?" I feel as if Jack had turned around and punched me

332

in the stomach. I swallow even though my mouth is suddenly dry. Finny hadn't kissed me just because he wanted to see what it was like to kiss a girl; he really had liked me. Even though we are alone, I lower my voice. "Has he said something to you?"

"No. He says you guys are just friends. But he said that last time, and it still took him forever to get over you," Jack says. I look down, afraid that I'm going to cry from disappointment. For one moment, my heart had leaped into my throat. "I didn't mean to upset you or whatever," Jack says.

"No," I say, "it's just not like that with me an' Finny." I swallow again and take a breath. Jack picks up the jug again.

"That's weird," he says.

"What is?" I say.

"You call him 'Finny,' like his mother does." I smile a little.

"Well," I say, "I've known him for almost as long as his mother has."

"I know."

"And that's what everyone used to call him. The Mothers sometimes call him Phineas, though, and I only call him that when I'm mad at him." I hear the back door open, and we both turn and look. Finny walks down the back steps. He's carrying a bag of pretzels.

"Don't say anything, okay?" Jack says.

"Of course not. And it's not like that with us anyway."

seventy-three

WE FELL ASLEEP ON HIS bed again. But I am awake now. The afternoon light from the window is streaming over us. On the floor next to the bed is our empty pizza box from lunch. His video game is paused. My book is on his nightstand.

Last night around three a.m., we got our blood pressure taken at one of those machines you stick your arm in at the grocery store. Finny's was perfect and mine was only a little high. We celebrated with a pound of gummy worms and what was left of the whiskey.

Tomorrow I'm going to have lunch with my dad, so we won't be able to stay out too late tonight. I wonder if Finny will stay up late without me or if he'll just go to sleep like me.

I stretch and roll onto my side slowly so that I don't jostle him. He's lying on his back with his hands behind his head. His mouth is a little open but he doesn't look silly, just relaxed and warm.

We had been watching the shadows of the tree outside his window and talking about my parents' divorce, and then how we should go to the art museum sometime or at least the zoo. Somewhere in there, my memory goes fuzzy, and I must have fallen asleep. I wonder if it was before or after him. Perhaps we fell together.

It's nice, looking at his face.

This close, I can see that he isn't exactly perfect. He has a tiny pimple on the side of his nose and a chickenpox scar on his cheek. We had the chickenpox at the same time. We spent a week in bed together, watching movies and eating nachos off the same plate. Finny was better about not scratching. He got better two days before me, but The Mothers let him stay with me anyway.

The longing to touch that scar is more unbearable than any itch I ever felt.

"I'm sorry," I whisper. "We used to even get sick together and I ruined it all."

If he were awake, he would say it was okay, and he would mean it. But it's not okay. Jack said that it took him forever to get over me, but that still means he got over me.

"I love you," I say to him, so quietly that even I cannot hear it. I close my eyes and listen to his breathing. I go back to the story in my head about how it could have been. I'm at the part where he is teaching me how to drive when I hear him take a deep breath, almost a gasp. I still remember that sound; it's the sound he makes when he wakes up, as if he is coming up from underwater. I let my eyes stay closed. He rolls over onto his stomach, slowly, the way I rolled onto my side. I expect him to put his hand on my shoulder or say my name, but he doesn't. I wait a little longer, and finally decide he's gone back to sleep. I open my eyes.

"Hey," he says.

"Hey," I say.

"I guess our late nights are starting to catch up with us," he says.

"Yeah."

We don't say anything else and we don't move and we don't look away.

I wish that this meant something. I wish I could hope that he is lying still and looking at me for the same reason I am, that he is thinking the same things I am.

"What's wrong?" Finny says.

"Nothing," I say.

"Are you sure?" he says, and then, "Autumn—"

And then his phone rings. He stiffens and sits up. When he picks up his phone, he looks at it and frowns.

"Hi," he says. "Isn't it like four a.m. for you?" I watch his frown deepen and then he turns away from me. "Just slow down, Syl—no, it's okay. Take a breath." He is quiet for a minute, and then he looks over his shoulder at me. He walks out of the room. "What did you have?" he says, and then he closes the door and I can't hear him anymore.

I lay my head back down on the bed and close my eyes.

When Finny finally comes back, it is to tell me that The Mothers want us for dinner. He doesn't look me in the eye. After we eat, I go back home. His window is already dark.

seventy-four

"IF YOU WANT ME TO, I can clear my schedule and go down with you and your mother when you move into the dorms," Dad says. We're sitting outside at the downtown restaurant he chose. He has a new red car that reminds me of Finny's, but his doesn't even have a back seat. "It's an important day," he continues, "and if you want me to be there, I will be."

"So if I don't want you to come, you won't?" I ask.

"If you want me to, I will, that's all I'm saying." Our appetizer comes, and my dad ignores the waitress as she sets the plates down. He doesn't even look up.

"Thanks," I say to her. She ignores me too and walks away from us.

"You don't have to make a decision right now, but the closer we get to the date the harder it will be." He dips his toasted ravioli in marinara sauce. "Not that I won't do it anyway." He takes a bite and chews.

"If it's what I want," I say. He nods. "And only if it's what I want. If you wanted to come and I didn't want you to, you wouldn't come anyway."

Dad wipes his hands on his napkin and sighs. "Honey, if you don't want me there—"

"What if I don't want Mom there? Can I just tell her not to come and then she won't?"

"Now, honey, your mom has to come. That is not optional."

"Why? Why are you optional and she's not?"

"You're saying that you want to move into the dorms without either of your parents there?" Dad says.

"No," I say, "that's not what I'm saying. I'm saying that—never mind."

We look back down at our food. It's too hot out to be perfect weather.

"Your mother told me about Jamie," he says after a while. The name startles me.

"Oh, yeah," I say. "It's not that big of a deal."

"Is that why you're upset?"

"What? I'm not upset."

"You're not upset?"

"No," I say. "I'm fine."

———————

When I get home, I don't call Finny. I want to, but I don't. At my desk, I write a couple of sentences, delete them, and close my laptop. I try to nap, but I'm not tired. I close my eyes anyway. The sun bleeds through, and all I can see is red. I'll wait for Finny to call me first. The afternoon passes.

seventy-five

A DAY PASSES. AND THEN another. I write a little; I read a lot. Finny doesn't eat dinner with us; he's out with Jack, his mother says.

On the third day, I watch him as he pulls the red car into the driveway. He hesitates before closing the door; he looks down at the keys in his hand for a long time. He doesn't move until Aunt Angelina comes out onto the porch and says his name. Then he slams the car door and looks up at her and smiles.

On the fourth day, my mother asks me if Finny and I have had a fight again.

"What do you mean 'again'?" I say.

"Well, I just mean that you were spending all this time together and suddenly—"

"What do you mean by 'again'? Who ever said we had a fight the first time? Maybe sometimes people stop spending time together and it doesn't mean anything."

"Okay, Autumn," she says. She lets me go up to my room.

Sasha calls me. I don't answer.

I wake up early in the morning, and I cannot sleep. I stare at his window until the sun is up and then sleep again.

On the sixth day, I call him. He doesn't answer. I lay my phone down on my nightstand and curl up into a ball. He must have seen it in my eyes.

I've managed to ruin everything again.

My cell phone rings. I pick it up. I look at it. It rings again.

"Finny?" I say, instead of coolly saying "Hello?" like I had planned.

"Hey," he says.

"Hey." We're quiet for a little while. I can hear him breathing. He clears his throat.

"I'm going to break up with Sylvie when she comes home."

"Oh," I say.

"Yeah. It's—it's gonna be hard."

I draw my knees up to my chin. I cannot start to cry right now.

"You want to come over and watch a movie?" he says.

"Okay," I say.

"Really?"

"Of course."

"Right now?"

"Sure."

After the movie, we go out for pizza. And we don't talk about Sylvie.

seventy-six

"DO YOU REMEMBER IN FOURTH grade," Finny says, "when we read *Charlotte's Web* in class and you cried?"

"Yes. Do you remember when that baseball hit you in the head?"

"Yes. Did you cry then too?"

"No," I say. We're sitting in his car. It's late at night again, but we aren't quite ready to go inside. The engine is off, but the dashboard light is on; I can barely see his face. I'm curled up in my seat. I'm so tired, but I don't want him to know.

"You were scared though. You said you thought I was dead."

"It was scary. You fell like a rag doll."

"Do you remember the Christmas it snowed and then iced over the snow?"

"We went to the creek."

"Yeah."

I lay my cheek on my knee. The windows are starting to fog up, but it doesn't feel like we've been sitting together all that long.

"Do you remember when you punched Donnie Banks?" I say.

"Of course I do."

"He said I was a freak."

"You weren't a freak. You were the only cool girl at school."

"How would you know? You never talked to any other girls."

"I didn't need to. Do you remember the Valentine's Day that my mother had the date with the bald guy?"

"Which one?"

"The creepy-looking one."

"I don't remember."

Finny turns in his seat to look at me. I struggle to make out the expression on his face. "Yeah, you do, we were plotting to throw a bucket of water from the window when they came home—"

"But the babysitter made us go to bed in separate rooms! I remember that, but I don't remember the guy."

"I do. He was creepy-looking."

"Or maybe you just remember thinking that he was creepy. Maybe if you saw him now, you wouldn't think so at all. Memory isn't objective."

"But you and I always remember things the same way."

"But that's because we always thought the same way back then. I bet we wouldn't remember—" I stop when I realize what I was about to say.

"What?" Finny says.

I shrug like it's no big deal. "We probably won't remember middle school the same, or high school."

"Oh. Maybe." We are quiet then, and I wonder why I said that and if he'll say that we should go in now.

"You were Mr. Laughegan's favorite," Finny says.

"Yeah, I know," I say. "But all the other teachers liked you better."

"That's not true."

"Yes, it is!" I say. I lift my head off my knees and sit up straighter. "Everyone always likes you. It was the same in elementary school too."

Finny shrugs. "I don't know about elementary school," he says, "but nobody liked me in middle school."

"That's not true."

"Yes, it is; I was nerdy and you were, like, the Queen."

"No," I say, "Alexis was the Queen. I was just a flunky." Finny shakes his head. "What are you talking about?" I say. "She was the leader of The Clique." I can't tell for sure because of the dark, but I think Finny rolls his eyes.

"But you were the one all the guys liked," he says.

"Oh," I say.

"Yeah, it was—weird. Hearing them talk about you like that, I mean."

"Oh," I say. The windows are completely fogged up now. I can only make out the glow of the streetlight coming through; otherwise, it could be any street in America out there.

"So why did you leave them?" Finny says.

"Who?" I ask. I'm thinking about the way he stumbled over his words when he said it was weird to hear guys talking about me.

"The girls. Why did you and Sasha leave them?"

"We didn't leave them," I say. "They kicked us out."

"That's not what they say," Finny says. I look up at him and wish I could see his face better. "They told me that after they joined the cheerleading squad you started talking about how cheerleading in high school was a stereotype and you wanted to be a part of something more meaningful. And you stopped returning their calls."

"That is not how that happened," I say. "They stopped being friends with us."

"But that does sound like something you would say," Finny says.

"Yeah," I say, "but they're the ones who thought they were too good for us."

"That's what they say about you," Finny says.

"But that's not true!"

"Memory isn't objective, right?"

"I guess so," I say, and for the first time I'm wondering what else might be different from Finny's point of view.

seventy-seven

WE'RE IN HIS CAR AGAIN, but it's under different circumstances. It's one a.m., and a police car has just pulled us over. It's the second time this week, but Finny has never done anything wrong. They just pull us over because we're teenagers in a red sports car.

"Do you ever wonder," I ask Finny as he gets back in after watching the policeman search his trunk, "if this car is more trouble than it's worth?" Finny shrugs. Behind us, the police car pulls away. Finny turns off his flashers and looks over his shoulder as he pulls out onto the street again. "Your mom says the insurance is really expensive."

"Yeah," he says, "but I like it."

"It is a cute car," I say.

"Don't call my car 'cute,'" he says.

I giggle. "Finny has a cute car. It's so cute."

"Shut up," he says, "or I'll stop driving you everywhere."

"Will not."

"Will too."

"You'd miss me."

"Not if you keep calling my car cute."

I laugh again.

"I should teach you to drive," Finny says.

I frown. "What? No," I say.

"Oh, come on, you can't go forever without learning to drive."

"Watch me."

"Take the wheel."

"Nope."

"Autumn, take the wheel."

I don't know if he's realized that I can't refuse him when he says my name like that, but it works. I lean closer to him and take over the steering wheel, and the car immediately begins to swerve to the right.

"Whoa!" Finny says. I start to take my hands away, but he places his over mine. He presses gently and turns us straight again. "There we go," he says. My heart is hammering, and I feel as if I am falling. "You have to make little adjustments as you go," he says. "Otherwise you'll end up going off to one side."

"Oh," I say. My voice is shaking. I swallow.

"You're okay," he says. "I'll catch you if we start to go too far."

He helps me turns us around a corner and then another. We circle several blocks and then he takes us back to Main Street.

"Do you want to go on the highway?"

"No," I say.

"Too bad," he says. His hands press down on mine as he forces me to turn us toward the on-ramp.

"Oh my God," I say. Finny takes my right hand off the wheel and places it on the gearshift. "Oh my God," I say again.

"It's okay," he says. "I've got you." He presses on my hand again and we change gears. My palms are sweating but his are hot and firm. The highway is nearly empty, and the road stretches in front of us uninterrupted.

seventy-eight

I'M SURPRISED THE NEXT TIME Sylvie calls when I am with him. I had somehow forgotten her. I had somehow forgotten that the world was larger than just us.

We're watching a movie on my couch. I pause it as he says "Hello," and that's how I know that it's her—the way he says it. He also says "uh-huh" five times, and "that's cool" twice. He says "nothing much" once and glances at me. I look back at him and keep looking after he has turned away from me again.

"Okay," Finny says, "I'll remember." He hangs up. "You can push play," he says to me.

"Was that Sylvie?"

"Yeah."

"Huh." I don't know what I mean by that, but Finny answers me anyway.

"I can't break up with her over the phone."

"I didn't say you should," I say.

"Well, you just—never mind."

"What?"

"Nothing," Finny says.

"I was thinking that it was weird how you're going to break up with her but she still calls—I mean, it makes sense 'cause she doesn't know, but it's weird."

"I guess so," he says. I look down at the remote control in my hands, but I don't push play.

"You never told me," I say.

"What?" His quiet voice matches mine.

"Why," I say. He doesn't say anything, and he doesn't shrug. He doesn't look over at me. He has not moved since he told me to push play. I wait.

"She's not who I want to be with," he says "She's not—that's all."

"Okay," I say, and I nod, as if he has said a lot more. He looks up at me now.

"Do you miss Jamie?" His question startles me; I can see Finny studying the reaction on my face.

"I don't know," I say, because I want to tell him the truth. "I don't want to say yes, because I don't want him back, but I can't say no, either, because I do care about him still. He's still Jamie."

"Do you love him?" I shake my head.

"I'm not *in* love with him." We are quiet again, and I think what a relief it is, how strange it is, to say that I am not in love with Jamie.

"Why are you smiling?" Finny says to me.

"I don't love Jamie," I say, and I laugh because it sounds so funny to say.

"I'm glad that you're happy," Finny says.

"I am," I say. "Actually, I've been really happy."

Finny's eyes soften, and we're looking at each other.

It was another moment when one of us could have said something, could have given us time, but neither of us did. We looked at each other until I couldn't bear it anymore.

"We should finish this and then go get something to eat," I say. We've invented a new meal, one that takes place after midnight and before dawn, and we rarely ever miss it. It's more time that we can spend together without saying what we should.

"Good idea," Finny says, but it isn't. Sylvie will be home soon.

seventy-nine

FINNY AND I STAND IN the driveway as the car pulls away. I wave and Finny just watches them. My parents' divorce was finalized today. Coincidentally, The Mothers are going to a winery for the weekend. They gave us a hundred dollars for just two days, and Jack is coming over later. We're going to have pizza and alcohol for dinner and probably stay up all night.

"This is going to be fun," I say.

"Yeah," Finny says, and it reminds me of the way he used to say "yeah" to Sylvie at the bus stop as she prattled on and on. I always suspected—no, I just wanted to believe—that he was bored with her.

"Is everything okay?" I ask.

"Yeah," he says. I look up at him. He's still staring at the driveway.

"I think I'm going to go over to my house and write," I say. He looks down at me then.

"Oh, okay," he says.

"Send me a text when Jack comes over," I say. "Or whenever you want me to come over."

"All right," he says. I turn and walk away then, and I hear him walking away too. I look over my shoulder. He closes the door. I turn away quickly.

An hour later I get a text. I take off my headphones and pick my phone of my desk.

When do I get to read it?

Never.

How about tomorrow?

Maybe.

Another few hours later, I get another text. I'm lying on my bed staring at the ceiling.

Jack is coming over in half an hour.

Ok

Why don't you come over now? I'm bored.

I smile and swing my legs over the side of the bed.

When Jack knocks on the front door, Finny and I are inside a tent we made of couch cushions, chairs, and quilts. We made it big enough so that all three of us would be able to stretch out inside of it, and we left one side open so that we can watch movies. Finny leads Jack into the living room. He's carrying a handle of rum and two liters of Coke.

"Hi, Jack." I stick my head out and wave.

"What is that?" he says.

"It's our cave," I say. Jack looks at Finny.

"Wow, dude," he says.

"Come on," Finny says. "I don't trust you to bartend." He tugs his arm and Jack follows him out into the kitchen.

"What are you talking about?' he says. "I'm a great bartender."

A few minutes later, Jack crouches at the cave's opening. He hands me my drink and says, "Okay, let's try this thing out then."

"You're going to love it," I say. I scoot over and he slides in next to me. He sits cross-legged and ducks his head down to fit.

"Okay," he says. He looks around the cave. The floor is lined with more quilts and pillows, so it's like a giant bed inside. "This isn't bad."

"Finny and I used to make these all the time," I say. "Every time one of us slept over. It was a tradition, and since I'll probably crash here tonight, it seemed appropriate."

I take a sip of my drink and make a face; it's way too strong. Jack laughs and shakes his head.

"That's weird," he says.

"What? That I made a face?"

"That your parents let you sleep together."

"Not like that!" I say. "I told you, it's never been like that with us."

"Hey," Finny says. I look up. He's bending down to peer inside. "Pizza will be here in an hour."

"Cool," Jack says. He scoots over and Finny climbs in. He stretches out next to me, three inches between us. I'm glad that he overheard me, in case he suspected something. As long as he doesn't know, I'll be able to keep him close to me.

Finny and Jack clink glasses and take long swigs.

"Me too," I say. Finny holds his tumbler out and I tap mine against his and take another sip. I shudder afterward and lick my lips.

"That was weak," Jack says. "We need to teach you how to drink."

"This drink is too strong," I say. Jack laughs. I look at Finny for support. He gives me his lopsided smile.

"Sorry," he says. "I'm with him on this."

My heart beats faster, and I take another drink.

The first time I wake up, I am still drunk and Finny is asleep next to me. He's lying on his back with one arm flung over his eyes. I scoot closer to him, slowly. I lie on my stomach with my forehead pressed into his armpit, nearly on his shoulder. I curl in a ball. My fingers touch his ribs.

When I wake up the second time, the boys are not with me in the cave. I know Finny isn't there before I even open my eyes. I feel cold and my head hurts.

"How could you have missed that game?" I hear Jack say somewhere in the room. I open my eyes. The light outside the tent is bright; it must be almost noon.

"Autumn and I were at the mall," Finny says. His voice makes me want to close my eyes.

"You never miss it when the Strikers are on TV," Jack says. Finny doesn't reply. I imagine that he has shrugged.

There is a pause, and then Finny says, "I'm going to break up with Sylvie when she gets home tomorrow." I stiffen, and my stomach rolls. I lay one hand on it. I didn't know that she was coming home tomorrow. He never told me the date and I never asked.

"I figured," Jack says. There is another pause. My saliva glands ache and my throat constricts. "Then what?" he asks. His voice is quieter.

"Oh God," I say. I climb out of the tent. Finny or Jack might say something to me, but I don't know; I am speeding past them and into the bathroom.

I'm still throwing up when Finny knocks on the door.

"Go away," I say.

"You okay?"

"Yes. Go away."

"Okay."

When it's over, I rinse my mouth out and look at myself in the mirror. I look like hell. I run my fingers through my hair.

When I come out, the guys are in the kitchen making toast. I slump down at the table and curl my knees up to my chest.

"Feeling better?" Jack says.

"More or less," I say. They continue their conversation without me. They aren't talking about Sylvie and I don't listen anyway. After a minute, Finny hands me a piece of buttered toast and I eat it quietly. My stomach protests but I keep it down.

Later we finish the movie we started last night, and then Jack leaves. I tell Finny that I am gonna go next door to take a shower. He says okay and doesn't ask when I'll be back.

At home, I huddle in the hot shower with my arms wrapped around my middle. I want him to break up with Sylvie. I don't want to watch him fall for another girl.

I want him to be in love with me. Like a movie montage I can't stop, scenes from the summer fly through my mind, moments when I thought, maybe, just maybe—

"Stop it, stop it, stop it," I say. I squeeze my eyes tightly. "It's not real," I say. And the need to write it down overwhelms me and I step out of the shower, dripping and shivering.

In my bathrobe, I sit at my computer and I write for a long time. At first I don't realize what is happening. I think that I will write a few pages and go back to Finny's. As the afternoon wanes, my mind starts to feel soft, but I keep pushing. I realize I want this over with. I can't do this to myself anymore.

I get up twice, once to get a glass of water, once to go to the bathroom. Both times, I rush back to write what I have been thinking.

Sometimes my hands are flying across the keyboard, other times I stare at the screen for long, silent stretches. Around dinnertime,

Finny sends me a text. I send him back one word. *Writing.*

It's late in the day now, but it's still mostly light out. I'm typing the last sentence, the one that's been in my head for so long now. I'm shaking. I click save. I stare at the screen.

That's it. That's all of it.

I'm still in my bathrobe. My hair is dry now. I feel numb, like I did after Jamie broke up with me.

I don't know how long it has been—it's starting to get dark, but isn't quite yet—when Finny knocks on my bedroom door. I know it's him. I figured he would come eventually. The door creaks as he opens it. I'm sitting on one end of my bed. I'm still in my robe.

"Autumn?" he says.

"Hey," I say.

"I came to check on you," he says.

"I finished the novel," I say, and I start to cry. I don't see him cross the room, but I feel him pull me into a hug. I haven't ever cried like this in front of him, at least not since we were kids. I lean my head on his shoulder and sob, but it doesn't last too long because I'm touching him, and he's holding me. Finny waits until I am quiet to say anything.

"Do you want to tell me what's wrong?" he says. He hasn't let me go. I sniffle.

"It's like they're dead," I say.

"Like who is dead?"

"Izzy and Aden," I say. "My main characters." I feel the tears building up again.

I feel Finny let out a breath. He laughs once through his nose.

"I thought something was really wrong," he says. Before I realize I'm doing it, I pull away from him in anger.

"Something is wrong!" I say, "Can't you tell I'm upset?" Finny laughs again. His right arm is still around my shoulders. I make a fist and punch his left one. He still laughs. "Stop laughing at me," I say.

"Sorry," he says, but he's still smiling. "It's just that it's really obvious that you're upset, and I meant I thought something was *really* wrong, like Jamie had called you."

"Who cares if Jamie called me?" My voice is shrill. "Who cares about *Jamie*?" Finny grins. I start to cry again. He pulls me into another hug. "You don't understand," I say into his chest.

"I know," he says. His voice is soothing; I close my eyes. "But I can't wait to read it," he says.

"You can't read it," I say.

"Why not?" he asks, and I can't answer him. He doesn't say anything else. He holds me even after my sniffling stops. It's dark outside now. I realize I want this over. I can't do this to myself anymore.

"Okay," I say. "You can read it after dinner."

eighty

ONCE UPON A TIME THERE were a boy and a girl named Aden and Izzy. They lived next door to each other and were best friends. Aden was smart and handsome, and Izzy was awkward and funny. Nobody else understood them the way they understood each other.

Aden and Izzy grow up, and Izzy doesn't leave Aden, and Aden isn't afraid to wait to kiss her until he is certain she is ready to be kissed. They go to high school, and they aren't just best friends anymore. When they undress at night they leave their blinds open so the other can see. Aden plays soccer, but Izzy doesn't do anything but watch him from the stands. They go to school dances sometimes, but mostly they just want to be alone together. They don't have any other friends, and they don't want any others because they're still best friends too. They steal vodka from Izzy's dad and go down to the creek where they used to play and get drunk. Aden learns to drive and then he teaches Izzy.

One night, Aden and Izzy have sex, and it is wonderful and scary.

Then Izzy is pregnant, but before anyone finds out, their baby dies, and it is very, very frightening but also a little bit beautiful, the way sad things sometimes are.

Sometimes people tell them they should make other friends or date other people, but Izzy and Aden never listen, because they know that it's just supposed to be the two of them, and it doesn't matter if no one else understands.

Then in their senior year, Izzy is offered a scholarship to study writing at a school far away from where Aden is going to go. Izzy really wants to accept, and Aden tells her she has to go. They cry a lot, and then they decide they don't want to ruin their perfect love by trying to stretch it across the distance. They think that they will be able to forever remember each other as they are now and never have to have arguments over the phone or wonder what the other is doing that night. When Izzy leaves, it will just have to be the end, and so they try to make the best of the last few months.

The day comes when Izzy is supposed to leave, and they are going to say goodbye at the airport. Aden holds Izzy for the last time, but when the time comes neither of them can let go. They keep holding on and the speakers are starting to call for Izzy's plane but neither of them moves, and they finally admit that they would rather ruin their perfect love trying to make it work because being unhappy together is better than being unhappy apart.

And then Izzy and Aden are finally able to let each other go.

And that's the last line of my novel.

eighty-one

FINNY SITS ON THE LIVING room couch while he reads off my computer screen. I read a book for a while, and the only sound in the room is the click of the keyboard as he scrolls down to the next page. Every time I hear it, I look at his face, but his face says nothing, nothing at all.

Around eleven, I turn on the TV and watch an old movie. Finny doesn't comment. Just before the movie is over, he gets up. I hear him drink a glass of water in the kitchen. He walks back to the couch without looking at me. The movie ends and another starts, and Finny is still reading.

But he's frowning now.

I stay awake for another hour, but my eyelids are heavy and my head is aching again. I turn off the TV, and Finny does not move. I stand and stretch, and he does nothing. I walk past him, out of the room, and up the stairs.

In Finny's room, I crawl under his covers and lay my head on his pillow. I close my eyes and breathe deeply. I thought I would feel jittery and want to bite my nails, but all I want to do is sleep; the act of giving it to him has exhausted me.

I sleep deeply, and I dream.

When I wake, it is either so quickly or so slowly that I cannot remember waking; I am just suddenly alert.

Finny is standing by the bed, his silhouette dark in the weak light. His hands are limp at his sides. I cannot see his face, but I do not doubt that he is looking at me. He says my name, and somehow I know that he is saying it for a second time.

"What?" I say. I sit up. My hair falls forward and I push it off my face and rub my eyes.

"Why did you have to leave me like that?" he says.

"I was tired," I say. "You were reading."

"No," he says. There is a slight tremble in his voice. "After we turned thirteen. Why did you have to leave *like that*?" The question hangs in the air between us, the way it always has.

"I didn't leave," I finally say. My words lack conviction; even I can hear it. "We just grew apart." Finny shakes his head.

"We did not just grow apart, Autumn," he says.

"I didn't mean to," I say. "I'm sorry."

"I already know why you did it," he says. "I just want to know why you had to be so cruel about it." My breath comes quicker.

"Okay, I was stupid and selfish that fall," I say. "And I'm sorry.

362

But everything would have gone back to normal if you hadn't kissed me out of nowhere without even asking. Do you have any idea how much you scared me that night?"

"I scared you?"

"I wasn't ready," I say. I wipe at my eyes with one hand. "And I didn't know what to think." Finny sits down on the bed, but he doesn't face me. I wrap my arms around my waist tightly and wait, but he doesn't say anything. I push the covers off my lap and crawl toward him. I lean forward and try to find his eyes.

"I'm sorry," I say. "I hate myself for hurting you."

"I'm sorry too."

"For what?"

"I'm sorry for kissing you."

"Don't say that," I say. "Don't say you're sorry for that."

Finny surprises me then; he laughs out loud and shakes his head. "I never know what to do to make you happy, do I?"

"You make me happier than any other person ever has," I say, but he still won't look at me.

"Do I?" he says. I nod.

"Every day," I whisper. My heart beats fast and my fingers close into trembling fists. We are both quiet for a few moments. I hear a lone bird singing outside; it must be close to dawn. I wish I could see him better. He still isn't looking at me.

"What if I kissed you right now?" he says. I can't answer him at first; everything inside me has gone still. I tell myself to take a breath.

"That would make me happy," I say.

It doesn't happen smoothly. First, Finny shifts his position so that he is facing me, and then I sit up straighter. We pause there, and I have to tell myself to raise my face for him. He reaches over slowly like he thinks any second I'll tell him to stop, and he lays his hand on the back of my head. I feel my whole body relax with his touch, and maybe he feels it too because it happens very quickly after that. Finny pulls me toward him and our noses bump. I turn my face to the side, and he presses his mouth against mine.

It's warm, kissing Finny, and sort of like my whole body is being stroked with a feather. He puts his hand on my hip and I want to do something with my hands too. I lay one on his shoulder, and the other on his knee. Finny's fingers tighten in my hair.

"Ow," I say, and I flinch away from his hand even though I don't want to, even though I want to pretend it doesn't hurt.

"Sorry," he says. Our noses are still touching, but he isn't kissing me. He starts to take his hands away.

"No, don't stop," I say. I pull on his shoulder. "Lie down with me." I lean back onto his pillows.

"Oh God," Finny says, and he crawls over me.

We kiss quickly at first, as if we're trying to make up for lost time, and then long and slow, as if we're daring each other to see who can last longer. My hands are on his back, trying to hold him closer; his are on either side of my face, holding me still.

I don't know how long we kiss like that; the only thing I am aware of besides him are the sounds I hear myself making from time to time; little sighs and moans like I have never made kissing anyone else.

It's never felt like this before.

It feels so natural.

It feels so right.

Finny.

I finally understand what's been missing for me all these years.

After a while, he draws his hand slowly, really slowly, down my shoulder and across the side of my ribs. He holds my breast, gently.

My Finny.

My eyes are wet again, and I feel one tear trail down the corner of my eye, and then another and another, and I realize that there may never be another moment more perfect than this for the rest of my life.

"Finny?" I say.

He stops kissing me slowly and then raises his head more quickly to look down at me. "Yeah?" he breathes.

"I want..." I say, and then realize that I don't know how to say it and the words trail off.

"Do you want me to stop?" he says.

"No!" I say. The thought fills me with panic, and I speak quickly. "I want the opposite of that." There is a moment of silence. I hold my breath.

"You want me to keep going?" he says.

"Yes," I say.

Finny blinks at me and stumbles over his next words. "I—I don't have—" he says.

"I don't care," I say. And I don't. All I care about is not losing this moment with him.

"Autumn," he says. "No—"

"Please, Finny," I say. I lean up and kiss his neck, right under his ear. He gasps sharply and his body shudders. "Please, Finny," I whisper between kisses. "Please. Please. Please."

Our mouths finally find each other again. After a moment, he pushes his hand under my T-shirt and up to my bra. I reach down and try to pull my shirt over my head without moving my lips from his until I have to. If we stop kissing, we will have to talk about what we're doing. He helps me and kisses me as I arch my back to unhook my bra.

I reach down and try to undo the button on his jeans, but I can't. He stops kissing me and pushes my hands away. I think I'm going to die until I realize he is undoing it himself.

There just isn't a way for two people on a bed to take off their jeans without being awkward and embarrassing. But it can still be perfect and wonderful too.

Finny sits up and pulls his shirt over his head. I can see all of him now, and for the first time, I am frightened. He looks down at me.

"Oh, Autumn," he says. I reach down and try to shimmy out of my underwear without looking silly, but I probably don't succeed. When they're past my hips, he pulls them down and off my ankles and tosses them on the floor. He's looking at me again. I feel like I've been tossed up in the air, and if I don't grab on to him in time, I will fall back down again. I hold out my arms to him.

"Can I tell you that I love you first?" Finny says. I begin to fall slowly, slowly down.

"Yes," I say. Finny leans over me again. One of his hands parts my thighs, and the other rests by my head.

"I love you," Finny says in my ear. I feel him touching me there, with his hand first, and then it isn't his hand anymore. "Oh God, I love you." He pushes into me just a little; it's a warning. I bury my face into his shoulder. "Oh God," he says. "Autumn."

I bite my lip and don't cry out. He moves slowly at first, and I know that it's for me; I can feel him holding back. It hurts, but not like I thought it would. It isn't a general blank pain; it's contained and exact, just like being ripped apart. I can almost hear it.

"It's okay, Finny," I say. "I'm okay." He groans then for the first time and moves faster. I close my eyes and rest my cheek against his. I think about lying in this room with him, drawing on each other's backs. I think about sitting next to him on the couch and watching TV. He moans and my arms tighten around him. I think of his hands over mine on the steering wheel. I think of us shining our flashlights in each other's windows at night.

It isn't long before I feel him suddenly stiffen. He cries out once and shudders. Tears sting my eyes again. Finny lets out a long breath and begins to shift away. I whimper only when I feel him moving out of me.

"Autumn?" he says. He looks down at my face.

"I love you too," I say. "I forgot to tell you." The tears spill over now, and Finny begins to kiss my eyelids and my forehead again and again.

"It's okay. Don't cry," he says. His words rush together and blend with his kisses. He kisses my cheeks and my tears. "Don't cry," he says. "It's okay."

"Will you hold me?" I ask. He rolls off me and holds out his arms. I wipe my eyes and lay my head on his shoulder. His arms fold around me and he presses me close.

"Like this?" he says.

"Yeah," I say. We're quiet as our breathing slows to normal. I watch the light get brighter in the room. There are more birds singing now, a whole chorus.

"I can't believe that just happened," Finny says. I almost laugh but somehow don't. A strange feeling is beginning to fill me now.

"Did you mean it when you said you loved me?" I ask.

"Of course I did," he says.

"You weren't just saying that because it's what the guy's supposed to say?" He doesn't answer me after that, and my stomach drops. Finny lets go of me and sits up on one elbow. My breathing halts.

"Come on, Autumn," he says. He makes a sound that isn't quite a laugh. "I know that you know I've been in love with you for forever. You don't have to pretend."

"What?" I say. He rolls his eyes.

"It's okay," Finny says. "I've always known that you knew." I sit up on my elbows too, pulling the sheet up to cover me, and look back at him. We frown at each other. I try to make myself understand what he's saying.

"What do you mean by 'forever'?" I say.

"You know. Forever. Since we were, like, what? Eleven?" he asks.

"Fifth grade? The year you punched Donnie Banks?"

"Yeah, you remember what Donnie Banks said."

"He called me a freak."

"He said, 'Your girlfriend is a freak,'" Finny says. "And he knew that you didn't want to be my girlfriend. And that I did."

"You liked me like that back then?" I say.

Finny looks like he finally understands what I'm saying. He sits up all the way.

"But isn't that why you stopped hanging out with me in middle school?" he says. "Because you got tired of me wanting to be more than just friends?"

"No," I say. "I had no idea you wanted anything like that."

"But after I kissed you, you knew," he says.

"No. I didn't know why you'd kissed me and it freaked me out. I thought maybe you were experimenting on me." Finny looks at me again. His mouth is slightly open, his eyes hinting at a frown.

"But this doesn't make any sense," he says. "If you didn't know, then why did you leave me?"

Now it's my turn to look away from him.

"It just felt so nice not to be the weird girl anymore. I liked being popular. We did *kinda* grow apart that year. I'm not saying it's not my fault. I'm just saying I didn't mean for it to happen."

"You really didn't know?" Finny asks.

"No," I say. "I really, really didn't."

Finny flops back down on the bed. He stares at the ceiling.

"And all these years I was terrified that you could tell I still… you know."

"Still what?" I ask.

"Still wanted you."

"Really?" I say. He doesn't answer me. He just stares at the ceiling with an expression that looks as confused as I feel. "What about Sylvie?" My voice has a hint of accusation in it, but I can't help it. Finny surprises me by laughing bitterly.

"The only reason I started hanging out with the cheerleaders after soccer practice was because I thought they were still your friends. I thought that maybe I'd have a chance with you then, that maybe I'd be cool enough for you to see me like that. Then when the first day of high school came, you didn't even say hi to me at the bus stop. And I found out that not only were you not their friend anymore, but you hated them. And then you started going out with Jamie, and Alexis was asking me why I was leading Sylvie on and I didn't even know what she was talking about—" His voice trails off and he is quiet again. I'm too shocked to say anything this time. He's still staring at the ceiling. I'm starting to feel cold without his arms around my shoulders. "Don't think that I never cared about Sylvie, because I did," Finny finally says. "She's not really like what you think. And she needed me to take care of her when you didn't anymore. I loved her, but I loved her differently from the way I've always loved you."

"Oh, Finny," I say. My voice is quiet, and I can't find the words to say anything else. After a moment, he turns his face toward me, but he does not meet my eyes.

"You said—you said that you loved me too." He's blushing, and I feel like I might faint.

"Yeah," I say. "I do." My voice is barely above a whisper and I cannot hide its tremble.

"Since when?" His voice matches my own.

"I dunno," I say. "Maybe since forever too, but I didn't admit it until two years ago." He raises his eyes to mine and I collapse back down on the bed. He wraps his arms around me again and I curl into him. Finny hugs me so tightly that it almost hurts, and then I feel his whole body relax. I close my eyes and sigh. It's so strange; it's such a revelation, this feeling of skin to skin all the way down my body. I reach one hand out and try to find his heart. He lays his other hand on top on mine and strokes my knuckles with his thumb.

"So," Finny says, but doesn't continue.

"What?" I say.

"It's you and me now, right?"

"Phineas Smith, are you asking me to be your girlfriend?" I can't help giggling.

"Well, yeah." He shifts underneath me. "Is that weird?"

"Only because it feels like we're already so much more than that."

He relaxes again. "Yeah, I know. But it'll have to do for now."

"You still have to break up with Sylvie," I say quietly.

"I know," he says. "I'm going to. Tomorrow."

"You mean today," I say. He looks over at his window.

"Oh. Right." He squeezes me again. "We should get some sleep, I guess."

"Yeah. I guess." I close my eyes, and we are quiet. The room is still and silent, and outside, the sun has risen on a hot August day.

eighty-two

I WAKE MANY TIMES. WE shift and change positions together; he nuzzles me, I move up against him. He holds my hands, my neck, my face. I dream, I wake, I see him, I sleep.

Finny's cell phone rings. He tenses and sits up. I am still and confused for a moment, and then I bolt upright. It looks like early afternoon. Finny is standing in the middle of his room, picking his jeans off the floor and digging through the pockets. I fold my arms over my breasts as I watch him. He opens his phone, looks at it, and presses a button. The ringing stops. Still holding his pants, he turns and looks at me. I stare back at him.

"Hey," he says.

"Was that her?"

"Does it matter?" He sets the phone on his nightstand.

"Yes."

"It was," he says. I look away, down at the covers on my lap. I hear his jeans hit the floor, and the bed creaks as he sits down. The blanket shifts as he climbs back in next to me. "Come here." He pulls me down next to him and holds me the way he did last night.

I think of Sylvie at some airport, excited about seeing Finny again soon. I think about how I laughed when Jamie told me he and Sasha had discovered they had feelings for each other. I realize how different this story must be from all of their points of view.

"Do you feel guilty?" I ask. He doesn't answer right away.

"Yeah," he says. "But I also feel like I've been loyal to something bigger."

His phone beeps. He has a text message.

"You should see who it is," I say.

"I don't want to."

"It could be The Mothers, and if we don't answer, they'll think we're dead and come back early." He sits up and looks at his phone. His back is turned to me as he types a reply. He doesn't say anything when he turns back around. He lies back down on his side and I curl up next to him so that we face each other.

"It was her again," I say.

"I told her that I won't be meeting her plane. I'll go see her after she has dinner with her parents."

"Oh. When?"

"We have a few hours. Go back to sleep."

"I'm not tired."

"Me neither." He reaches over and strokes my hair. I close my eyes but do not doze. His fingers are gentle on my scalp and I shiver once. "Do you regret it?" he asks after a while. I open my eyes again. He looks worried.

"No," I say, "but—" I lower my face so that I can't look at him. "I wish it had been your first time too," I say. He stops stroking my hair and his hand drops on to the bed between us. When he speaks, it is slow and haltingly.

"The first time—we were both so drunk neither of us can remember it. And then it turned out—" he pauses and frowns "—that she couldn't do it unless she was drunk. And if she was drunk, it felt wrong to me. It didn't happen often or even go well when it did. So—I mean—in a lots of ways, it was a first for me."

"What do you mean she couldn't do it unless she was drunk?" I ask.

Finny looks away and mumbles. "Someone hurt her once."

"Oh," I say. We are quiet for moment. I reach over and cover his hand with mine. He turns his palm facing up and our fingers twine together. Our eyes meet again.

"I wanted something better for you," Finny says. "That's why I made you promise not to do it when you were drinking. But really, the idea of you ever doing it with anybody made me mad. You remember how you told me that you were going to after graduation, and then the day after you were sitting on the porch and you said you were waiting for Jamie?"

"Yeah?"

375

"I went up here and punched the wall. I'd never done that before. It hurt."

"You thought—"

"Yeah," Finny says. He still holds my gaze, but his expression shifts into some mix of emotions I can't quite figure out. "Then after I found out you guys had broken up, it was hard to see you miserable over him when I was so happy I wanted to pick you up and spin you around," Finny says.

"You were sad that time Sylvie broke up with you," I say. "I was so angry at her for hurting you that I thought about pushing her in front of the school bus."

"I was sad," Finny says. I can't help the sliver of jealousy that pierces my stomach. "But it was my own fault," he adds. "I told everybody that I didn't like it when they made comments about you and Sylvie got jealous. She asked me if I had feelings for you and I told her to drop it and kept trying to change the subject. She could tell."

"Why did you get back with her?" I ask the question even though I'm not sure I want to know the answer.

He pauses for only a second before answering. "You loved Jamie all this time too," Finny says. "Didn't you?"

"Yeah," I say.

"Then why don't you understand? I wanted—I tried to love only her. When I told you last month that I was going to break up with Sylvie, it wasn't because I thought I had a chance of being more than just your friend. It was because loving you from a distance was

376

one thing, but it wouldn't have been fair to her if I were in love with my best friend."

I sit up and pull the blankets with me so that he can't see my body. I can't look at him. Everything he has said has made me so sad and so happy and more than anything else, I am so frightened.

"Autumn?" I hear the bed creak as he sits up too, but I hang my head and refuse to look at him.

"What if you see her and realize this was all a mistake?" I say.

"That will not happen."

"It could."

"It won't."

"If you love her—"

"But if I have the chance to be with you—God, Autumn, you're the ideal I've judged every other girl by my whole life," Finny says. "You're funny and smart and weird. I never know what's gonna come out of your mouth or what you're gonna do. I love that. You. I love you."

I raise my head a little. He's staring at me with an expression I've never seen before. I watch his eyes study my face.

"And you're so beautiful," he says. I duck my head back down and try to hide my face. My cheeks are warm. Finny laughs. "Now, I *know* you already knew that."

"It's different when you say it." He laughs again.

"How?"

"I don't know."

"You're so beautiful." Finny puts his hand under my chin and turns me to face him. He looks me in the eye. "Last night was the best thing that ever happened to me, and I would never think it was a mistake unless you said it was."

"I would never say that."

Finny leans his forehead against mine. "Then everything is going to be okay. We're together now. Right?"

"Of course."

Again, Finny laughs at me. I pull my face away from his and look at him.

"I never, ever thought this would happen," he says. "And then you say 'of course' like it's the most natural thing in the world."

"Doesn't it feel like it?"

He laughs again, quietly this time, and the tone is different. "How did we ever get here?" he says. I don't know what to say to that. So I just look at him. And then he smiles at me and pulls me toward him again, and I sit on his lap with his arms around me and it is the most natural thing in the world.

eighty-three

FINNY IS SUPPOSED TO LEAVE in a few minutes. He's in the shower, and I'm in his room, dressed and waiting. I made his bed and tried to cover up the bloodstain, and now I'm sitting in the middle of it with my knees curled to my chest. The sky has clouded over, and even though it is still early evening, it looks almost dark out.

I hear the shower stop; I rest my chin on my knees. It takes forever for me to hear him in the hall. He comes in fully dressed and rubbing his wet hair with a towel. He looks at me.

"It's going to be okay," he says.

"Can't you wait until tomorrow?"

"I want it to be over," he says. "I want it to be just us." He drops his towel on the floor. He takes a baseball cap off his dresser and covers up his wet head, then takes it off and runs his fingers through his hair. He turns back to me.

"Walk me out?" he says. I nod, and he holds out his hand to me.

I follow him to his car, and then we stand looking at each other.

"I promise you," he says, "I'll come back as soon as I can. It may take a while though."

"Please don't go," I say. He puts his hands on my shoulders and pulls me to his chest. "I have to do this," he says. "You know that, Autumn."

I can't answer him because I know he is right. He lays his cheek on the top of my head.

"Here is what we'll do," he says. His voice is soft and light, as if we are making the sort of mischievous plan we made as children. "When The Mothers get home, you go to bed early, and when I get back I'll sneak in your back door and come to your room. And then I'll hold you all night."

I raise my head to look at him.

"Okay," I say. He smiles and leans down to kiss me. He kisses me once, and then I lean in for another. We kiss for a long time after that. I lean back against his car and he presses into me. Both of us are breathing harder. If I can just keep kissing him, then he'll never leave.

A car door slams. We both look up but we don't separate. The Mothers are in the other driveway, unpacking cases of wine from the trunk. They are pointedly not looking at us.

"Do you think they saw?" I ask.

"Definitely," he says.

"Oh God," I say.

"I think my mother has a special bottle of champagne hidden away for just this occasion," Finny says.

"Oh God," I say again. Finny looks down at me and smiles.

"I'll be back to help you fend them off."

"Okay," I say. This time I resist the urge to tell him not to go. His smile slowly fades and he takes a deep breath. My arms drop from his neck reluctantly. He kisses my mouth quickly and takes a step back. He turns to open the car door and I take a step back too. He looks at me again, and just before he gets inside, he smiles again.

"After this," he says, "things are going to be the way they were always supposed to be." Then he climbs inside and closes the door.

He starts the engine without looking up at me again. I stand in the yard and watch his car until it is gone.

It begins to rain.

eighty-four

***

LATE IN THE NIGHT, I hear footsteps in the hallway. I roll over and look at the door. It opens slowly.

"Finny?" I say. There is silence.

"Oh, Autumn," my mother says.

eighty-five

On August 8, Phineas Smith died, and I can imagine every detail of that night. I can see his face and the curl of his fingers around the steering wheel. I can hear his breathing and I feel the race of his pulse.

I know what he was thinking about as he took that turn too fast.

I know what they had been arguing about before the little red car spun out.

I know that Sylvie's face was already streaked with tears when she crashed through the windshield.

It'd be wrong to say Sylvie killed Phineas. She was the instrument of his death, but not the cause. If he had been with me, Finny would still be alive. If he had been with me, everything would have been different. But whose fault is it that he wasn't?

I see Finny sitting in the red car, perfect and untouched. Rain falls through the hole in the windshield but he does not feel it. He feels nothing. He thinks nothing. He is alive.

Stay. I whisper to him. *Stay in the car. Stay in this moment. Stay with me.*

But of course he never does.

Suddenly, as if he has been punched, his senses come back to him. He feels the warm leather seat beneath his jeans, and the steering wheel clutched in his fingers so tight that his knuckles are white. He sees the glass glittering around him and the gaping hole in front of him. And through that hole where the windshield once was, he sees her. Through the blackness and the rain he sees Sylvie lying in the road, still and quiet.

Stay, I whisper.

Just as suddenly, his hands unclench from the wheel and he is taking off the seat belt that spared his life, opening the door and running down the road toward her.

I see the puddle of water by her head even though he does not. I see the black glistening power line that the storm has torn down draped through the water. Finny does not; he only sees her, what he thinks is his destination.

Sylvie lies on the other side of the puddle, safe and unmoving, only serving her purpose.

He kneels before her. He says her name. She does not move. He is filled with a fear and panic that matches my own in watching this moment. To steady himself, he lays his left hand down by her head.

Death happens to him more suddenly than I can describe to you or even care to imagine.

eighty-six

———————

IT'S LATE SEPTEMBER NOW. WITHOUT talking about it, we all knew I wouldn't be going away to college this year. I stay in my room most days and tell The Mothers that I am reading. Aunt Angelina still sleeps over here every night, but my mother no longer has to beg her to eat. My father takes me out to lunch once a week; he thinks that he's distracting me when he talks about taking me with him on his next trip abroad.

I had to go see Dr. Singh again. He asked me a bunch of questions and I told a lot of lies. He upped my prescription and let me go.

I haven't taken my pills in a month now.

Today is the day halfway between our birthdays and the leaves have begun to change. I lie in bed and look at Finny's window. This September was so hot and dry that some of the leaves have already turned brown and died, and in this setting, the beginning of autumn is dull brass instead of gold. I can see some of the roses still blooming in my mother's garden. Brown on the edges and bright in other colors, they open and unfold, their petals drooping downward, dying just as their lives have begun.

They've stayed past their time, and I've realized that I have too.

In the end, my decision comes down to one thing: I think Finny would forgive me. It wouldn't be what he wanted for me, but he would forgive me. And if I continue to try to survive without Finny, there are paths I could go down that he would think were much worse than this.

The afternoon passes into evening and then night. I wait until I can no longer hear The Mothers talking together before bed. I step carefully on the stairs, avoiding every creak I can remember. In the kitchen, I leave the note on the table. It took longer to write than I thought it would. I finally had to accept that I wouldn't be able to say all of the things I wanted. I go to my mother's butcher block, and this is the only I time I ever pause, and it is to consider if I should take the biggest knife since it is what I imagined, or if I should be practical and choose the one that would do the best job. But if I am caught with this note, I will have to tell lots of lies for days or maybe weeks until they will leave me alone long enough to try again, and so I decide that if I am determined enough, it won't matter which knife I take, and so I take the big one.

As I sneak out the back door, I spare a moment to glance at the backyards where we played together, at the tree where we never built our tree house. But I hurry across the grass to his yard, and run past the spot where he kissed me first.

Aunt Angelina is always losing her things, so she keeps an extra house key under the empty flowerpot on the front porch. After I unlock the door, I put the key back so that maybe she won't realize I used it and blame herself. It's the least I can do; this is already not fair to her. But the temptation to be close to him one last time is too great for me to resist.

The house is quiet, empty, shadowy. The stairs creak as I go up, but there is no one to hear and I relish the sound, remembering how we ran up the stairs together.

The door to Finny's room is closed. I knew it would be. No one has been in there since he and I walked out of it holding hands.

I use clear tape to hang the sign I made on the door.

Please, do not try to break down the door. It is too late for you to do anything. Call the police and let them handle this part.

And I come into this room and lock the door behind me.

eighty-seven

IN BOOKS, PEOPLE ALWAYS WAKE up in the hospital and can't remember how they got there, and then it all slowly comes back to them.

I opened my eyes and thought, "Oh shit."

I sit cross-legged in the middle of the bed, wearing a scratchy blue nightgown. The hospital blanket is depressingly small and thin, more like a beach towel. I have an IV in one hand and my wrists are so neatly wrapped and taped that it makes me wonder about the person who bandaged them. I study my bandages as the nurse takes my blood pressure and asks me if I know what day it is.

"And do you remember why you are here, dear?" the nurse asks me. I dislike her voice. "Autumn?"

"I remember," I say. I remember much more than I wish I did, since I am planning on doing it all over again.

She asks more questions. I mumble answers. I shouldn't ask about the person who did the bandages because that would be weird, and I need to get out of here as soon as possible. Finny would forgive me. No, Finny will forgive me when I get to explain to him afterward. I touch the cotton wrapping with one finger.

"And when was your last menstrual cycle, dear?"

For the first time in weeks, everything within me goes still and silent.

"On what day did you last have your period, Autumn?" I look up at her face for the first time. She's younger than I thought.

"I can't remember," I say. She frowns.

eighty-eight

FINNY WOULDN'T APPROVE OF ME trying again if I am pregnant. I could argue with him all I wanted, but he wouldn't budge. Finny couldn't stand to let worms die on the sidewalks; I would never be able to convince him that it would be for the best.

I can see the expression on his face. His frown of disapproval. I try to explain to him and he just raises his eyebrows at me.

People do things like this. Aunt Angelina did.

We could live with The Mothers at first; they would be happy to have us. I could wait tables and save money and go to college a few courses at a time. I could still write at night, maybe not every night, but still.

Just because something seems impossible doesn't mean that you shouldn't try.

And of course, it wouldn't be like having him back. Not really. But it would be better than not having him at all. I remember him holding Angie's baby at the hospital, the way he stared in wonder at that small face.

And Finny smirks at me because he knows he has won.

eighty-nine

It's hospital policy, dear," the nurse says. I blink at her.

"What is?"

"The test."

"Oh. Okay."

"Now, I am leaving the room for just one minute. The ward is locked. Are you going to behave yourself and wait right here?"

"Yeah," I say, "I'll wait." She leaves me. I wrap my arms around my middle and press until my wrists ache. My eyes close. I'll wait. And I'll be okay.

And for the first time in years, I feel like things are going to turn out the way they were always meant to be.

acknowledgments

My husband, Robert, held my hand both literally and figuratively as I struggled to achieve this dream. Baby, we've done it.

My parents, Gary and Susan Nowlin, raised me to love myself and to love books. Mom, thanks for giving me a passion for beauty in all its forms. Dad, thanks for being exactly the opposite of Autumn's father.

My big sister, Elizabeth Nowlin, is awesome. Thanks for toughening me up.

My in-laws, Jay and Tina Rosener, are two of the most loving and generous people I have ever met. Guys, I could not have done this without your support.

My agent, Ali McDonald, made this dream come true. Thank you. Thank you so very, very much.

And thank you, God, for these and all the many blessings you have given me.

about the author

LAURA NOWLIN holds a BA in English with an emphasis in creative writing from Missouri State University. When she isn't at home agonizing over her own novels, Laura works at the public library where the patrons give her plenty of inspiration for her writing. She lives in St. Louis with her musician husband, neurotic dog, and psychotic cat. Thank you for reading her book.

FIREreads

🔥 #getbooklit

Your hub for the hottest young adult books!

Visit us online and sign up for our
newsletter at FIREreads.com

 @sourcebooksfire

 sourcebooksfire

 firereads.tumblr.com